PURPLE DOVE

J A CRAWSHAW

XYLEM
PUBLISHING

CONTENTS

Published by XYLEM Publishing

978-1-917019-09-5 Paperback

978-1-917019-08-8 Ebook

Trigger Warning: This book contains themes of narcissistic control: physical, emotional, sexual (non-explicit), and psychological manipulation.

Cover image/design by Xylem

Editor: Jill French. JFEditorial

Proofreader: Sadie Robertson

MY FREEDOM FROM DYSLEXIA

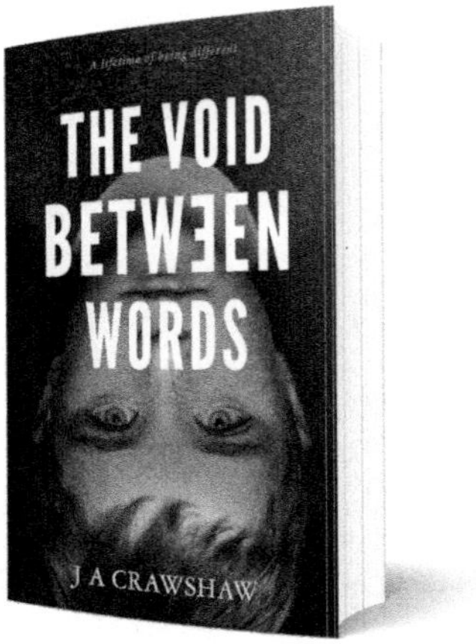

Personal Memoir

The inspirational true story of how I overcame dyslexia and 50yr fear of words and reading to write this novel.

Available on all platforms and bookshops. Hardback Paperback Ebook and Audiobook & Dyslexic friendly format.

Personal Signed Copies

https://www.jacrawshaw.com/bookstore

TRIGGER WARNING

This book contains themes of narcissistic control: physical, emotional, sexual (non-explicit), and psychological manipulation.

PROLOGUE

'What would you be without me? Do you think you'd be living in a house like this, overlooking the sea, with an acre of gardens and the envy of the village? They look up to us here and do you know why? Because we have high standards.'

'You make me sound ungrateful.'

'A machine fitter's daughter. You were destined to work in that cafe for the rest of your life. If I hadn't walked in that day, you'd still be there.'

'I'd be happy,' she shouted.

'So, you are ungrateful? After everything that I do for you, and you say you'd be happier earning a pittance and living in a damp flat somewhere in York. I doubt it.'

'Why do you have to be so cruel? I run this house, grow our own produce, have your dinner on the table every day without fail. I clean, show up at events as the doting wife and pick up your dirty pants from the floor.'

'I'm saving the world. Haven't you realised that? Do you

have any idea what chaos this country would be in if I weren't doing my job?'

Heather's stomach wrenched. His voice, like his angry fist, squeezing it tight. 'They will see you for who you really are. The truth will come out.'

Angus laughed. 'The truth!' He brought his face up to hers. 'The truth is, I keep vermin off the streets. The truth is, you don't get to my position without the respect of the people and, since I donated my kidney to the Lord Chief Justice, I'm now a saint. Untouchable.' He stood up straight and pushed his chest out, like a triumphant warrior.

Beads of sweat formed on Heather's forehead, and she vomited in the sink. His arrogant smile hid nothing. The attention-seeking schoolboy, obvious beneath his overweight, middle-aged facade.

'Why don't you run along and make us some tea? I have case notes to read,' he said, catching himself in the mirror.

1

AGAINST THE TIDE

Days like this were bittersweet. The rock pools swirling with the incoming tide made Heather realise it was time to go, but her eyes, transfixed by the horizon, glued her to the rock like a limpet clinging on for survival.

The current surged its way between the stubborn rocks and almost touched her feet. She didn't want to leave, and revelled in her defiance against its force. She knew another minute or two and she would be cut off from the beach and at the mercy of the open sea.

Heather smiled as she watched the tall sail of a yacht breach the waves on its way out of the harbour, setting course for a journey to freedom. *Where was it going? What would it be like to weigh the anchor and have nothing to hold you back?* She thought as she watched its sail billow with optimism, and the gleaming paintwork and chrome look joyous in the reflection of the low autumn sun on the crystal-picked ocean.

She turned to observe the rising water as it covered the last remaining crossing points back to the beach. The rocky headland was as far out to sea as she could get and where the air was freshest. She felt her cheeks tingle as the salty air pushed her back to safety. She resisted its force, still watching the boat head further into the great unknown. A deep sigh, thrust back into her mouth as the wind buffeted her and threw her off balance. With the sea now covering all possible routes, she pondered staying to let nature take her where it wanted. *It might be easier that way?*

The black heads of two seals popped out of the water and watched her, intrigued. Their kind expressions and knowing smiles looked like old souls on baby faces. Their eyes seemed to ask questions they had already answered, and their whiskers bristled with adventure as they swam together under the arch beneath the sheer white cliff. They were a partnership; that seemed obvious. Guiding each other with a calm, yet playful, reassurance and mutual trust, they navigated the turbulent waves with ease, unity and love.

Heather wasn't a strong swimmer, and her rock-climbing skills amounted to an indoor wall with the Brownies some thirty-five years previous. She remembered that didn't end well! A broken arm and weeks in a cast were not an option now.

A ledge, as wide as a shoe at its widest, was her only option. It led to where the boulders were closest together and the narrowest point for jumping over the fast-flowing insurgence. Tucking her dress into her knickers, she grabbed the chalky rock and teetered along the ledge. Not daring to look down, she persevered, knowing that one slip would mean falling into the crashing waves below.

The leap to safety is as wide as two deckchairs laid side by side. She weighed up the distance between. She'd jumped that many times when she was a girl, no problem, and although her gymnastic abilities were still good in her head, they were compromised somewhat by a forty-six-year-old body. But there was no other choice. With no run-up available, and a crumbling, shaley landing point, she grit her teeth and leapt.

The raw beauty of the dramatic cliffs and the energy of the sea meeting the unforgiving, jagged rocks and battling against the wind made her feel alive. It was dangerous and thrilling, yet comforting and secure. Familiar, yet always different. It was freedom.

The blood dripped from her knee onto the pebbles and then vanished like it were an insignificance. And it was. Tiny droplets on a vast beach where shipwrecks had been eaten up, and centuries of fishing and piracy cleansed away as if they had never happened. Her peril, as inconsequential as a discarded fish and chip wrapper on a deserted promenade. It made her feel empty.

Her phone, cut off from any signal, at least offered its clock with a stark reminder she couldn't be late home and triggered an anxious twitch in her neck, which she tended, by fiddling with her pendant.

Hobbling over the pebbles to soft sand, she sat to examine her wound. The warmth of the sand felt safe. It was just a gash, nothing serious, nothing broken, but it was beginning to swell. She looked at the many steep steps up the cliff. It was knee-jarring enough without an injury, but it was her only exit. She sighed and then smiled. A female pirate would be able to ascend the cliff, injury or no injury, she thought, as she chuckled to herself, then winced as her knee twisted.

Letting the blood clot in the salty air, she stood up. Her graceless walk to the steps was painful. Her mind focused on one step at a time, and she tried to banish any thoughts of the entirely uphill walk back to the house.

. . .

A strategic wooden bench at the halfway point was a welcome resting place, and she took a moment to catch her breath and attempt to clean the rivulets of blood from her shin. She began to shiver.

'Are you okay?' A masculine voice surprised her.

'I'm fine thanks,' she replied abruptly.

'I saw you hobbling and you look cold? I can get help, or carry you up,' he said with a smile.

He was younger than Heather, early thirties maybe. Tall and his shoulders broad. He looked like the kind of man who could indeed carry her to the top.

'As I said, I'm fine. Just taking a moment to catch my breath.'

He didn't reply, just looked at her.

'I just need a moment,' she said, breaking the uncomfortable silence, and covering her legs with her coat.

He knelt. 'I see you're bleeding, let me take a look.'

'Don't touch me!' she cried, tightening her coat around her legs. 'I told you, I'm fine.'

He backed away and nodded. 'You're at the halfway point; there's a hundred steps to go.'

Heather stayed rigid on the bench. 'I will be fine. Please respect that,' she said, avoiding eye contact by staring out to sea.

He courteously took a step down. 'There's a cafe at the top. I'm sure they will have first aid kit if you need one?' he replied as he set off down the steps.

Watching him disappear, she broached the first step. The pain was bearable until she put weight on it. She looked back, wishing she had said yes to his kind offer, but he was gone. She had to erase the pain from her brain and just get on with it.

This was a case of mind over matter, and she knew she was good at that.

Continuing on, each step tested her resolve as she remembered her mother's condescending voice. 'Pain is all in the mind,' she would say. 'Life is meant to be painful, so learn to live with it.'

Glad she's dead, Heather thought as she closed her eyes and tried to imagine each step was the last, and each having her mother's face on as she stamped her foot.

'I can't bear to see you suffer. Please, let me call someone for you.' The young man's voice, familiar and kind in tone, was right behind her.

'I thought you were heading to the beach?'

'I was, to see the seals, but I can't bear to see anyone in pain. Please let me call for help,' he said, looking at the ring on her finger. 'Do you have someone to come and pick you up?'

'NO!' she shouted. My husband doesn't know I'm ... No. Really. I'm fine.'

'Doesn't know what?' he asked, shaking his head.

'It's nothing. I shouldn't have come here, that's all!'

The man offered his hand. 'Well at least let me assist you to the top?'

Her knee had almost seized up, and despite her frosty barricade, her heart was crumbling too. 'Just to the top. But make sure no one sees us,' she replied, standing on one leg and looking to see if anyone else was around.

Expecting his arm as an aid, she was taken by surprise when he scooped her up into his arms like a baby. He was strong, very strong and although her heart was trembling, she had little choice but to accept his help.

'Just relax,' he said, smiling. 'I'll have you to the top in no time.' And so he did, with ease. Each step compounded her guilt at needing his help, not to mention being in the arms of a total stranger.

His heart thumped against her arm as he man-handled her to the top and courteously deposited her on a seat below the whitewashed lighthouse.

'Did you have a car?' he asked. 'Because I don't think you should drive.'

'No. I'm local. I walked from home at the top of the hill. I'll call a taxi.'

Checking her phone, she could see she was connected to the real world once again. But worried, she was already late.

The man waited patiently until he knew the taxi was on its way and wished her well as he proceeded to walk along the verge.

'Wait! I didn't catch your name? And thank you. I ... appreciate it. I must have weighed a tonne?'

He stopped and turned. 'You were as light as a feather. Hope the knee gets better soon.' He carried on walking and then turned again. 'The name's Will.'

~

'Drop me here please,' Heather said.

'I can take you to the door, madam,' the driver replied.

'No. Here is fine, thank you.'

She knew Angus was home. He was meticulous like that and three missed calls made her cringe. Why did she have to push it too far? It wasn't worth it, and a cover story was needed once again to conceal her tracks. Her only undetectable entry onto the property was through a small inconspicuous gap in the hedge. The double row of beech allowed her to slip in undetected. There were no cameras, unlike at the gate, and he had no clue of its existence. She slipped in quietly and hoped her thumping heart was not audible to the outside world.

Rubbing soil onto her knees to disguise any remnants of blood, she picked up the wheelbarrow and trundled it to the greenhouse, making as much noise as possible. She scraped the metalwork upon the stone path and noisily closed the windows of the greenhouse, or orangery, as she called it. It was a large and impressive Victorian glasshouse with a high roof and stuffed with potting tables, irrigation pipes and autumn's plentiful fruit and vegetable harvest. The orangery was an impressive structure and also Heather's safe haven and sanctuary.

'I shouted, where were you?' he said with his arms supporting his thick-set body within the doorway.

'Angus! You surprised me. I've been down in the orchard doing some pruning.'

His glare made her neck twitch.

'The front door was locked!' he said.

'I knew I'd be at the bottom of the garden, and didn't want to have it on my mind.'

'Mmm,' he replied, still glaring into her eyes. 'I called you.'

'Oh! Sorry, my phone died and I left it in here.'

'And there's no dinner either.'

Trying her best not to look flustered, she took a subtle but deep breath. 'I thought we'd order in for a change. I've been quite busy and ran out of time, before I'd even noticed,' she said, edging down one of the aisles.

'You know I don't like takeaway food. Especially on a Wednesday.'

Grabbing the brush, she pushed it between them in a half-hearted attempt to clean the floor. 'Well, there's a new Thai place opened up in the village and I thought we'd give it a try.'

He grabbed a tomato from the vine and, while shaking his head, bit into it and gobbled it down as if he hadn't eaten for a month. 'You know, it amazes me sometimes how complicated you can make things,' he replied.

'It's not complicated. It's simple really.'

He shook his head and smiled. 'In your head maybe, but to everyone else it looks disorganised, like you don't care. It's not a problem to me, we'll have takeaway, but it is my duty to protect you, especially if you're becoming more forgetful or slap-dash. Do you understand?'

'Yes!' she replied with a compliant smile.

'I'm doing this for you, Heather. You know that! Keeping standards high,' he said, staring at her.

She carried on brushing the floor.

He smirked and leaned in towards her. 'It's funny! I was only thinking the other day about your father, working for a pittance at the factory and boozing his life away, and what you might have become if we hadn't met.'

Heather stopped and looked him in the eye. 'We have a fabulous life here Angus. I know that. I'll do better next time.'

Angus grinned. 'Green curry and jasmine rice for me then,' he said as he took another tomato from the vine and crushed it in his fist.

2

HIGHCREST

His car left the drive, and the automatic gates closed to leave the entire house and gardens to herself. She toyed with the silver pendant around her neck. A beautiful dove in flight, within a simple silver ring. The solitary diamond that formed the dove's eye dug into the skin of the finger as she watched the car vanish. Then a smile broke across her face as Benny the cat weaved his way around her legs and brushed his cheek against her. 'Come on, let's feed you,' she said, lowering her hand to catch the tip of his tail.

Painkillers and anti-inflammatories had helped to keep her knee moving, but it had been a painful night concealing the injury. He would have asked more questions, and it wasn't worth the aggravation. A bag of frozen peas around the swelling made her wince as she sat on the chair and finished her coffee.

The house stood alone within an acre of formal gardens and featured front and rear lawns and a variety of trees, including ginkgo, horse chestnut, silver birch and an impressive Atlantic cedar which shaded the rear lawn. A paved terrace overlooked the harbour, and a small orchard and kitchen garden accommodated the productive elegance of the orangery.

Victorian in style, Highcrest House dominated the village below. A grand house with stone bay frontage, white woodwork and curious attic windows. It was worthy of a High Court judge and his wife, and each room had a formal theme. William Morris influenced most of the downstairs, while the upstairs rooms had a contemporary feel. Especially the master bedroom, with its sophisticated combination of white stone walls and green smoke feature panels, contrasted with a blackened fireplace and small, delicate, seemingly trying to be understated, crystal chandelier. Heather enjoyed making it a home; it was important to her both as a woman and as a wife. As a young girl, she dreamt about living in such a house and growing her own produce. The three remaining bedrooms lay mainly unused, unless guests stayed over following a party or New Year celebration, but she kept them pristine, just in case. Fluffy towels and fresh flowers from the garden were always on display, and she would often just open the doors, let the air in, and spend a few moments in each, filling her pride bank and contemplating yet another redesign or linen revamp.

Benny was grateful for his bowl of jelly-rich mackerel morsels and jumped up onto the worktop, as she washed the breakfast dishes. He was a loving soul and a good listener too. Well, he always looked like he wanted to hear her thoughts and troubles! His brother, Top Cat, had sadly died the previous year. Well, that was the assumption – one day, he left the house and never returned. Heather often pondered where he might have gone and why he never came home. Benny's purring made her smile as she stroked him under his chin and dabbed soap bubbles on top of his head in jest.

He followed her into the sitting room, but when she sprayed wood polish onto her duster, the hairs on his back sprang to attention and he bolted for the door. *How could so much dust accumulate in such a short time?* She moved the photos on the solid-wood mantel above the fire. Angus didn't like an untidy house, and he had a dust allergy. Taking hold of the photo of their wedding day, she examined every detail. He looked handsome in his blue tartan kilt and high socks. He didn't smile, not that day or any other day, but she could see he looked proud as he stuck his chest out confidently. It was his confidence that had first attracted her to him, notwithstanding his heavy accent. She had smiled at how her dress clung to her slender figure. She was young then, twenty-eight and her long red hair glistened in the sun. Her Scottish heritage was from her grandparents, and she remembered brushing her grandmother's auburn hair in front of the fire in their tiny cottage in Oban.

The wedding was in York. Her parents had moved there before she was born, and that's where Heather and Angus met. His promotion to District Judge, at the age of thirty-five, was impressive and not only did it afford them a modest house to the north of the city, and a life of well-to-do parties and ceremonial events but also responsibilities for her as his wife which she had not expected. Angus being ten years her senior was something she never considered. He was chivalrous and charismatic, but above all, he was ambitious, and she admired that. Her humble life as the daughter of a machine fitter at the chocolate factory was a complete contrast, but she did her best to make it work. Heather picked up Angus's empty whisky glass and smelled the remnants of stale Scotch and his breath around the rim. It reminded her of her father, and it sent a shiver through her entire body. They were worlds apart, yet similar in the way they drank away their troubles and brandished their frustrations with a heavy hand. Another shiver ran deep in her veins as she looked at the large photo of Angus in his red robes, white collar and wig. He was all man and now in his mid-fifties, but she could see the frustrated boy within his eyes. He too had been on the receiving end of severe beatings from his father, and it had made him, in many ways, an island. An impenetrable soul with an egotistical cover plan, which he wore with arrogance and status.

But who was she without him? Just a plump, plain Jane, strawberry blonde, machine fitter's daughter with no prospects and low self-esteem. There were no photos on display of her as a child. Her strict 'no chocolate in the house' rule, coincided, and neither were allowed to be seen, ever.

Looking around nervously, Heather isolated a photo of herself, taken in the grounds of Castle Howard by friends when she was thirty-five. Carefully, she removed the backing plate and a layer of paper to reveal two hidden photos. With another cursory glance at the door and a couple of breaths for courage, she looked at the first one. It was a black-and-white ultrasound image of a baby. Heather brushed her thumb over the image as if to connect with the tiny body. 'Verbena,' she whispered. 'Verbena.'

Closing her eyes, she took a moment to reflect, and then a tear trickled down her cheek. Verbena didn't make it into the world. She was not meant to be, and although Heather had a sliver of gratitude in her heart, the loss weighed heavily on her shoulders. Propping the photo up against another, she took the second image. It was almost identical to the first. A black-and-white picture of an unborn foetus. Her tears were now uncontrollable as she once again ran her thumb over the tiny body. 'Hello Daisy,' she said, barely able to speak. 'You are never forgotten. I love you both. You are my strength and, in my heart, forever.' Her tears dripped onto the photos as she kissed them, almost wanting her DNA to bring them to life.

3

SWEET ALYSSUM

With apples and pears to harvest and an intended pumpkin and squash casserole for dinner, her swollen knee was a huge inconvenience. Scrabbling around in the vegetable patch was out of the question, well, for today at least. Instead, there were the last of the tomato crop to use and, combined with some stewing lamb, would cook one of Angus's favourites, lamb tagine. *He'd like that, and a shrewd plan to move on from the Thai takeaway debacle.* She hobbled to the orangery. Benny accompanied her and, oblivious to her injury, did his best to trip her up as he darted back and forth around her legs.

October on the east coast of Yorkshire could be drizzly and cold or, bright and warm. Total opposites, but either way, you could guarantee Highcrest would be the first to know. Heather buttoned her cardigan as she made her way along the stone path. The sun had a warm optimism as it sluggishly appeared from behind the horizon, but there was a chill in the air. Opening the door of the orangery made her smile. Sheltered from the breeze and already warmed by the early sun, she savoured the astringent smell of ripe tomatoes, the honey-like fragrance of sweet alyssum and the underlying tone of earthy compost. This was her sanctuary, her safe place, and her pride and joy.

Benny established himself on his favourite cushion in the warmth of the sun and Heather placed the pile of letters and post of the day on the bench, switched on the radio in anticipation of Woman's Hour and proceeded to harvest the tomatoes into her basket. They were at their sweetest straight off the vine, and she bit into one, closed her eyes and relished not only the taste, but her success at nurturing such a fine crop. For half an hour, Heather lost herself in watering, dead-heading, pruning and picking flowers for the house. A small kettle accompanied by hand-painted tin boxes for the tea and coffee looked like something you'd find in a shabby chic hotel room. The flower-adorned containers, painted by her in acrylic paint and labelled on the front, sat perfectly upon a scrap of rough-cut birch wood. The click of the kettle switch made Benny's ears twitch, and Heather made herself a steaming mug of black coffee and sat on her stool. Gathering the post, she turned up the volume on the radio and took a tentative sip of coffee. 'In today's programme, we discuss coping after losing an unborn child, and strategies for moving on.' She immediately turned it off and sat in silence while the aroma of coffee filled her nostrils. Her head rocked back as she looked up into the sky, watching the clouds edge their way across the gap in the chestnut tree canopies.

Her fingers involuntarily drumming on the mail in front of her, brought her around. There was a lot of post today, some of it for Angus and some for her. Letters to him, usually looked official and sometimes, even had a red wax seal! She never opened them, instead, placing them in a pile ready to deposit back at the house. Heather's post consisted of the monthly bill from the butcher, the lawnmower repair invoice, an invitation to the opening of a new women's clothes shop in the village and numerous items of junk mail. But there was one more. A large white envelope. She knew what it was, but enjoyed prolonging the opening while she took another sip of coffee. Once a month, this was an indulgence, and one she savoured.

Opening it with her garden knife, she cut the envelope into tiny pieces and, while swivelling on her stool, sprinkled them onto the compost heap and mixed them in with a trowel. And there it was. A dazzling brochure of enticing azure water and whitewashed romantic getaways. Luxury villas set among swaths of lavender and cosy mountain hideaways surrounded by wildflowers, cattle with huge bells and snow-capped peaks. Holidays, getaways, adventures and life-changing views and excursions. Every page a new and exciting destination and a wonder of the people, the smells and the tastes of foreign lands. Heather devoured every page and, using her pen, circled places of most interest, while finishing her coffee and imagining she was ensconced in a little taverna or chic cafe with everyone wondering why she was there, alone.

The last few pages drew her in most. The Greek islands by catamaran. White sand, lush pine-clad coves and dolphins playing freely in bow waves. It looked fabulous. But Angus wasn't a sailor, nor a flyer. Both seasickness and claustrophobia put paid to anything in the brochure being possible. Scotland it would be again next year, as it was this, and she wasn't in a position to be ungrateful, she knew that, but it was all about Angus's love of golf and shooting deer which drove them there year on year.

She loved Scotland, of course. The air was clean, and the nature sublime. She'd traced her heritage and Angus's right back to the Celts, and there she always felt inspired to paint watercolours and sketches of the landscape. She was no Constable, but did enjoy the freedom of her hand and mind when she allowed herself the time to paint. Not that it was difficult on their holiday, because Angus would be busy for hours chasing a ball around a links course or, if he wasn't shooting helpless deer, waist deep in a freezing cold river, fly-fishing. None of that appealed to Heather. She was disgusted with him for persecuting defenceless animals, and although he claimed it was his instinctive right as a man to hunt, she found the leery smile which would accompany his defence, foul and repulsive. They would, of course, be staying at the usual five-star hotel just down the road from Balmoral, and with indulgent spa facilities, exquisite food and private access to the river. That was a treat, and there were classes to attend, and also the chance to explore the culture and nature of the area. She leaned forward and placed her elbows on the bench and, while resting her chin in her hands, stared at the azure water of the Mediterranean and sighed. *Hint at a cruise next year, perhaps?*

Benny distracted her. Stretching his paws into the air, he rolled over, stood and moved to the shade of a seed box and curled himself into a tortoiseshell ball. Heather smiled and stroked the top of his head. 'I'll take you with me,' she said, picking up the brochure. Her eyes focused on the house and then scanned the entire garden. She ended up double-checking the driveway and took a deep breath. A weathered, sap-green door in the brick wall that formed the back of the greenhouse had a knob that turned the wrong way. There was something joyful about the irony and as she opened it and adjusted her eyes to the darkness inside. There was barely any light, just a glimpse of daylight visible through a gap in the boarded-up window and what came in with her from the greenhouse behind her. The dark, cool environment offered the perfect place to hang the onions and garlic and force rhubarb in the spring. Heather negotiated the hanging strings of produce to the far-left corner and to a heavy-duty wooden cabinet with the word 'seed' visible on the front. A large bag of grass seed lay on top, and piles of plastic seed trays teetered precariously to just above head height. Another glance at the door made her eyes squint and then take a moment to readjust to the darkness once again as she removed the plastic trays and placed them on the bench. She gritted her teeth, picked up the heavy bag of seed and placed it alongside the trays with a grunt. Keeping her back straight, she grabbed the edge of the large wooden cabinet and pushed it along the floor. Her knee made her cringe as she did. A scraping noise was unavoidable on the flagstone floor; she had tested every kind of action. Fast and loud, slow and painfully audible and a mixture of both while coughing in an attempt to muffle any kind of giveaway to her actions. Wheels or sliders would eliminate that, but that was exactly the point. It was designed to be difficult, and hopefully, no man, in his late fifties would attempt it, let alone have any reason to try.

The cabinet to one side revealed a redundant and boarded up, narrow Victorian fireplace, with a wood panel blocking the opening. Heather reached above her to the roof joist and instinctively took the cold metal key, which lay discreetly on top. Placing it within a tiny hole in the panel enabled her to unlock it. The torch on her phone allowed her to view the contents inside.

Removing a sealed plastic box, she placed it on the floor and then took today's holiday brochure and added it to a pile of others, which had been stacked neatly. There were so many, the pile formed a substantial knee-high altar within the void.

She took the plastic box and removed the lid. Rolls of £10 and £20 notes bundled together with elastic bands forced their way out. Nothing to add today, but the rolls of cash were beginning to make the lid difficult to close. *It did no harm to check the cash,* she thought, as she listened intently for any hint of a noise. A shoebox filled the void at the back. Placing one hand on it, she looked back at the door, then drew it closer, hesitated while her eyes adjusted from the glare and then calmly pushed it back into place. *Not today.* Neither necessary nor timely, she thought.

Systematically, Heather put back all the elements of her stash, leaving no sign of disturbance, and confidently re-entered the bright warmth of the orangery and closed the door behind her, turning the handle the wrong way and listening for the click of the latch. Giving Benny another stroke on the top of his head, she picked up her basket of vegetables, Angus's letters and headed back up to the house to prepare her husband's dinner.

'I knew I'd catch you in at some point!' A voice shouted from the gate.

'Sally! How lovely. So sorry I didn't respond to your text. It's been hectic recently.'

'I was just passing. Is the kettle on?'

Sally ran the cat rescue centre and had introduced Benny to Heather not long after they moved in. An absolute heart of gold, but, boy, could she chat. It was always better to pop in on her with an 'I only have ten minutes' excuse ready to present on entry and a keen eye on the clock, rather than an ambush on home soil! Heather had managed to avoid her a couple of times recently, but this was a fair and square, unavoidable, 'you got me and I have nowhere to escape' attack.

'Absolutely. Was just about to make a coffee. How are you?'

Sally plonked herself at the kitchen table with a huff. They were of similar age, but Sally always looked worn out and as if weighed down by something. 'I had a cat to see just up the road. New 'parents'. A follow-up visit just to make sure everything was going okay. How's Benny?'

'He's fine. Loves his cushion in the orangery. It's always warm and cosy there.'

'He was tiny when he came to me. Someone found him abandoned at the back of the fish market. I never knew who his mother was?'

'Well, I'm glad you found him, because some days he's the only one who'll listen to me.'

'Tell me about it, Heather. At least you have that amazing husband of yours. I just have twenty-six cats."

'Yes, but I bet they all agree with you?'

Sally laughed. 'Not always! Anyway, I went on a date a couple of days ago.'

'Oh, yes?'

'I joined that dating app. Paws For Love. You know, like-minded people. Well, that was the plan. Anyway, his name is Alfie, lives at Boggle Hole and has two Munchkins and a Ragdoll.'

'Are those his children?' Heather laughed as she poured the coffee.

'Actually, like me, he's never been married.'

'Sorry, Sally, that wasn't a funny joke. So, what happened?'

'Well, we met at the cafe by the harbour and had tea and cake, then walked on the beach. He's an interesting man.'

'Do I need to get a hat? Is romance in the air?'

'Well, he asked me for a second date and I said yes.'

'That's fantastic. Where are you meeting for that one?'

'Well, he suggested meeting at his place, so I can see the cats and then walk from there.'

Heather placed the coffee mugs on the table. 'Are you sure that's a good thing? You don't really know who he is?'

'He's a cat lover Heather, anyway, he has his mother living with him, so how bad can it be?'

Heather's eyes rolled. 'Just trust your gut instinct and call me if you need an escape plan.'

'What are you going to do if I do? Send up a flare and get the coastguard in?' Sally said.

'Just be careful. That's all I'm saying. You don't want to be getting mixed up with anything ... well, you know what I mean.'

'The app is all verified. Anyway, he was very gallant and friendly.'

'I'm sorry Sally. I didn't mean to pour cold water on it. He sounds like a lovely guy and hope date two is purfect!' They both laughed and chinked their coffee mugs.

Heather reached for her purse and handed Sally £200. 'Here, take this. You do a fabulous job with the cats and to be honest, feel a little guilty I don't have more here. I would but ... Angus ... you know.'

4

DUTIFUL

'How many people will be there?' Heather asked.

'We've been every year for the last fifteen years. You know how many will be there.' Angus replied from the en-suite bathroom.

'I just need to know that I'm wearing the right thing.'

He strode into the bedroom, adjusting his black tie. 'How does the number of people affect what you wear?' he said, shaking his head and tutting.

'It just does!' she replied, zipping up her over-the-knee, black velvet dress.

'Well, it doesn't matter whether there is one person or a thousand, you're not wearing that!'

'What do you mean?' she said looking down at the dress and thick black tights.

'You look like a frumpy old woman. Like one of those hippies from Greenham Common.'

'Greenham Common doesn't exist anymore,' she replied, raising her eyes.

'You know what I mean. I'm receiving an award tonight.

This isn't the usual Christmas dinner dance; it's a stepping stone to something greater. An honour. The King. Services to justice. Do I have to spell it out?'

'It's an internal award, not a knighthood!' she said, looking at herself in the mirror. Seeing her body, she realised he was right, and she *was* old and frumpy. Her hair was flat and boring; she was putting on weight, and her breasts were virtually nonexistent. He was always offering to pay for enlargements, but she couldn't bring herself to accept. It seemed ... unnatural. The dress was comfortable and perfect for 'blending in' she didn't want to stand out or, if truth be known, be there at all.

'Are you going to let me down again?' he said. 'I'm a High Court judge not a hippie schoolteacher. Wear that red dress I bought you a couple of years ago. The one with the slit up the side.'

A shiver ran up her spine. 'It's too clingy. I can barely sit down in it.'

'Edgar Horton's wife will be in a dress with a split up to her cute little arse.'

Heather looked him in the eye. 'Edgar Horton's wife has been fucked by the entire judiciary and probably half of the criminals too. Do you want that reputation when you meet the King?'

Angus sneered and looked her up and down. 'I want you to show me some respect and be a good wife, so that I don't look like an idiot.'

~

The annual Christmas dinner dance was always held at the end of November and close enough to the big day to count.

Heather hated it. With all the pomp and ceremony of the awards and then the drunken backslapping and unspoken-about dance-floor groping, it always felt to her like an above-the-law and immaculately dressed sex party, with everything except the sex. Well, on view, anyway! But it was her duty, and as he said, if she were a better wife, he would be proud of her.

'Well, if it isn't Heather Sinclair, in a stunning red dress!' A voice greeted her.

'Oh Judy. Thank you. I really need to lose some weight though. I'm worried the split will continue up to my armpits. I'm so glad to see you here. I thought you moved to Cornwall.'

'We did, but we're back. Bertie has landed himself the High Court job in Leeds.'

'He's done well. Really well,' Heather replied.'

'He has, but they couldn't do it without us. You know what I mean,' Judy said, raising her eyebrows.

Heather smiled politely.

'What about Angus, how's he getting on?'

'He's moving on up too. Tenacious as ever. I'm not supposed to mention it, but there's an award tonight and the prospect of more to come.'

Judy put her hand on Heather's shoulder. 'Don't worry, I won't say anything. Anyway, how are you?'

Heather nodded vigorously, shrugging her shoulders. 'Good. Yes ... very good. As I said Angus is excelling and we've talked about moving, although I have the house just as I like it now.'

'I remember. The lovely Victorian place up on the hill?'

'That's right. Keeps me fit, just walking into the village and back.' She laughed.

'So, life's good?' Judy said, scrunching up her cheeks.

'Yes,' Heather replied. 'Never better. It's idyllic.'

Heather held the trophy on her lap as the taxi took them home. Angus snored for most of the way back. He could drink, but copious amounts of champagne and then whisky and cigars into the wee small hours had taken their toll. She was glad, though. He was difficult to handle when he was drunk. One year he exposed himself in the taxi and demanded she 'finish him off' on the back seat! She managed to fend him off with her sequin purse, but she regretted it later, when he told the driver she was frigid.

Meeting Judy had helped make the evening enjoyable. They danced together while the men hogged the bar and behaved like bald and overweight schoolboys on their first ever night out. Judy was a good woman. Stronger and more capable than Heather in many ways. She knew that. With Bertie wrapped around her finger. She had a confidence about her that Heather admired. One thing was for sure, and that was Judy had convinced her that the responsibility of a judge's wife was to facilitate his career and maintain a stable home. Judy did that so well, and Heather could do a lot more to be the perfect wife. *All it needs is a fresh impetus and a conscious decision to find her inner Judy.*

5

MIZZLE

Free range poached eggs, smoked streaky bacon, sausages, mushrooms, homegrown tomatoes and tattie scones were lined up and ready for Heather's final plating up. She had also pulled out all the stops with her homemade sourdough bread, which she toasted and cut into triangles. Up before dawn and despite only a few hours' sleep, she wanted to provide a breakfast fit for a king. It had involved her dashing all the way down the near-vertical hill to the butcher's in the village, and back up again, but it was worth it not only for the bacon and the black pudding, but the eggs too, and all while her bread was proving.

The winter air was cold, and the sky dull, as if it were too much effort to change. No bright warm sunshine, just a miserable grey, sea-fret mizzle, which appeared inconsequential but drenched her to the core. A stark reminder that the weather was totally out of her control so to grin and bear it was the only way to survive. The sound of Angus coughing upstairs and then, running water from the shower hurtling down the pipework raised the alarm. *Perfect timing*, she thought as she continued cooking and serving the full Scottish breakfast.

He appeared in the doorway. His eyes struggling to adjust to the main light of the kitchen.

'Can you remember what happened last night?' he asked.

'You drank a fair bit, that's why I thought you'd like a cooked breakfast.'

'Is it Scottish?' he asked taking his chair at the table.

'Aye,' she said. 'Although we have lived in England longer than both of us combined in Scotland, so we could drop the tattie scones if you felt brave?'

'Never!' he replied, looking at her with complete contempt. 'I remember receiving the award, but nothing much after. On that note, where is it?'

'Your trophy?'

'Yes.'

'I put it on the mantlepiece beside your official photograph.'

He nodded. 'Thanks. You know, I don't know what I'd do without you.' He paused and stroked his clean-shaven chin. 'Actually, I do know, but it scares me.'

Heather nervously toyed with her pendant and averted her eyes.

'It's only a county award but it shows eyes are on me and a good few bottles of Balvenie with Dickie Granger won't have done any harm. He's the mover and shaker at supreme level these days.'

'I saw, but didn't come and interrupt. It looked like you were engrossed.' Heather muttered as she served up the gargantuan feast.

'You looked good in that dress. Reminded me of you in your thirties,' he said, tucking into his sausage.

'I need to lose some weight,' she said, flattening her stomach with her hand, and catching a glimpse of herself in the window.

They sat at opposite ends of the table and ate their food in silence. Handing the salt and pepper pots to each other, their only communication.

'It was a good breakfast. You've done well. I was starving,' he said, pushing his plate away.

Heather smiled and finished her meagre poached eggs and one rasher of bacon on toast. 'I've made fresh coffee too and managed to get the Saturday paper.'

He looked up and nodded. 'A day of doing nothing seems very appealing and a good start to my three days off.'

Heather poured the coffee. 'I wondered if you'd help me in the garden?'

'I'm playing golf tomorrow,' he said, raising an eyebrow.

'How about Monday? We need to do some cutting back and the beech hedge needs trimming; I can do all the other things.'

Angus sipped his coffee and rolled his eyes.

'It would mean that the garden is ready for winter.'

He rolled his eyes again.

'I could get someone in to help. Save you having to bother and they can take all the cuttings away too, so we don't have to rake and man handle them to the compost?'

Angus peered out of the window into the mizzle. 'No. I'll do it. I don't trust anyone else. They're all crooks, those tree surgeons. Can't tell you how many I've sent down over the years.'

Heather shook her head. 'Like all the car mechanics and estate agents?'

His face remained stern. 'I told you about the tree surgeon

who kept his wife captive and then dismembered her body with a chainsaw, didn't I?'

Heather looked at him with disgust. 'A thousand times and I told you I don't want to know.'

'Well, anyway. It's safer me doing it. As long as you do the raking up.'

Heather took his empty plate and stacked it in the dishwasher. 'Raking is the hard bit.'

'But you like gardening. You never stop saying how much you love the plants and could never leave this place because of the garden.'

'I just appreciate a bit of help, especially on the larger jobs,' she replied.

Angus stood, walked over to her and cupped her face in his hands. 'You're my little garden elf. Of course I'll do the hedges,' he said and then kissed her on her forehead. Heather smiled and put her hands on his. 'Thank you.'

Angus turned to exit the kitchen and spoke as if addressing an audience out of the window. 'It's what makes this house a proud house. Its history and garden,' he replied, looking down onto the village with his arms behind his back.

Heather assembled her gardening equipment and heard the rasp of a petrol engine in the garage. The hedge trimmers were heavy, and although she knew all about the two-stroke 5:1 petrol mix ratio and maintenance of the reciprocating blade, she was happy to hand it all over to Angus. He was taller than she was which meant she didn't have to risk using ladders.

She giggled to herself when she saw him walking down the path in his cerise Ralph Lauren polo shirt, green wellingtons and bright orange chainsaw helmet. His portly belly, flopping over his belt and his chubby face peeking out from under the mesh visor, finished off the 'weekend-arborist' look with an out of sorts arrogance and comic-strip humility. That was Angus to a tee. He was a born academic, with private school, dorm-room humiliation deep within his driving force to succeed. But she was grateful he was helping her and that the garden would be ready for spring. She followed him as the cuttings fell to the ground. Raking them up was hard work, but her focus on reducing her waistline kept her going. Wheelbarrowing them to the compost area was tricky but fun. There was a set of three steps to negotiate and a narrow path along the side of the pond. Heather loved the challenge of keeping the contents within the barrow and even sped up just to make it more thrilling. She emptied the cuttings and turned to watch Angus brandish the trimmer. Her heart thumped in her chest. A deep, contented beat, which brought a lump to her throat, and a tear, which welled slowly and then ran down her cheek.

'Tea up!' she shouted above the noise of the trimmers as she waved a steaming mug in front of him. He nodded and finished off the small section ahead of him. Turning off the engine and resting the trimmers on the ground, she noticed his polo shirt had ridden up over his belly, and she laughed uncontrollably. He removed his helmet and revealed his bemused look with raised eyebrows. She pointed at a beech leaf, which was stuck in his belly button and looked like a little brown tongue sticking out. His serious face made her stop immediately, and her leg began to twitch as he looked down at his paunch and then back at her. She wanted to laugh again, but maintained her composure. Her eyes wandered down once again to the leaf, and so did his. He then proceeded to stick his belly out even more and shook his head. Heather nervously took a step back and eagerly watched his stern face. His lips crinkled as if he were sucking and biting the inside of his cheek, and he lifted his head. She pushed the mug of tea towards him and was greeted by laughter. Joyous laughter in all its beauty. His belly rippled as he gave out the surprising laugh. His face turned red as he continued to see the humour in the little tongue sticking out of him.

What a joy! She hadn't seen him laugh like that for a very long time, and she joined him. Pointing at the leaf, and both of them shaking their heads and letting go in their moment of humility. He took his tea and plucked the leaf from his belly button. Heather smiled. She was glad she'd asked him to help and elated at their shared moment of fun. It reminded her of when they were first dating. Giggling on the back seat of the cinema and being told to be quiet before they were thrown out. Heather handed him an apple, and he munched it while finishing his tea. She placed her hand on his shoulder, smiled, and then carried on with the raking. Only stopping to watch three long-tailed tits skitter along the hedge line and disappear into the orchard. She smiled again and gave a little chuckle.

On went Angus's helmet and ear defenders. The repeated turning over of the petrol engine, as he tried to restart the trimmers, brought sighs she saw as steam from his mouth. It wouldn't start, and he became more and more vigorous in his pulling of the starter cord. The noise of the despondent engine sounded choked as she registered that the engine was flooded and how he needed to let it rest and let the petrol evaporate within the carburettor. Her grandfather had shown her this with his chainsaw when she was a girl. She loved visiting him in his workshop and helped him cut large timbers to build his boat. *Let it rest*, she said to herself, as he pulled and pulled. *Let it rest!*

Suddenly, she saw him drop the trimmers and let out an almighty cry. He stooped over, holding his back. 'I can't move,' he shouted. 'I can't move!'

Heather rushed over. 'Are you all right?'

'No!' he cried. 'I'm sodding well not alright. It's my back.'

Heather grabbed her phone as she watched him keel over onto the lawn. Calling for an ambulance, she described what had happened, and she saw that he was in agony. 'They say they'll be here as soon as they can,' she said, panicking. Rushing to the orangery, she grabbed a blanket and an old coat and placed them over him. He winced and cried out again in pain. 'I told you I shouldn't have done the bloody hedge trimming. Why did you make me do it?'

Heather didn't answer. Instead, she dashed once more into the orangery and exited with some horticultural fleece, which she placed under his head. 'Don't move. They said not to move.'

6

WAVES

W*aves never stop, do they?* she thought. It's not as if they switch off when the sun sets and restart in the morning. They just keep going. Even on the calmest of days, there are waves. Nature's powerful heartbeat, in a way. Constantly beating against the shore in a relentless reminder that energy is life and life is ticking away with each and every wave, either violently crashing against the jagged rocks or as a silent, solitary ripple up the beach. Sitting on the harbour wall, with her legs dangling over the edge, Heather listened to the creaks of the fishing boats and the rattles of the sailboat masts as they jostled each other as floating equals, yet secretly vying for importance within the dock. The tide was in, and everyone was afloat. When the tide was out, they lay awkwardly on their sides and appeared abandoned and neglected. But when the water rose, so did they. Their masts and flags confident and ready for the next adventure, they impatiently awaited their skippers and anticipated new and exciting co-ordinates.

One thing was for sure. Looking east, the sun was about to

introduce itself to a brand-new day. The same old sun, but with a new lustre. Like it had been dipped in the egg yolk of new life and its taste, deep in honesty and rich in courage. She had those random thoughts. Meaningless in many ways, and confusing too, as she knew deep down that new life, and courage was not part of her destiny. In reality, the sun had a melancholy taste for her. Enabling her to cast shadows and hide within the darkness, while showing courteous teeth to the rays, like she was grateful!

But she was grateful. The house, the garden, the fresh, salty air. There were people living in cardboard boxes who had no choice other than to scavenge for discarded food in dustbins. Cold and wet and without the privilege of nurturing their own produce and sleeping in an oversized pocket-sprung divan.

'You might get washed away if you stay there much longer,' a voice said.

Heather lifted her eyes to see the rosy cheeks of Barry the butcher with a ribcage of meat slung over his shoulder.

'Hello Barry. I just thought I'd have a minute before I attempt the hill. Where are you going with that?'

'To the hotel. The chef likes to butcher his own.'

Heather nodded and pursed her lips.

'How are things up there? Haven't seen that husband of yours in a while. Is he still playing golf?'

'Yes, very much so.'

'It's just, we're planning a charity golf day and wondered if he might be interested in joining us. There's me, Harry from the barbers and Larry the accountant, we just need a number four?'

Heather laughed. 'Barry, Harry and Larry! Why didn't you ask Garry from the post office?'

'We did, but other than a round of crazy golf on the promenade, he wouldn't know a birdie from a bunker shot, and he has to work Saturdays.'

Heather continued laughing. 'I can pretty much rule Angus out I'm afraid. He's suffering with a bad back at the moment.'

'I thought I hadn't seen him in a while.'

'He's usually so busy with work, and has time for little else. I'll let him know you asked. Oh, I nearly forgot. Did you prepare my order?'

'Yes, it's ready. It weighs a fair bit though. Do you want me to deliver it for you later this afternoon? I have to come up your way.'

'*No*! I'm fine. It will keep me fit. I need to lose a few pounds,' she said, hiding her stomach with her bag.

Barry nodded. 'Some might say you look pretty good as you are. Don't go losing any more. I'll put a few extra sausages in for you.'

Heather felt her cheeks flushing. 'That's very kind, but ... you know. Age is cruel sometimes.'

'There's many a man in this village, would be knocking at your door, given the chance Heather. I'm not talking out of school here, I'm a happily married man, but an attractive woman like you, can still turn heads.'

She turned her head to the side with a coy, Princess Diana kind of response and said nothing.

With her bag ladened with shopping, Heather worked her way up the steep cobbled road. The variety of brightly coloured houses and tiny passageways with stone steps and occasional wooden benches lifted her spirits. She passed the grocer's shop with its lush green fake-grass display and loaded with local fruit and vegetables. Past the post office, she cut through a narrow snicket and over the wooden bridge that spanned the river. A natural verdant valley, with hazel and alder, were a reminder of what the whole valley would have looked like before the village was built. *A testament of how nature could still hold on to its beauty and its dignity despite human intervention,* she thought as she stopped on the bridge and rested her elbows on the handrail. A pied wagtail hopped from rock to rock. Bobbing its tail up and down, as if it were excited by life itself. She watched as it flitted downstream and then under the bridge.

The shortcut up a steep flight of stone steps brought her back out onto the road and on to the newsagents. A small shop stuffed with books, magazines, sweets, fishing nets, inflatable pink flamingos, beach towels and everything else to make a seaside holiday the best ever. Heather loved going in there, whether she needed anything or not. But that was the ethos of the shop. Everything you want, but you really don't need! A frivolous foray of fun and, of course, a source of news! There was another reason she liked to indulge herself. Rebellion. Defiance against the weasel words of her father. 'It's all Japanese rubbish. We're not buying any of that!' he would say. No brightly coloured bucket and spade. No beach ball or kite to have fun with on their holidays. But he would always buy a newspaper for himself, and would occasionally treat her with some wine gums. But that was the extent of his generosity.

Heather picked up a gold, sparkly windmill on a stick and blew hard to make the sail spin. It made her smile as she spun around herself, becoming dizzy. She steadied herself against the newspaper rack and carefully placed the windmill back in with the others before focussing her eyes on the papers and choosing the *Financial Times* for Angus.

'The windmills are for children of *all* ages.' Mr Biernacki said with a raised eyebrow.

'I was just looking,' Heather replied, handing him the newspaper.

'We are all the children we once were, just with the weight of an unnecessary burden on our shoulders,' he said calmly.

'What do you mean?'

'I mean, we shouldn't lose sight of who we are deep inside, whether we are adults or children. A windmill is free to spin even if it is unable to run. I lost myself following my wife's death some years ago. Couldn't imagine getting back on my feet, but knowing deep down that one day you will have the energy to turn the sails again, is enough to make it happen.'

Heather smiled politely, paid him for the newspaper and thanked him for his wisdom. *He had a kind face, Mr Biernacki and a calm voice,* she thought as she exited the door onto the street. She looked up the steep hill and took a deep breath. It was an abrupt climb back to the house and a bittersweet one at that. Not one to relish, but good for mind, body and soul, once conquered. She put the paper in the bag with the meat and grabbed the handle tightly, setting off up the hill. Then, to her own amazement, she turned around and walked back into the shop. She picked up the windmill and placed the money on the counter. 'It will go nicely in my vegetable patch. Thank you, Mr Biernacki.' With that, she walked with purpose to the door while blowing vigorously and watching the sail spin joyfully.

Before she could get to the door, she noticed a card on the 'Local Businesses' board. This one slightly bigger than all the other cards advertising laundry, plumbing, baby sitting and taxi services. This one had the silhouette of a cedar tree and a lawn mower and the words. 'No job too large or too small' in bold lettering. 'Will's Garden Manetenence'. She smiled at the spelling mistake. *A gardener didn't need to be able to spell,* she thought. He needed to be able to mow lawns and rake like the devil. The bottom line convinced her to take the phone number. 'Honest, local and reliable. I'll be there when you need me. A garrentee!'

7

OVER MY DEAD BODY

'Did you get my *Financial Times*?'

'Yes, and a few extra sausages for your breakfast. How's your back?'

'Killing me. You've been a long time.'

'Barry from the butcher's asked if you wanted to play in a charity golf match. They are looking for a fourth player.'

Angus laughed. 'I think I'm a little out of their league.'

'Well, I told him you had a bad back anyway, so you're definitely out of their league.'

Heather felt him staring at the back of her head as she sorted the laundry. 'I also bumped into Mrs Drake from the tea shop, and she said that her husband's back took three months to sort itself out, and the doctor said he was carrying a bit too much weight.'

'What do doctors know? Anyway, you can tell Mrs Drake to mind her own business.'

'I also called a gardener to come around and give us a quote for finishing the hedges. I saw his card in the newsagents. He's coming to have a look at eleven o'clock.'

'Over my dead body are we having some unknown 'Handyman' sniffing around here. You can tell him not to bother.'

Heather carried on putting the laundry away in the respective drawers. 'It's too late, he's pushed another job back, and unless you can come up with a better plan for finishing the hedges, then I need some help to keep this place ship shape!'

Angus huffed and winced as his head rocked back in pain. 'Well, I want references, and I'll have the final say. And where are my goddamn painkillers?'

Heather calmly passed him the box of pills and pointed to a glass of water by the bed. 'I'll make you a sausage sandwich, and where do you want to meet him, up here?'

'I don't want him anywhere near the house, do you hear me?' He moaned.

Heather turned as she exited the door. 'We can do it all in the orangery, if you can make it down there?'

~

Feeling the compost between her fingers was heaven. Second-best to sand between her toes, but it lifted her spirits and gave her something to focus her mind. She distributed it into seed trays and then planted onion seeds in anticipation of the spring. One of the benches was heated through the winter. Not only did it supply perfect over-winter temperatures for the seedlings and plants but also a cosy refuge for Heather and Benny. She felt the warmth against her belly as she filled up the trays. Then, out of the corner of her eye, she spotted a silver pickup truck pull up on the drive. Quickly cleaning her hands with a cloth, she exited the orangery and noticed a tall lad in a woolly hat, blue checked lumberjack shirt, which was untucked, khaki shorts and steel toe-capped boots.

'Hello. Mrs Sinclair?' he asked as he strode boldly towards her.

'Yes. Heather. You must be Will?'

He gave a single nod. 'I've passed this house many times but never seen the garden in detail.'

'Well, it's not at its best in the winter. On that note, isn't it a bit cold for shorts?'

He looked down at his knees. 'I don't feel the cold,' he replied. 'Unlike you!'

Heather took a step back. She wasn't expecting such a retort. 'I beg your pardon?'

'If I'm not mistaken. The last time we met, you were shivering and had blood dripping from your knee.'

Heather examined his face closely. His hat was covering most of his head, and other than a few sprigs of dark hair – the penny finally dropped. 'You carried me up the steps?'

'How is your knee. It looked pretty swollen?'

'Oh, erm ... fine. It's back to normal now, thank you.' Heather felt uncomfortable at his direct questioning and slightly guilty she had not recognised him, and it made her heart beat fast and her head, light with confusion. An insecure tingle in her hands and feet, a sign she was in fight or flight mode. It was an official meeting. One of hedge trimming and garden duties, yet it seemed overly personal and compromising. She glanced up at the bedroom window and saw the bulky silhouette of Angus peering out. *The painkillers are at work!*

'I'll show you the jobs I need doing and if you could give me a quote, that would be fabulous. My husband has expressed that he would like to meet you and that you provide references.'

Will shuffled on his feet. 'I don't have anything written down, but I can give you the numbers of other clients to call.

I've been doing the Sampson's garden at the end of the road for ten years and Mrs Sampson is Costa Rican, so you can imagine how knowledgeable she is about plants and gardening.'

Heather led him out of view of the window and to the unfinished section of hedge. 'I'd appreciate it if you didn't mention our encounter at the beach. He can get a little jealous and I wouldn't want us to get off on the wrong foot,' Heather said, quietly.

Will looked back towards the house. 'Is he dangerous?' he asked.

Heather paused and also looked back at the house. 'No. He's a judge and often wary of strangers.'

'Well, I've seen everything in this job. Neighbourly disputes often manifest themselves in the trees on the boundary and I've witnessed quite a few punch ups while I've been harnessed within the very trees themselves.'

'You haven't?'

'I have. But generally, my customers are lovely and care for plants and nature.'

'So would you say *you* care for plants and nature?' she asked.

Will's smile reached from ear to ear and showed off his white teeth. 'Absolutely. It's in my veins. I think it's the grounded energy or the wonder of the new shoots and how incredible nature is. I don't know. I just love all things wild.'

Heather's smile reached her ears too. 'Well, you'll fit in well here then. I'll show you what I need doing to the hedge, and if you do a good job, there might be a few extra things too, at least until my husband's back issue is resolved.'

They strolled around the garden, and Will reassured Heather that finishing the hedge was a straightforward job and wouldn't take more than half a day. They agreed to a few other tasks, including the picking up of all the debris dropped from the cedar onto the lawn so that the crocuses in the spring would be unhindered in their glorious display, to make it a full day.

'The whole lawn is covered in a carpet of crocuses every year,' Heather explained. It's probably my favourite feature of the garden and such an inspiring sight after the winter gloom.'

'I bet,' Will replied with open eyes. 'I love the sea of purple and yellow.'

'Me too,' Heather said.

'Just remember to let the foliage dieback completely before mowing and they should look after themselves,' Will said and then spotted something out of the corner of his eye. 'It's an elm. Rare, very rare. Did you know you had it in the garden?' He pointed to the slender tree on the edge of the wooded area.

'No. I had no idea. I thought it was a hazel.'

He picked a leaf that was still hanging on and showed it to her on his palm. 'It's like a hazel, but the lobes of the leaf as it joins the stem are uneven. Asymmetrical, I think they call it, and another way to tell is the roughness of the underside.' He turned it over, and they both ran their fingers over the ridges.

'Wow, that's such a surprise,' Heather said, marvelling at the tree.

'Well, there aren't many left in the UK. Dutch elm disease has almost wiped them out, but there are some survivors, especially along the coast.'

They walked towards the house, up the steps by the pond and to the kitchen door. 'I'd like you to meet my husband. Please let him know about the references and I'm sure he'll be fine.'

Will nodded obligingly.

Angus was sitting at the kitchen table.

'Mr Sinclair?' Will introduced himself politely.

'You up to the job young lad?' Angus blurted out.

'Absolutely. Just a half day and we've discussed a few extras to round it up to a full one.'

'Don't go ripping us off.'

'I won't sir. I haven't been in business this long by ripping people off.'

'Can you supply references?'

'I explained to your wife ...'

Heather cut him off. 'He will supply us with the phone numbers of other clients, including the Sampson's at Southview House.'

Angus murmured under his breath. 'So, nothing in writing then?'

Will responded quickly. 'I'm not so good with writing and paperwork, but I am good with my hands.'

'I'm sure you'll do a fabulous job,' Heather replied.

'I'll be doing a police check. Any issues with that?

'No sir.'

'What's your surname?' Angus quizzed as he tested a ball-point pen on the edge of his newspaper.

'Calvert, sir. Will Calvert.'

'Mmm. Calvert. Norse heritage, I believe. So, you're from these parts?'

'Yes, my grandfather and his father before that as far as I'm aware.'

'The name sounds familiar. You ever been to prison?' Angus asked with a stern face.

'Never!'

'That's enough now Angus,' Heather said. 'I know Will has other appointments. You'll supply us with a quote I assume?'

Will nodded. 'I'll drop you an email, and you can decide if

you want to book me. I'll include the phone numbers and my liability insurance details as well.'

'We look forward to it,' Heather said, ushering him out of the door before Angus could interrogate him any further. She walked with him to his truck and thanked him for his time.

'I'm so sorry my husband was like that. As I said, he's just protective about who comes into the property. You understand?'

Will clambered into the driver's seat and wound down the window. 'Absolutely. It's not a problem. I'll be in touch.'

Heather came up to the window. 'Did you see any seals? You know, the other day?'

Will started the engine. 'Yes, there were two down by the archway into the cove.'

Heather put her hand on the door. 'I saw those too. I think they're a couple.'

'Ah, yes, they looked like they had each other's backs.' Will said, smiling.

Heather sighed. 'Thank you. I appreciated what you did. It was very kind.'

'You're welcome and thank you for the opportunity to work with you in such a lovely garden. Well, fingers crossed.'

8

THE WALRUS

'I'm not having some young lad using my tools.'

'He brings his own. That's the point. He makes light work of it. Takes the strain out of your back. Both our backs!' Heather replied.

'I'll be back on my feet again soon.'

'Backs take time Angus. I think you'll be off work another few weeks. To be honest I was surprised to see you downstairs. How did you manage?'

Angus gesticulated with a nod to the crystal-cut whisky glass and empty painkiller box.

'We need to get you fit. In fact, we need to look after both our backs and our health. We're not getting any younger. I'm putting us on a healthy eating programme. No more sausages and the booze won't be helping,' she said, taking his whisky glass.

He grabbed her arm. 'I'll decide whether I have a drink or not. You make it look like I have some sort of problem.'

Heather prized her forearm from his grip, only to see him

wince and then hold his back. 'Let's get you back upstairs, and I'll bring you a cup of tea.'

He looked like a three-year-old shuffling upstairs on his bottom. Heather's patience wore thin as she helped move each of his feet after every shuffle. 'I'm blaming you. You know that,' he snapped.

Heather gritted her teeth and smiled. 'Remember, the doctor said not to move at all. Let's get you back in bed so you can rest until it improves.'

'You and your damn hedge.'

'It's our hedge and the envy of the village. As you said, we have a responsibility to this house and its history.' Her voice wavered as she once again lifted his foot and placed it on the next step.

'Time off work won't look good at senior level. Your hedge might cost me my knighthood.'

Heather bit her lip and held back a tear. 'I'll do everything I can, to get you what you deserve, and all I ask, is that I get some help in the garden. It means a lot me.'

'Garden, garden, garden. It's all you ever think about. You're obsessed with that goddamn garden.'

His words jabbed at her, like a knife, but she remained calm as best she could. It felt like he had his grip around her heart and was twisting it. She momentarily closed her eyes and felt her teeth almost biting through her lip. 'Because I care for everything here. The garden, the plants, the house and you. It's my life.'

A hug is what she needed. She craved a hug to make it all okay. But she couldn't ask. He never hugged her, and even when she cried, he mocked her. There was no point in crying or reacting. It didn't do any good, just made her feel worse.

'With you around more, I need to get more supplies. Can I

have some additional money?' she asked. Her toes were scrunched up tight in her shoes. The pain of scrunching them so tight, the only thing stopping her tears.

He looked at her and made her wait for his answer. The disdain in his eyes made him look ugly, but she could see that he relished making her wait.

'There's some cash in my office drawer. A hundred pounds.'

'Thanks. I'll bring you tea and I'll head into the village,' she said, trying to retain her dignity.

His office was in the attic. Squirrelled away under the eaves and with a single window overlooking the front door and the harbour. Rammed with papers, box files and golfing trophies, the centrepiece was his desk. Solid wood with red leather inset. Heather opened the top left-hand drawer and instantly saw the roll of £20 notes. Without hesitation, she put it into her pocket, slid the drawer shut and walked over to the window. A floorboard creaked under her feet. *Must get that fixed,* she thought.

Rain droplets ran down the window. Slow at first and then gathering momentum as they joined forces and ran together. Heather looked up into the sky. Black clouds dominated and weighed heavily in the sky. Pushing down onto every living thing. Repressive and menacing. Selfishly lightening their own load by dropping miserable rain onto anything vulnerable below. Placing her hand on the glass, she brought her face up close and attempted to look through one of the droplets, which was hanging precariously. It offered a distorted view of the landscape. Magnifying it, yet blurring the edges, like she was in a weird dream. She pulled away and peered at all the rooftops below and the distant boats in the harbour, jostling each other in the wind.

Creeping down the stairs, and on passing the bedroom, she looked at him sleeping. He hadn't shaved in days and resembled a walrus stranded on a beach. His snoring caused the crystal droplets around the lampshade to jangle. Touching the wad of money in her pocket, she turned and crept out. Fastening her coat up and deploying the hood, Heather set off through the gates and strode purposefully down the road. At its steepest, the road had stone steps and a black wrought-iron handrail. Heather didn't bother using them. Instead, she walked directly down the centre of the cobbled road. Her eyes became distracted by a waving arm in front of the brightly coloured row of cottages to her left. It was Evelyn. She was the unofficial gatekeeper. Her red house was the third one in and was flanked by both yellow and blue. Resembling a sentry box in Heather's mind, nothing came in or out of the village unnoticed.

Evelyn's cries of 'You hoo' were unavoidably distracting. Heather looked over and waved back. She didn't want to talk to anyone, let alone the village gossip. 'Don't usually see you out in the rain,' Evelyn shouted.

'Just nipping into the village for provisions,' Heather replied mid-stride.

'He's keeping you busy with that bad back then?' Evelyn shouted.

'Oh yes, absolutely! Gotta dash.'

The jungle drums beat heavily in this part of the village. Barry must have mentioned it, and being the butcher, knew everyone. The gateway to the village was one thing. But things changed as you descended further. The eyes and ears of a village steeped in maritime history, but also smuggling, were ever vigilant and selectively close-knit. The nearer to the water, the narrower the snickets and the tighter the secrets. Heather headed down towards the harbour. The rain now much lighter, and the black clouds above relenting into a grey blanket of mild misery.

'How are you keeping?' The high-pitched tones of Amy Armitage met her at the corner by the grocer's shop.

'I'm good thanks,' Heather replied. 'How are you?'

'Fine, fine. Looking forward to spring and some decent weather. How are things up there in your eagle's nest?'

'Just wonderful,' Heather said, not able to ignore her ample chest and thin waist in her pink and black 'jogging' gear. 'I still can't believe we were lucky enough to find that place.'

'It certainly is a magnificent position up there,' said Amy.

'It's perfect, and the garden takes some looking after but it's my passion,'

'And what about that wonderful husband of yours? I see him occasionally on the golf course when I'm walking the dog. He always waves.'

Heather admired her curvy bottom, slender legs and pink trainers. 'I don't know what I'd do without him. He's been working on some big cases recently, but is suffering with a bad back at the moment.'

'Oh dear. Hope he's going to be alright? Let me know if I can help with a massage. I have my level three now and have set up a small business. You know, aromatherapy, hot stones and deep tissue, that kind of thing.'

Heather smiled politely. 'I'll let him know, but its bed rest for him at the moment.'

Amy put her hands against the wall and stretched her hamstrings. 'Lovely to see you Heather, let's catch up properly sometime? Anyway, gotta dash, I'm training for the East Yorkshire half marathon.'

'Well, good luck with that and ... yes, we must catch up soon!' Heather said as she inched her way down the stone cobbles. Amy Armitage was the last person she wanted to 'catch up soon' with.

On passing the grocery shop, she cast her eye over the array of root vegetables, beetroot, artichokes, celery and brightly coloured peppers. She paused, as something different caught her eye to the left. There it was. A beautiful shop frontage in white and a hand-painted name and logo above the door in sandstone pink. 'DUNE' The highly anticipated women's clothes and accessories shop. Heather paused, walked sideways for a couple of strides and then straight in through the front door. Large sun-hats, brightly coloured beach cover-ups and bikinis, sandals, stylish flip-flops and a selective couple of dress racks made her head spin. It had a summer, beach vibe, but a classy sophistication which excited her. She once again, touched the money in her pocket. She loved everything in there and instantly knew, it was her kind of shop. Made for her, in fact. Even the beach towels and the hair scrunchies were to her taste.

'Hello,' a voice said.

Heather looked around to see a tanned lady in white pedal-pushers and a Breton-style stripy top with the sleeves rolled up.

'Welcome to Dune. I'm Lesley. Have you been in before?'

'No, but you haven't been here long, have you?'

'It's my second week.' Lesley said.

'Well, congratulations. You have some lovely things in here. You obviously know my taste.' Heather laughed.

Lesley smiled, exposing her bright white teeth. 'It's my taste too and I always dreamt about having a shop with all the things I love.'

'It looks beautiful. You've done a good job of it. I wish you every success.'

'I appreciate that ...'

'Heather. Heather Sinclair. I live up on the hill.'

'No way! I love it up there, such lovely houses. There's one up there with a fabulous cedar tree.'

'That's mine. Highcrest.'

'Yes. Highcrest. I remember driving past. Looks like you have a beautiful garden?'

'It's ... idyllic. The house is beautiful and the garden ... well, it's my sanctuary, if I'm honest. You obviously know your trees.'

'Not really. I just remember we had a cedar in the garden when I was a child, that's all. It was there when we moved in.'

'Lucky you,' said Heather.

'It was a good place to live, despite my parents.'

Heather smiled one of those 'I'm happy for you, but I'm holding back my entire life behind these lips', kind of smile and lifted a purple dress from the rack. 'You're welcome to call by any time for a coffee and see the garden.'

'Thank you so much,' Lesley said, bowing her head slightly. 'That would suit you. Deep purple and auburn hair. You'd turn some heads in that for sure.' Lesley said, pointing to the changing room.

Heather couldn't resist trying it on and eventually stood, wearing the dress, in front of a full-length mirror.

'Wow!' Lesley shouted. 'I probably would have picked emerald green or black for you, but the purple, your eyes and hair together, it's such a powerful look. Here, try it with these black heels.'

Heather put on the one-inch heels and walked back to the mirror. She'd never felt as good in her entire life. The colour was stunning, but the fit of the dress was exquisite. *Made for her.* Elegant, yet fun and with a very sexy low-cut back, it effortlessly defined her figure without making her look fat or flat-chested. And to top it all, the shoes made her feel like she wanted to waltz around the shop. So, she did. Catching herself in the mirror now and again and feeling free.

Lesley stood with her arms folded and giggled while shaking her head. 'I don't think anyone could carry that dress off like you. You look like a princess.'

'How much is it?' Heather asked.

'Well, with the shoes one hundred and twenty pounds. But, as you're a new customer and I can't see anyone else in that dress to be honest, let's call it one hundred.'

Heather's heart thumped fast and strong. She could feel it in her feet and her temples. 'One hundred?'

'Yes,' Lesley said, smiling her biggest smile.

Heather returned to the changing room and examined her face in the mirror. *It was an indulgence. Could she justify it? But would Angus like it?* It was a bargain though and too good to dismiss. With the dress back on the hanger and the shoes abandoned on the floor. She took the cash from her pocket and counted it. One hundred exactly. The money for Angus's food. She looked again at the dress hanging beside her. It was perfect. It looked beautiful, and it felt exquisite to wear, and it made her feel free. Free to waltz, free to spin, free to fly.

'Is everything all right in there Heather?' Lesley's voice sounded concerned.

She'd lost track of time and hadn't realised she'd been looking at herself in the changing room for so long.

'Yes, all good. Just making up my mind about the dress.'

'Stay in there as long as you need. No pressure from me.' Lesley's voice now, sounding genuine and sweet.

Heather exited with the dress in hand and walked over to

Lesley at the till. 'Sorry I took my time. It's just I hadn't seen such a lovely dress in my entire life.'

'It suits you, Heather. You looked radiant and full of life in it.'

'Thank you. It is perfect.'

'Do you want me to wrap it for you?'

Heather's eyes dropped to the floor as her hand touched the cash in her pocket. 'I can't have it. I can't take it.' Her voice trembled with guilt.

Lesley smiled. 'If it's the money, don't worry, we can work something out. Pay in instalments, whatever suits you.'

'It's not that. It's just ... I'd rather leave it for someone who deserves it, someone who will wear it often and cherish it. Anyway, I'm not sure the hem line was for me, but thank you all the same.' She felt Lesley's eyes burrowing into her brain as she walked to the door, leaving the dress and heels behind.

Lesley opened the door and gently took her wrist. 'You're a beautiful woman, Heather. You are the person who deserves this dress, and don't let anyone else tell you otherwise. We are all worthy; don't forget that. Let me know if you want a coffee and a chat sometime.'

9

THE GARDENER

'You're paying me to do the job and no other customers follow me around with the rake.' Will told her.

It was a strange feeling. Normally, Angus flailed around with the trimmers, and she dodged his often-exuberant swings and raked and collected the aftermath. Heather had to tell herself to stop flitting around him like a guilty nightingale and go and do other things instead.

One of those things was taking Angus a cup of tea. His back was on the mend, and although he wasn't on his feet, his rate of painkiller consumption was on the wane.

'He's here.' Heather said, placing the mug on the bedside table.

'I can hear. Such an irritating noise! Does he look competent and trustworthy?' Angus asked in his gruff and very untrusting tone.

'He has all the equipment. Safety helmet and the earmuff thingies.'

'Ear defenders!'

'Yes, that's right. And he wouldn't let me do any raking.

Said he had a large bag, you know, like the ones you get gravel and sand delivered in, and that he would collect it all at the end and put it in the back of his pickup truck.'

Angus pursed his lips and shrugged. 'Whatever works best for him. Make sure he does a full day, and that he doesn't go away with any 'extra' tools.' He growled.

'I don't think he's that kind of man. You called all of his references, didn't you?'

'Mmm,' he said, taking his tea. 'But they're probably the type that don't keep an eye on him.'

Heather huffed. 'You're always so suspicious. He wouldn't have worked for them for ten years if he'd stolen from them. There are some good people in this world you know!'

He didn't reply.

Heather made tea for Will and took it to him. He was finishing the last part of the hedge, and she made sure she caught his eye as she approached. With a few upward strokes of the trimmers and a finishing run along the top edge, he turned off the machine and removed his helmet.

'That was quick,' she said, handing him the tea.

'When you do it day in day out, it becomes second nature. Thanks for the tea.'

'I didn't know if you brought a flask or not?'

'Some days, if I remember, but a fresh brew is always welcome. Anyway, I'll have this raked up in no time and I can move on to the other jobs.'

'Well thank you for agreeing to do the work, it's a great help.'

Will guzzled his tea. 'To be honest, I wasn't sure if your husband wanted me to come. I wasn't expecting the call.'

'The truth is, he's beyond this kind of work now, but too

stubborn to admit it. We need someone like you to help with the heavier tasks.'

'Well, I don't want to step on anyone else's toes.'

Heather sipped her tea. 'Well, let's see how we get on. Do you think you'll be able to prune the apple and plum trees today?'

'Of course,' he said. 'But you'll have to show me again, how many there are, I've forgotten.'

'There are three of each which need pruning. I'll leave the others for now. I am quite fussy about the pruning though.'

Will laughed. 'Like all my other customers. How about I show you what I know, and you see if it fits with what you want?'

'Perfect!' Heather replied.

He just got on with it. No fuss, no drama and tidy. Very tidy. The raking, which would have taken her half a day, took him half an hour, and the lawn was left in an immaculate state. Heather had plenty to get on with in the orangery. Seedlings to prick out and general cleaning and maintenance, but she kept the tea flowing. A couple of times she saw Angus at the bedroom window with his hands on his hips, but the last time she took him tea, he was fast asleep. Benny adopted the same plan and accompanied her in the orangery for most of the day. She was just flicking through a seed catalogue when Will appeared at the door. Heather leapt into action in an attempt to stop him before he could enter. As she stood, her pendant tore from around her neck. It had hooked itself around a nail in the wooden racking. 'Ouch!' Heather cried as she heard it hit the floor.

'Yes!' she said in a panic. No one entered her safe place. It was the law and even applied to Angus, unless personally invited.

'The pruning is done. I wanted to know if there was anything else down there before I drag all the cuttings to the truck?' He spotted Benny curled up on his cushion and took a step through the door to take a closer look.

'*No!*' she said, blocking his entry with her entire body. Will took a couple of steps backward and looked bemused.

'I mean, no, there are no more jobs down there.' She took a step forward, making him retreat even further. It was important to her that her sanctuary remained sacrosanct. Benny, was an honourable guest, but that was it.

'No problem. I'll tidy up in the orchard and I seem to remember we talked about clearing debris from the main lawn, ready for the crocuses?'

'That would be amazing if you would, and then that's just about everything.'

Will turned, but Heather interjected. 'Apologies if I was a little rude?'

'Rude? When?' he asked.

'Just now ... it's just ...'

Will cut her off. 'I understand. It's your space. You have it just the way you want it, without a stranger intruding. I'm exactly the same at my workshop where I'm building my boat.'

'You're building a boat?'

'Well, kind of. I inherited my grandfather's boat and I'm doing the repairs to get it seaworthy again. It had been neglected for many years and much of the hull was rotten and it needs a brand-new mast.'

'Sounds like a project? So, you have a workshop?'

'Yes. I rent a space by the harbour. I have it set out just the way I like it and can lay my hand on any tool at any time. I don't want anyone coming in there and 'tidying' it up, so I know exactly what you mean.' He laughed.

Heather smiled. 'Thank you Will. I appreciate that.'

She didn't watch him return to the orchard. Instead, searched on the floor for her pendant. It was partially wedged between the table leg and the watering can. She picked it up and instantly noticed that not only was the chain broken, but the mount that held the dove within the circle had detached too. Soldering and a new chain were needed from what she could see, and although she would miss its protection around her neck, it looked salvageable. At least, she hoped so.

Will left the orchard tidy, and she couldn't help but marvel at him lugging the giant bag of cuttings on his back as he took them to his truck. *They'd done the right thing, getting help*, she thought, and then pondered whether it might be useful to employ him for the spring and summer jobs too?

He'd only been raking the lawn a minute or two, when he came up to the glass of the orangery and gained her attention with a wave. 'The crocuses are just coming up. I can rake lightly so we don't damage any, but just wanted to run it by you before I go any further,' he said through the glass.

Heather gave him the thumbs up and then sat back watching him get back to the raking. *How polite of him and thoughtful*, she thought. He'd never stopped all day, other than to have a cuppa or check something with her, and he made such light work of it all. Impressive to say the least, but something he said kept replaying in her mind. 'So, we don't damage any!' he said. *'We don't damage any.'* Holding that thought, she took a spare rake from the tool store and joined him on the lawn and began raking.

Will smiled at her and gave a nod of approval, and she smiled back. No words exchanged, just teamwork happening, and she felt a sense of satisfaction fill her mind, which made her rake with vigour.

It was almost dark when they'd finished. The lawn looked pristine, and not a single crocus had been harmed. Heather took him to the house, where Angus met them at the door.

'Hope you haven't been slacking?' He growled condescendingly.

'He's done a fabulous job, and barely stopped for a cuppa,' Heather replied.

'Do you have an invoice?' Angus asked.

'No sir. I don't usually do invoices. Everyone else just pays me cash.'

'Cash! That sounds dodgy to me. I like to see a written invoice before I part with any money.' Angus persisted.

Heather barged in front of him. 'He's done everything we asked for, and more. I think we can pay him now, Angus.'

'What's your full name again lad?'

'Will Calvert, sir.'

'Mmm. Calvert. I'm sure that name rings a bell. Are you sure you have a clean slate?'

'I do sir,' Will replied.

Angus looked down at him. 'Fortunately, I have some cash, and seeing as it's a one-off, you can write me a receipt now and I'll pay the full amount.'

Heather didn't hesitate in running into the kitchen and grabbing a sheet of paper and a pen. She wanted him to be paid and save any further embarrassment for the poor man.

Will took the pen in his hand and stared at the paper.

'It's Mr and Mrs Sinclair.' Angus said, pushing him to get on with it.

Heather could see that his hand was shaking holding the pen. 'That's S, I, N, Sinclair, No E,' she said, knowing that most people were unsure of the Scottish spelling.

Will wiped his brow with the back of his hand and hesitated again.

Angus looked stern and, despite his back, rose up on his toes. 'What's up lad, you totting up the extras?'

Heather noticed the beads of sweat on Will's forehead and his hand shaking uncontrollably.

'No receipt, no pay!' Angus insisted. 'Don't you want to get your money?'

Will dropped the pen onto the paper and straightened his back. 'Sorry sir. I struggle to read and write!'

10

A FAILURE

The smell of change was subtle yet thrilling. Green-tipped optimism turned into blossoming glory as the snowdrops and crocuses poked their heads further into the chilly air. *How did they know spring was coming? How did they know when it was their time to shine?* Heather pondered how mystifying nature was. How such delicate flowers had the energy and foresight to emerge at this time and rise up into the optimistic sunshine. The ground looked frozen and impenetrable, with pockets of ice and a hard frost in the shade on the lawn. She sat on the edge of the stone trough on the fringe of the lawn and said hello to each green flower protruding through the grass. Her denim dungarees gave little barrier to the coldness of the stone, as she poked the frozen water with her finger and marvelled at the array of tiny bubbles trapped within its solid state. A stark reminder that winter still had a firm grip and the longer, warmer days of summer were held within the tight buds of the trees, as if trapped against their will and only able to flourish when time allowed.

She finished welcoming each crocus and took a deep

breath. It was her birthday. Her forty-sixth. Nothing special. No milestone, but edging closer to the big five O. They'd been to Scotland for her fortieth. A golf and spa hotel in the highlands, surrounded by wild nature, Caledonian pine forest and hillsides of her namesake, into which she'd immersed herself fully. Despite the cold conditions, Angus managed to play golf, and Heather read. She couldn't remember how many books, but at least five. It was a pampering birthday more than anything, and Angus treated her to facials, aromatherapy massages and even a colonic irrigation. Subsequent years had faded into insignificance, but today was different. She was cooking a meal, and he had said that he had a special surprise. He was capable of surprising her. In their early days, he swooned and courted her as if she were a princess. Lavish gifts and things she didn't really need, but which were flattering and expensive. A river cruise dinner, trips to the theatre and even dancing into the night. He had been fitter then. They both were, but he liked to show off by spinning her around the dance floor and ordering obscene amounts of cocktails.

It was all planned for his return from work. Figs with goat's cheese, drizzled with heather honey. *A nice touch,* she thought. Seared duck breast with myrtles and cassis accompanied with sugar snap peas, tender-stem broccoli and dauphinoise potatoes. To top it all, her absolute favourite pudding. It always was and always would be – Manchester tart. A homemade, blind-baked pastry base, jam, spread across the bottom, sliced banana, all with set custard and sprinkled with desiccated coconut. All her favourites in one sitting. The Manchester tart was made and, in the fridge, so all that was left to do was the preparation of the starter and main. Angus was due home from work at 6.30pm, and she had dinner planned for 7.30pm.

Enough time for him to shower, change and then her final preparations.

Her bottom ached with the numbing cold from the stone, but she lingered to ponder what she was going to wear. *A black dress perhaps?* The one she had bought a couple of years ago and never worn. Part of her 'virtual' wardrobe. Items that were eagerly awaiting the light of day but were frustratingly kept in the dark. She liked that dress. It had two long ties, which wrapped around her waist and then fastened at the back in a bow. Discrete but elegant floral embroidery finished off the neckline, and she could wear thick tights and her low heels to give a sense of glamour, but enable her to move around the kitchen without too much trouble.

The postman caught her attention as his red van pulled up by the gate. He'd disappeared by the time she got to the box, which was integral to the gate pillar. Two letters. Both addressed to her, one with beautiful old-fashioned handwriting and postmarked Oban, and the other without a stamp and just her name.

Auntie Sheila. They were overdue for a visit, and a pang of guilt made Heather close her eyes and remember her tight hugs and salty porridge. She would mention it to Angus and plan a trip soon. Sheila was her only surviving relative. Her mum's sister and a true Scotswoman. Hands like shovels and a heart softer than the inside of a deep-fried Mars bar. She was a strong, capable woman. Lost her husband out at sea in a fishing accident and, after a brief spell as a nun, set up a donkey sanctuary on the west coast. Angus didn't like her. Said she was a bitter man-hating witch, but she wasn't the only one to be branded with the title.

She ran her finger over her name on the second envelope. Heather Sinclair, it said printed in capitals. Opening it, she found a hand-painted card of the bay, surrounded by the white chalk cliffs and the archway into the cove. The steps down to the beach bordered by the pinky-red of bloody cranesbill, purple viper's bugloss and grass fronds blowing in the wind. 'Happy Birthday from Will' the card read. Succinct and to the point, he'd obviously asked someone to write it, but she could tell he had painted the picture as there was a 'W' in the corner.

Will's card was placed on her bench in the orangery, and Aunt Sheila's card, took pride of place, on the mantelpiece in the sitting room. Angus would have left it to the last minute for sure and would bring his on his return, no doubt. *Why change a habit of a lifetime?* she thought as she cut noggins of goat's cheese ready for stuffing into the figs.

Heather sang to herself as she busied herself in the kitchen. No particular song, just making it up as she went along. 'Honey in the hive, you make me come alive. Figs on the tree, will you marry me, do da da deee.' She wasn't even thinking about the words; they just came out, and she enjoyed the skittish freedom of letting her subconscious write the song. Myrtles and cassis into a casserole with five-spice, cinnamon and herbs. She loved the depth of the sweet, savoury taste and the fatty duck breast set against the garlic, creamy sauce of the potatoes. Her heart beat faster, and her singing became louder as she conjured up the image of the dinner table with candles and bulbous glasses filled with Argentinian Malbec.

Buzz, buzz, the gate intercom alerted her, and she downed her tools and rushed to the gate. 'Flowers, for me! Who would buy me flowers?' She gasped.

'There's a card inside,' the lady said and then jumped in her little van and sped off. Heather took the flowers inside and undid the wrapping. White lilies offset with eucalyptus and blue-green thistle heads. They were beautiful and just to her taste. The card read. 'Happy birthday, Heather. Wishing you a fabulous day. Look forward to seeing you soon. Lesley. 'Dune' Fashion Shop.'

It was such a kind thought. She'd only been in there once and hadn't bought anything, and there she was sending flowers. She turned the card over. 'PS. Here's a 15%-off voucher for your next visit.'

That was kind too, but she didn't deserve it. She put the voucher with the card, placed the flowers in a cut-glass vase and displayed them as a centrepiece on the table.

The overcast day did nothing to lift the temperature, so Heather headed to the orangery. Opening the door brought life into her face, and before she knew it, Benny raced from some hiding place within the garden and wove himself around her legs. She smiled. 'Happy birthday Mum,' she said in her cat voice. 'Thank you, Benny,' she replied. 'How thoughtful of you. You're not just interested in mice, sleeping and mackerel morsels after all!' She giggled to herself and stroked the top of his head, before he headed for his cushion.

Sitting for a moment at her bench, her hand involuntarily went to toy with her pendant. It was at that moment, if she were a smoker, she would automatically light up, or a drinker, instinctively pour a secret tipple or, some other type book in for the next tattoo. She wasn't that daring or rebellious to want any of that, but playing with her dove pendant and feeling the solitary diamond cut into her callused finger, brought about peace, security and a familiarity she craved when she spent time in her own mind. A strong wave of anxiety filled the veins in her neck and chest, like vinegar replacing her blood. She was missing her pendant, but remembered that it was due back from repair that evening. Angus had promised he would collect it from the jeweller and bring it home with him. That would be the best birthday present ever, as it was inherited from her grandmother and had become her only real source of strength. 'It will bring you peace, and when you need it most, you can rub the diamond and I'll be there with you, for courage and for hope.' Her grandmother would say.

Not having it around her neck felt weird and made her feel vulnerable. She hadn't realised how important it was as a shield against anything threatening, but also as an intrinsic part of her being, and almost the DNA of her grandmother on a silver chain. Her hand felt her neck and collarbone. The lack of a pendant enabled her to explore elsewhere, and she looked down at her bat-wing arms. It was shocking to see the body of an older woman before her. Not the twenty-year-old in her mind but a woman on the wrong side of forty-five. He used to tell her she was attractive and sexy, but not for at least ten years. She stood and searched for her figure's reflection in the glass. People told her she was the perfect shape, and some even said a little too thin. But she felt saggy and like she could always lose some more. Untying her hair from her ponytail, she zhuzhed her red hair on top of her head and let some of it fall down at the sides while posing like a catwalk model and looking at herself in the reflection in the glass. *Shall make an effort tonight*, she thought. A special effort. For her birthday. Bring back some of her youth. Surprise Angus. Not with thick wool tights, but stockings, high heels and the attitude of a red-haired vixen.

After all, Angus always said that she could do better as a wife, and with the striving came happiness. She had to believe him. He was older and wiser in many ways. Dealing with the world at such a high level, he had a better understanding of it, and she knew he had her best interests at heart. Well, at least that's what he told her. The black dress it would be, as a thank you for sorting out her pendant, but also hopefully to rekindle some passion.

Back in the house, she prepared the potatoes and set the table in the dining room with a flame-red tablecloth she'd never used before, but found in the bottom drawer of the sideboard. White napkins, silver cutlery and rose-wood candles. It was her birthday, after all, she kept reminding herself, and they were going to enjoy it. She added sprigs of dried lavender into a small glass vase and then headed upstairs for some serious pampering.

A bath would not only warm her up and clean away any hint of greenhouse, but allow for a bit of 'me' time and some substantial hair management in all departments. Lavender and bergamot bubble bath made her feel calm and added an element of luxury as she lowered herself in. A bath in the afternoon felt not only decadent, but downright naughty, and Heather loved it. Immersing her entire body in the water made her toes and hands tingle. Under went her head, and her shoulder-length auburn hair followed suit. This was a top to toe operation with conditioner and the works.

Eventually, the bubbles began to subside, and Heather enjoyed part-drying her hair. Working the soft towel into her thick locks and massaging her scalp. The hairdryer would do the rest, she thought, but this was the next best thing to someone coming and giving her an Indian head massage. She lay half submerged and contemplated her shoe choice. There were options, and, given the black dress decision, plenty of them. She rarely wore her three-inch heels. She used to wear them all the time and enjoyed the attention from Angus, and others sometimes. Black were the most obvious choice. Red, were too garish. It just wasn't that kind of evening. The white pair were weddings only really, but the gold ones had been her favourites for a long time and they were open toe, so added a fun element without saying total slut. Gold it would be, with neutral stockings and the beautiful black dress. Her heartbeat quickened as she envisaged the outfit in her mind, and then pulled the plug, letting the water drain from around her.

She hadn't allowed herself this much pamper time in a long while, and it felt good. Time to indulge in herself, use the copious amounts of creams and fragrances which usually stood on the bathroom shelf awaiting liberation. It was definitely something she wanted to build into her life moving forward, and she hoped Angus would respond favourably. It was all part of being a good wife, all part of being the best form of herself and showing that not only did she care about him, but herself too. There were things to heal between them. Some of them were big things, but she knew she was determined to make it work.

A scream from outside made her wrap the towel around her and dart over to the window. A woman and two toddlers walked in front of the gates. They were jumping up and down on a frozen puddle in their tiny, bright yellow Wellington boots and screaming with joy. Heather stared at them. Their miniature coats and bobble hats looked warm and cosy, and their unity together, jumping hand in hand, made Heather's knees shake. Her legs felt heavy, as if all her blood had drained into her feet, leaving her lightheaded and dizzy. They were the cutest things she'd ever seen. Bundles of bundled-up joy and without a care in the world. But the pain inside Heather's heart was unbearable as she wrapped her arms around herself and endured the agony as she focused in on their happy little faces.

She would never be a good wife. She was unable to do what a wife should do. Bear offspring. Provide the next generation, the heir to the family name and the legacy. A failure and a letdown. She knew that. There was no getting around it. The proof was there, and Angus was disappointed. Naturally. He was a man of principles and pride, and he chose her to give him a family he could be proud of. Instead, she once again fell short of the expectations. Her mother's face, once again, filled her mind humiliating her in front of her friends when she failed her exams. It wasn't that she didn't have the knowledge or understanding to pass; it was the pressure to succeed, while being told she was never good enough.

She was crippled by failure and a total letdown.

11

PENDANT

Naked in the mirror, her stomach looked odd. Fat, but unused and empty. Heather rubbed it gently with her hand. No cellulite or stretch marks, just a boring and barren shell. In reality, she was ugly. No real shape, no child-bearing hips or ample breasts, just empty skin and bone. Unlovable and useless. Redundant and becoming old. She hated her body and felt like an oversized match no one wanted to strike. A pale, dispensable, redheaded, Celtic misfit.

She entered the bathroom and scrutinised her face in the mirror. The lines and crow's feet seemed to increase tenfold overnight. Her green eyes darker than ever before and the occasional grey hair, which she plucked immediately, becoming more occasional than just a few months ago. *Was she washed up and redundant? Would she ever feel the inner peace and happiness she had always sought?* Her mother *was* right. Life was never meant to be easy, and moaning about it didn't do anyone any favours. She had to pull her socks up and get on with it. Being selfish was the quickest way to a sad, lonely and early grave! She was right about that too, despite being the most selfish woman she'd ever known. The memory of her miserable face in her coffin at the age of forty-eight, a stark reminder that life is short and that it is our duty to make it the best it can possibly be.

Contradiction after contradiction. She'd battled all her life, not feeling good enough. But this was her special day, and if she was going to defy her mother and her father, now was the time. Her black dress stared at her from its hanging place on the wardrobe door, and the gold shoes shimmered as they stood to attention on the floor.

'Come on,' she said to herself. 'What do I have to feel selfish about?' she said to Benny as he strode in and jumped on the bed. 'Look at where we live. We have everything. And it's my birthday. Did you know it was my birthday?' She quizzed Benny while picking up both his front paws and initiated a little dance. He didn't look amused, or in the slightest way impressed. He released his paws, rolled over and stretched his body out fully, in anticipation of a tummy rub. 'Well, we're going to have a party,' she said.

The heels were put to one side while she seared the duck breasts and placed the broccoli into the steamer. Thirty minutes and he would be home. The duck would go into the sauce and then be braised for a further forty minutes, and the steamer lit when they sat down for the fig starter. It was a juggling act, where perfect timing was essential, but it was all ready to roll. She would get him to open the wine, but everything else would be effortless. The smell from the lavender candles was subtle yet sublime. Removing her apron and swapping her slippers for the gold high heels, she looked down at herself and recalled the last time she had worn them. *Not recently, that was for sure.* It was his forty-second birthday. They'd been out to an Italian restaurant in Whitby. He wore a pinstripe suit, and she a gold, shimmery dress and the matching heels. He kept spanking her bottom, which she loved. They made love that night. She remembered him unzipping her dress in the hallway to reveal her new black underwear. It was thrilling. He was charming over dinner, and they kept touching knees under the table. In the hall; they kissed passionately as he lifted her feet off the floor and carried her upstairs and threw her onto the bed. He was strong then, full of intention and exciting. Her heels stayed on throughout, and they made love. It felt naughty and frivolous, yet deep and fulfilling. *Maybe the heels could have their day again.* She touched the solid-wood worktop.

With ten minutes to go, she touched up her makeup and checked the duck breasts. They smelled divine as they bubbled away in the rich, sweet sauce, which was caramelising on top. She knew he would love it, and she couldn't wait to tuck in either. She placed the wine bottle on the table and caught her reflection in the window. It was dark outside, and the shoes sparkled in the light of the candles. *If she had any redeeming feature, it was her legs*, she thought, turning her right leg on the tip of the shoe and examining her calf. *6.30pm.* He would be arriving home any minute. One final check of the duck, potatoes and lipstick and she was ready. *Now 6.40pm, where was he?* She opened the front door, but his car was nowhere to be seen. The traffic could sometimes be awful, especially if there had been a crash. Heather reduced the heat in the oven and slid the figs onto the top shelf. *Now 6.45pm.* She checked her phone – nothing. He didn't like being called or texted while he was driving, so she resisted. As the goat's cheese was beginning to melt into the baking figs, she checked the front door again – nothing.

Benny walked into the kitchen and sniffed around his

bowl, so she fed him. She knew the duck breasts would be overcooking, and the figs were becoming soft as she peered in through the oven door to see the honey bubbling on the tray. *Now 6.59pm*, she checked her phone – nothing again. *Should she be getting worried?* Taking her phone upstairs, she positioned herself in the window overlooking the drive. There was still no text or call. Defying him, she sent a text. 'Dinner is almost served. Hope you're, okay?'

There was no reply. At 7.06pm she watched the road for any sign of him. At 7.12pm she returned to the kitchen to find the figs browning a little too much and the potatoes ready to be served. Turning the oven off, Heather paced the kitchen and sent another text. 'I'm getting worried. Let me know you're, okay?'

Heather watched the long hand on the kitchen clock tick onto 7.30pm. *The dinner could still be rescued,* she thought, but was now scared something had happened to him. *A fatal car crash or driven off the road, perhaps?* She called his phone. 'Angus here. Sorry I can't answer your call, but leave a message and I'll get back to you as soon as I can.' His answering-machine message sounded upbeat and friendly. 'I'm worried Angus, please let me know you're all right!'

At 7.45pm it was calling-the-police time. They reassured her there had been no accidents on his usual route and asked whether he was a missing person. She said, not exactly and they advised her to wait a little longer and then call them back.

How long do you wait for a missing person? she pondered. *An hour and a half, two hours, four?* She couldn't go looking for him as she had no car.

At 8pm, she sat at the table. Her heels discarded and with the worry he was dead constantly moving between her heart and her brain, which made her rock back and forth. She dialled 999 and before she could press the call button, a text came through from Angus. 'Just finished work. Damn hearing overran. I'll be home by 9pm.'

Heather snivelled as she took a deep breath. Tears ran down her face, as relief filled her veins. Closing her eyes, she shook her head and instinctively went to toy with her pendant. Her naked neck, once again a reminder that she was laid bare and vulnerable.

Opening the oven door, she stared at the wizened food. All heat from inside now gone, she continued to stare. A numb stare. A stare of no consequence and a stare which – just stared. The only thing tangible was her slow heartbeat in the back of her eyes.

It could have been two minutes or an hour. But she closed the oven door and witnessed her sad face in the glass. In one turn, she took the bottle of Malbec, thrust in the corkscrew and popped the cork. Glugging the wine into her glass, she didn't hesitate in filling it almost to the brim.

Positioning herself sideways on the windowsill in the bedroom, she put her back against the recess wall and tucked her knees tight to her chest so that she was entirely within the window. The wine tasted raw. Acidic at first, then mellow and warming as she swallowed and felt it go into her aching stomach. It wasn't the first time this had happened. In fact, all of her birthdays had been ruined somehow. Either Angus completely forgetting or some other kind of drama. She sighed. This time it wasn't intentional. He had no control over the overrunning of the trial, and she knew he wouldn't have his phone in the courtroom, but nevertheless, he always managed to turn her birthday into something about him.

She waited. Guzzling the wine like a teenager. The light-headedness came without a care. A peaceful numbness! That's what it was. A void of ... nothing, except an increasingly bitter taste and blurring vision. It must have been an hour at least, when she opened her eyes and saw the headlights of his car pull up in the drive. The courtesy light, then showcasing the signing of her birthday card. She bit the inside of her cheek and pondering his mood, wondered if there would be a gift. Not that she wanted anything, but this was about thoughtfulness, not about stuff.

She was at the kitchen table when he walked in. 'Smells good,' he said, placing his briefcase on the dresser.

'It's ruined!'

He nodded silently. 'You've been drinking.'

She nodded and folded her arms.

'The trial overran,' he said, removing his jacket.

'You could have let me know somehow.'

He took the wine bottle in his hand and examined the label. 'I don't know why you're making such a big deal of it.'

A whiff of whisky took Heather by surprise. 'You've been drinking!'

'Just a quick one after we finished.'

'So, you went for a drink instead of calling me?'

'It was a murder trial. A tough one. Don't you realise, I'm protecting the world here. Do you not realise what I do for a living? You can't send someone down for life and not have to have some kind of leveller.'

Heather shook her head. 'A leveller. Is that what you call it? A High Court judge drink driving.'

He poured himself a glass of wine and took a swig. 'I wasn't over the limit.'

'Well, you're over the limit here. I had dinner ready for 7pm and I made an effort, and everything.' Her voice wavered as she held in her emotions.

'I was two hours late. It's not a crime and here you go again, turning everything into a drama.'

'It's my birthday Angus.'

'It's not a special one. Everybody has a birthday, every year. I don't get the big deal?'

'Yours is always a big deal. It's always about you Angus. It's always about you.'

'Now you're sounding paranoid. Like I'm deliberately out to get at you.'

'I know what's going on,' she replied.

'But, do you?' he said shaking his head. 'It looks like you're having one of your 'moments' again. It's the drink. Blowing everything out of proportion. You imagining everyone is out to get you. I've said it before, maybe you should consider talking to someone about it.'

'It's my birthday Angus. Does it not count for anything?'

He thrust her card towards her. 'Happy birthday. I even wished you happy birthday this morning and got you a card and you throw it back in my face! You make it sound like I don't care.'

Heather opened the card, which had a picture of a Highland cow on the front. 'Happy birthday, love Angus x,' it read.

She bit the same raw patch within her mouth. 'Thanks.'

'That's better,' he said, swigging back his wine. 'Is there anything edible to eat?'

'Yes!' Heather said, striding to the oven and opening the door. Reaching for a spatula and a plate, she chiselled the figs off the tray. They resembled baked walnuts, surrounded by a black carbonised halo. Combined with a shrunken duck breast and a spoonful of blackened potatoes, she made it into a portion worth having.

She slid it in front of him and then busied herself at the

sink. Not daring to look at him, from the corner of her eye, she noticed he'd pushed it away and was staring at her.

His eyes burrowing into the back of her head were unbearable. But she bore it anxiously. She could see her hands shaking, and her legs felt like they were about to give way. The back-of-the-head treatment was silent torture. A submission, like running away from a lion but knowing you had already lost the game. *How could you describe contempt in a stare?* Impossible, and however hard you tried, it would never stand up in a court of law. It was like the devil's resting face. Calm and collected, but with the fire burning at maximum heat, and the branding iron of ownership ready to sear her heart and burn the core of her very soul.

'Smash!' She dropped a glass, and it splintered across the floor. Quickly grabbing the dustpan from under the sink, she heard him tut.

That was it! The infernally hot branding iron was now burning its way through her self-esteem, and then three more. 'Tut, tut tut.' The sound of his wet tongue, like a gleeful snake about to inject its venom.

Fragments of glass cut into her knees as she frantically swept up the mess. Under the table, he didn't move his polished black Oxford brogues. Instead, making her search for every last piece around his legs.

Emptying the shards into the bin, she felt for her pendant. Feeling the solitary diamond dig into her skin was what she needed. It was the heart of her grandmother and her only source of strength. She missed not having it there as protection, and this was when she needed it most. Clenching her fist, she gathered everything she had inside and looked at him.

'You're becoming clumsier,' he said.

'Did you collect my pendant?' she asked while stroking her throat with her finger.

He leaned back in his chair like a cocky schoolboy. 'I've done one better than that.' His smirk made her stomach turn.

His arm reached into his jacket pocket and produced a black velvet box. Brushing the top of the lid with his finger, he raised both eyebrows and smiled. 'Don't ever say I don't love you.'

'Did they fix it?'

His smile widened as he opened the lid. 'Let's just say, I made them turn it into a pendant worth owning.'

Heather's heart stopped beating, and she felt the blood drain from her veins. Empty was not the word. Desolate, abandoned and alone sounded joyous compared to the gut-wrenching despair that consumed her entire body.

Gone was the single diamond from the dove's eye, and so was the elegant yet simple circular surround. Replacing it was a complete ring of diamonds. Big, brash and ostentatiously repulsive.

'Trying not to acknowledge his smug nodding, she picked up the pendant and placed it on her palm.

'Eighteen diamonds. One for each year of our marriage. I thought you'd like a surprise on your birthday.'

'Did they keep the original diamond,' she asked while searching for it amongst the others.

'They said it was worthless and removed it.' The dove's eye was now represented by a small ruby instead. 'It's in the box somewhere,' he said, shrugging his shoulders.

Heather lifted the felt insert and found the diamond lying on its side in the corner of the box. It looked like a wounded star. Discarded and lying on its side, and no longer able to shine its bright light.

'Do you like it?' he asked, glugging back some more wine.

Heather said nothing. The shock, too much to contemplate.

'I knew you would. There are not many people down there, have eighteen 1.5 carat diamonds to wear around their necks,' he said while pointing down towards the village below.

Heather nodded and then vomited all over him.

'You stupid, stupid bitch!' he said, wiping sick from his eyes.

12

WHITE CLIFFS

Its purpose was to protect, to oversee and warn off impending trouble but the lighthouse's position high on the cliffs made it a dangerous place to be, especially in gale-force winds. The only other person attempting to brave the horizontal rain and unrelenting wind, was a woman, bundling two soaking wet cockapoos into a car. Heather watched the door slam hard as the wind caught it and, with effortless brute strength, made the car almost lift off the ground. Heather took the narrow path in front of the lighthouse. It wove its way along the top of the sheer white cliffs. She was unprepared. No coat, no boots, just jeans and a jumper. The urge to escape the house was overwhelming. She hadn't contemplated what was ahead, just waited for Angus to depart to work and then headed down the hill, navigating only by the bright flash of the lighthouse.

In places the path had slipped into the sea. Slices of chalk cliff vanished, leaving no trace of the path, except for the jagged edge of the four-hundred-foot vertical drop onto the rocks below. Heather's head was down, and she was looking no further than her feet. The chances of walking off the edge were high, but she didn't care. You don't care when you feel useless or you stop feeling anything, when you know you are worthless. Angus was right. Of course he was. He was frustrated with her. *Not his fault, but entirely hers.* It didn't matter how hard she tried; she was never going to give him the children he wanted. He was mean sometimes, and it hurt. The bruise around her eye was sore in the biting wind, but she understood his anger. His father didn't care. Angus was never good enough in his eyes. He'd never said that, but she'd seen how he was with him before he passed away. A fully grown adult behaving like a schoolchild. Trying to please, and trying to prove himself. Searching constantly for approval and finding disappointment, the only reward.

He became angrier following his father's death, and Heather, of course, was at the forefront of his despair. But that was her job. To soften the blow and absorb his frustration. She knew that. If she couldn't be a mother, she could be a good wife. Her mother had driven that home every day of her childhood. 'The best you can hope for, is to be a good wife. Loyalty to our husbands is our greatest achievement.'

Her father beat her mother. Heather rarely saw it, but she heard the screams as a child when she was in bed of an evening. But they stayed together, and she wept as his coffin disappeared into the ground. 'Don't expect anything from life Heather. Men will let you down, they always do,' she would say.

Angus was a provider, that's for sure. The house, food and clothes and a holiday in the Trossachs every year. Although happiness was never mentioned. Gratitude and loyalty were the mantras of a marriage which lasted, and although she'd often seen her mother in pain, her words were ingrained within the inner cortex of Heather's brain.

With no horizon to be seen, Heather stared out into the grey mist. The only thing visible, the violent white water below as it crashed relentlessly onto the unforgiving rocks. An occasional black-headed gull and gannet braved the turbulent air, but most others clung to their safe perches on the rock. She watched them twist and turn, swooping and then rising fast on the updraft. *She could join them, why wouldn't she?* The jump to freedom, just one stride away. Easy to just step off the edge and liberate herself completely. Free to fly wherever she wanted and free to shed the shackles of her past. She put one foot over the edge and balanced against the fierce gusts. *Did she have the courage?* she asked herself. *But what was courage?* 'Suicide was cowardice,' her father used to tell her, and the last time was not four days before he ended his own life. He was a hypocrite and a coward. She could have saved him if she'd tried. But she kept it hidden, or just didn't bother to see. *Maybe she was the coward?*

She leaned further into the wind and raised her arms like the wings of the gannet. A gust of wind hit her face and flung her backwards into the grass. She didn't move. Just lay there, partially protected by the tall grass. The rain fell forcefully onto her body and face, which eased the swelling. She would talk to Angus. Explain her unhappiness at his recent anger and ask how she could do better. It was the only way. She would do it that evening. Brush aside the events of the previous few days and ask him outright. She'd read something somewhere that communication within a relationship was the key to success and that women should take the lead when in search of their happiness.

She removed the pendant from her pocket and examined it

closely. The simple silver circle of unity, which housed the beautiful dove in flight, and the single diamond, which represented her grandmother, had been destroyed beyond recognition. Now, the simplicity and elegance were gone and her grandmother seemed discarded. The simple ring, melted down and replaced with grotesque and ostentatious items of filthy arrogance. It repulsed her. The one thing that helped her through her struggles, and it was no longer sacred. No longer the talisman of hope and no longer wearable on her person.

13

TONED POSEIDON

Cold to her core, Heather's thumping heart drove her back to the house. Her clothes weighed heavily with the rain as it continued to run down her face. Hastily removing them at the door, she abandoned them on the steps and entered the house. A towel in the downstairs bathroom warmed her skin as she wrapped it around her, and another accommodated her soaked hair as she tied it around her head.

He was watching her. Peering through the gap in the door. Their wedding photograph visible in the living room and his beady eyes following her every move. Her heart was thumping fast. The thrill of the clifftop, defying the storm, had invigorated her. She walked towards the photograph. Her eyes fixed on his. Taking it in her hand, she moved her focus to herself. In her white dress she looked young, naive and vulnerable. And she was. He had rescued her, and she was indebted. Her life back then was about to totally change, but she knew! On that very day, she knew he wasn't the right man. He'd raised his hand once or twice while they were courting, but she put it down to the stress of the wedding. The bruise on her face skilfully hidden with makeup and her smile drawn on with gratitude.

She gripped the photo tightly in her fist, and then it happened. *Red mist, blinded by rage, a loss of control?* Whatever you want to call it, but now it was her turn. She drew back the photo and threw it against the wall. The glass shattered on impact, and the photo and frame fell to the floor with a clatter. It felt rebellious and outrageous, as the sound of the glass hitting the wooden floor made her cringe with delight. She knelt to pick up the pieces and then stopped. Standing again, she took a controlled breath and felt the bruise on her face with her fingers. Next went the photo of him in his wig and gown, deliberately hurled at the wall. This time, Heather purposefully listened for the shatter and, unsurprisingly, relished the clatter of the pieces as they fell against the hard floor. It felt dangerous. It felt lawless, and it felt liberating.

Suddenly, the doorbell rang. Heather hurried into the hall to find the front door still ajar and the figure of a man peering through.

'Mrs Sinclair? I'm so sorry. The gate was open and I'm sure we agreed 12.15pm? I can see you're taking a shower. Please forgive me.'

Peering through the narrow gap, she partly hid her face. 'Will. You surprised me. Erm ...yes. I'm sorry too, it completely slipped my mind.'

'And the blood?' Will asked, pointing to her hand.

'Oh! Hawthorn. Damn prickly blighters, aren't they?'

Will nodded and took a step back, as Heather nervously secured her towel around her. 'Why don't you take ten minutes to familiarise yourself with the garden, while I get myself dry and I'll come and find you?'

Will smiled and then offered her the clothes that were on the step.

Taking them through the gap, she closed the door and then squirmed with utter embarrassment. Walking past the sitting-room door, she paused. Looked at the photo debris on the floor and carried on walking.

'We'll pay you cash after each day and my husband has prepared a printed receipt so all you have to do is sign with your name, is that okay?'

Will nodded. 'That's absolutely fine and I'm sorry for any misunderstanding. Is everything okay with your face?'

'I walked into the shower door. I should have laid off the red wine last night,' she said, hiding it with her hand and realising she hadn't done a thorough enough job with the heavy makeup.

'Well, like I say, I hope your husband wasn't offended?'

Heather shook her head. 'He just likes everything to be by the book. As a county judge, he has to show that he's doing everything right. How much can you read?'

'Not much, to be honest. The odd word and my own name, sometimes! I ducked out of school at fifteen and set up my business.'

Heather couldn't believe what she was hearing. Everyone she knew could read and write. 'Well, it's a very brave thing to do. How long have you been doing it?'

'Sixteen years.'

'Well, if you work as hard as you did a few weeks ago, I'm sure all your customers are happy.'

'I'm grateful for the opportunity of working with you again Mrs Sinclair. Thank you.'

'Well, that's good. So, two days per week, pruning when needed, grass cutting on both days through the spring and summer and whatever else I think you could help with. Is that okay?'

'It sounds perfect. Thank you. What would you like me to do this afternoon?'

'It doesn't look like this rain will ease. Are you okay with turning over the compost heaps and maybe cleaning off some of the tools? They're going to get wet anyway.'

Will looked into the grey sky. 'I carry my waterproofs in the truck; I'll get stuck in.'

'Oh! Thanks for my birthday card by the way. That was very thoughtful.'

'I remember you mentioned it and I always think it's nice to receive a card. I had to get my friend to write it, but hope you liked the scene?'

Heather smiled.

Forking the compost and cutting the lawns were the jobs Heather hated, and Angus did too. The manual, heavy-lifting jobs and maintenance. It would give her more time to do ... other things. She handed Will the tools, and watched him disappear down to the bottom of the garden.

Listening to the rain hit the side of the orangery, she'd make him a brew in half an hour, and while the coast was clear, she turned the knob the opposite direction and entered the store. Leaving the door slightly open to let in some light, she removed the bag of seed and with all her might, slid the cabinet to one side. Checking the door again, she reached for the key, unlocked the secret panel and reached in for the plastic box. In went two twenty-pound notes and then she closed the lid.

She reached further in and touched the shoebox. Her hand slowly pulled it forward and lifted the lid. Dangling the pendant and solitary diamond, which she'd taped to the chain.

She made space by rearranging the contents. Her pristine and never-used passport was a top-secret item. Angus had never allowed them to have one. 'Why would we go abroad to filthy countries and stifling temperatures when we have our beloved Scotland?' he would say, but Heather had claimed hers without his knowledge. Just touching it made her heart race. Next to it, a brown envelope with 'Certificate' handwritten on the front. She nodded, proudly, but left it unopened. Instead, she poked her driving licence with her index finger. She didn't want to touch it with her bare hands, as beads of sweat made her forehead cold, and she shuddered while closing her eyes. Her hand continued moving items to one side and the distinct shape of a whistle made her open her eyes and focus again on the contents. She really wanted to blow it, but refrained. Instead, she swizzled the bezel on the compass and set the course due south. A bus timetable and a torn-out page from her holiday brochure of Valletta harbour in Malta completed the stash.

With the lid back in place, she embarked on closing everything up and resuming her position in the orangery and put the kettle on.

Mixed feelings swirled in her head. She hated herself for doing it. Having secrets, but Angus wouldn't understand. Going abroad for him was inconceivable, and if he knew she'd ordered her own passport, he would have gone ballistic. It was her getaway plan. There was no denying it, and on days like today, it was a comfort to know she could easily put the contents into a rucksack and walk out of the gate, simple! But that was the problem. It wasn't simple, and the secret contents were really a stupid dalliance with freedom. A joke. They would never be used; she didn't have the courage. Instead, just a weird game of secret defiance and hope, in which she was the ultimate loser.

Of course, with no money of her own, she was forced to squirrel away cash. *Every housewife must do that, surely?* she thought. It was her only tangible form of freedom, and the bonus of dealing with Will meant cash, and cash was king. He couldn't read, so an extra twenty pounds on the bill and no one needed to know. A few hundred pounds was not enough for complete freedom, but it was enough to ease her mind and allowed her to treat herself to guilty pleasures, when she was struggling to cope. It made life bearable, and that was the best she could wish for.

The rain made no sign of relenting, and the pathway was slippery when she took Will a cup of tea. He was busy digging the compost heap in waterproof trousers and no shirt. Just his bare torso. Negotiating the steps by the pond, she couldn't help but notice how effortless it was for him forking the steaming pile of garden waste. His thin waist and ribs evident as he dug deep into the compost using his muscular arms. She approached and held out the mug of tea. He stood up straight and jabbed the fork into the ground before wiping his sweaty brow with his forearm.

'You must have read my mind?' he said, taking the mug.

'It's thirsty work. You're obviously fit enough to manage?' she said, pointing at his handy work.

'Day in, day out. It keeps me fit. Especially this and the tree climbing,' he replied, thrusting his hips and pulling down with his arms as if managing a climbing rope.

Heather raised her eyebrows at his action. She could smell him. It was the same smell as when he'd carried her up the steps to the lighthouse. Masculine, musky and manual. 'I remember how strong you were when you carried me up the cliff. I was impressed.'

'I thought we had to forget about that,' he said raising an eyebrow.

Heather didn't know what to say. She could see that he was being professional, but also playing with her. Testing and looking at her for the response.

'You're doing a fine job. Thank you. When you're finished, give me a knock on the orangery door and I'll pay you.'

'Right you are,' he replied, picking up the fork with one arm, ready to get stuck in. Heather gasped and pretended not to ogle. He looked like a young and very toned green-fingered Poseidon brandishing the fork like that. Handing her his mug with the other hand, he didn't hesitate getting back to work.

Heather set off back to the orangery and couldn't help looking back one more time as he plunged the fork into the ground.

14

IMPULSE BUY

Poor old Benny! Getting the blame for knocking over the photographs. She would have to keep the sitting-room door closed from now on.

When he asked her about her pendant, she explained that she found it a little too heavy now that the new diamonds were in place and that she would save it for best. He rolled his eyes, poured himself a large whisky and then drank himself to sleep in the chair.

The following morning, the sun hitting her eyes woke Heather. The house was one of the sunrises earliest occupants and lit up the room with a pinky, orange glow. Angus was like a bear with a sore head. 'If we can't trust that damn cat in the house, it will have to live outside,' he said, staring at her. It felt like he was on to her by the way he prolonged his stare and waited for a reaction.

Heather negotiated his growls and negativity by presenting him with Will's gardening receipt and a request for his next payment and money for her hair appointment later in the morning. She didn't ask where he got the cash. That's the way he liked it, and who was she to argue? It was his way of keeping tabs, and although an inconvenience to keep asking, it meant she could spend it or 'divert' it as necessary. On this occasion, her hair was a priority as it was Angus's birthday in three days' time and, of course, there was a party organised through work. They did that. Any excuse for a drunken knees-up where the other judges and partners could let off steam and get criminally drunk. Of course, Heather was dreading it. She knew exactly what to expect, but at least his birthday was about him, and so not usually a drama.

Zeta welcomed Heather into the salon. It was a small place with two chairs and a large wall mirror with lightbulbs around like a movie-style dressing room. A fuchsia-pink sofa and floral displays in pots and hanging from the ceiling gave the place a fun, almost, tropical feel and Zeta's service was impeccable. Always a glass of fizz on entry and of course a shampoo and mini head massage before the cut.

'The colour of your hair Heather never ceases to amaze me. At first glance it looks ginger, but there are so many different colours in there. Various shades of red, some almost brown, others blonde and a few grey ones in there for wisdom,' Zeta said, massaging.

'I don't know about wisdom, more like stress,' Heather replied while she sipped her prosecco.

'A lady of leisure like you, stressed?'

'Well, a demanding husband, and, on occasion a busy social life has its moments.'

'What's this occasion?'

'Angus's birthday. A party in Leeds which, to be honest, I'm not looking forward to.'

'Are they all snobs?' Zeta asked. She didn't beat around the bush with her salon chat.

Heather laughed. 'Yes! And egos. It's a joy, trust me. They're dealing with criminals day in day out and often serious ones at that. They see the world very differently to you and I. Puts a skew on decency and honesty.'

'I'd never thought of that. Thank goodness we're hiding away in our little fishing village and where the most serious crime is painting your house pink.'

'Well, you did it.'

'Only on the inside and the front door. I'm not an organised crime unit you know!'

They laughed together. 'It's a good place here, and us women need to stick together,' Heather said, indicating the level of her preferred cut, just above her shoulders.

'On that note. I loved the carrots, leeks and other vegetables you brought me the other day. Do you have any more?'

'It will depend on what I have available and when you want them.'

'Well, I was thinking on a regular basis. You know, like a veg box and I'll pay you.'

Heather shook her head. 'You mean weekly?'

Zeta laughed. 'Yes, but not if you haven't much to spare.'

'I'm not sure? That sounds like a business and I wouldn't have a clue about that.'

'Well, let me know. It might put a little extra money in your pocket.'

A cut, blow dry and a hint of a curl gave Heather a warm feeling of femininity, and Zeta had not only worked her magic, as always, but had also instilled in Heather a little confidence. She knew that it was her job to give compliments, but she sounded genuine when talking about her hair, complexion and cheekbones. It all helped to make her feel better about herself, and that a pamper shouldn't just be for her husband's birthday, but for her own health and wellbeing. Anyway, there was something else on Heather's mind, and that was the veg box. *Could she do one every week?* she thought. There was always too much for herself, and if she were prepared to pay, then even better. Thanking Zeta, she walked with a skip in her step as she followed her nose towards the harbour. Caught off guard by a wolf-whistle behind her, she turned quickly to witness two grinning builders in a van. She scowled at them and then carried on walking with a ... well ... just ... a flutter inside her, that's all!

Sheltered from the open sea, the harbour was a welcome home for a myriad of different vessels. Rowing boats rubbed hulls with yachts, and puffin tour ribs jostled with heavyweight trawlers. There seemed to be no discrimination amongst them, and Heather loved the bright colours and the smell of an industrious port. She watched with interest; the yellow-clad fishermen loading tangles of turquoise and orange nets onto stocky, no-frills boats, which looked like they could handle themselves in any conditions, and they had needed to. Men in Breton-style blue caps scuttled around with diesel cans and crates, while skippers in more formal attire boarded with important-looking briefcases. *What a thrill to be immersed in such a spectacle of colourful vocation,* she thought. In many ways it was like a marine pantomime, which entertained every sense. The salty, fresh-catch smells combined with an orchestra of industry, and the sun, spotlighting the rippling stage and, with lobster pots, rusty ladders and tall sails, an unmistakable maritime backdrop. To top it all, the boats appeared confident in their abilities and eager to fulfil the next leading role. Heather let her senses explore every detail and was content to sit on the wall, all day, taking it all in.

She followed a swooping seagull with her eyes and watched

it perch on a weather vane above a little workshop. One of the double doors was wide open, and she could just make out Will working on his boat. She'd wondered where his workshop was when he mentioned it. And there it was, so she decided to take a closer look and set off walking along the harbour wall. The keel of a clinker-built wooden boat and piles of fresh wood shavings on the floor came into view, as well as the back of Will's head as he put all of his might into planing a long section of timber, in a T-shirt with no sleeves. She wanted to remain unnoticed, but was transfixed by his strong command of the plane and his artisanal style of woodwork, which reminded her of her grandfather. *He must work on the boat on his days off,* she thought.

She could have stayed for hours watching him work and absorbing the vibrant harbour energy, but she didn't want to be spotted and the potential of an awkward conversation about not stalking him! It was best for her to move on, so she deliberately walked behind the workshop and out of sight.

Sally caught her eye rattling a collection box outside the pub. Heather marched over and thrust £20 into her hand. 'I don't like to think there are any strays out and about going hungry,' she said.

'You're always very generous, Heather,' Sally replied.

'How was your date?' Heather asked.

'Maybe I'll pop up for coffee sometime and tell you all about it.'

'Was it that bad?'

'Can't tell you right now, but it wasn't what I expected!'

Heather thrust another £5 into her hand. 'Be careful, won't you?'

Sally nodded. 'I'll just stick with the cats I think, but then I see someone like you, happily married and it makes me envious. Sorry, I shouldn't say that.'

Heather searched in her purse and drew out another £20 note. 'No one knows exactly what's going on in people's lives. You'll find someone who loves you. Just don't lose sight of that.'

'Thanks Heather, you're such a together lady. Everything sorted in your life and generous too.'

Heather smiled courteously. 'Loneliness hurts at times, but guilt will kill you in the end. Make sure the cats get some extra treats.'

Dune was not only a beautiful shop, but unmissable in 'every' way, thought Heather. Its position on the corner by the harbour access, made it visible from everywhere. No matter where you were going, you had to pass it, notwithstanding the colourful window display. *A stroke of genius on Lesley's part,* Heather thought as she made a B-line for it.

'Hello Heather,' Lesley called from the doorway.

'Hello Lesley. It's a beautiful day.'

'Your hair looks good, have you—'

Heather cut her off. 'Yes, this morning. Just a trim.'

'It looks fabulous. Any special occasion?'

'Angus's birthday.'

'How lovely. Your purple dress is still in here, by the way. To be honest, I can't see it suiting anyone else,' Lesley said, placing the back of her hand to the side of her mouth as if telling a secret.

'Oh, no, I can't justify it Lesley. It's a wonderful dress, but—'

Lesley cut her off. 'You can always use your voucher, even if you've left it at home.'

Heather stopped, looked back and paused. 'I could just

have another look at it. If that's okay? And thank you so much for my card.'

Lesley smiled and opened her arms to welcome her into the shop.

'Just a look mind, nothing else. Angus wouldn't let me ...'

Lesley interrupted her. 'We have a strict policy of not letting men have any influence within this shop or, indeed, having any kind of authority when it comes to a lady's personal wellbeing. If you know what I mean.'

Heather smiled and paused. Lesley was such a confident woman. She could see it in her face and demeanour. The things she said were as if she didn't care about other people's opinions. No games, just straight talking, and with a calm, assured voice, which captivated Heather.

'Where do you get your confidence?' Heather asked. 'Have you always been like this?'

Lesley laughed. 'No! Far from it. Shall I put the kettle on?'

Heather nodded and rummaged among the hair scrunchies in a basket by the till.

'The truth is,' Lesley said. 'I was confident until I started school and then I was bullied. We had no money growing up and my school uniform was free from the local council. On the surface it was the same as everyone else, but there were subtle signs that gave it away. The buttons on the white blouse were yellow, not white. The shoes were clunky with a thick heel and were lace up. And don't get me started on the skirt. A-line with pleats! For heaven's sake, when everyone was in short, straight ones. I tried to make it shorter by rolling it up around my waist, but it looked awful. So, I turned to food to make me feel better.'

'You are joking?' Heather said. 'I wore that same council uniform and was ridiculed. Kids can be so cruel. I had exactly the same. Those yellow buttons were the bane of my life. My mother used to say that they were off-white, but they weren't, were they?" Heather said.

'No way! I can't believe you had the same. They were puke yellow. No hiding them. I'd binge on chocolate and sweets and then feel awful about it. I'd make myself vomit, of course, but it didn't stop me feeling bad about myself, and I put on weight.'

Heather looked her up and down. 'But you're so slim. In fact, I don't think I've ever seen anyone as beautiful as you.'

'That's very kind of you, Heather, and yes, I feel good about myself now, but it had to get worse before it got better.'

'What do you mean?' Heather asked.

'I'd seen this boy in my late teens. He was a bad boy. A rebel. I liked that. Thought he might be my ticket out of the mire, so I starved myself. Got myself that short skirt and became his trophy. I was cured. Slim, attractive and we went everywhere on his motorbike. Life had begun for me and he proposed to me at the funfair, and we were married the following year, at seventeen. It was legal then. I do hope I'm not going on too much?'

Heather shook her head. 'So what happened?'

'I found out that he'd slept with every girl under the sun, including my best friend. I was back on the treats and secret snacking and he left me for Tracy Longshaw. The tart. You know the type. Big chest, peroxide hair and the scruples of a dustbin.'

'And then, what?'

'Well, I'd lost myself in the marriage. Abandoned who I was, just to be loved by him. You probably don't understand because you are one of the lucky ones. You found a good man. A man who loves you and has a moral backbone. But I chose badly and the breakup made me ill.'

Heather choked on her tea.

'Are you okay?' Lesley asked.

'I'm fine. Just taking it all in.'

'Well, I've probably said too much. I don't want to bore you with my life history.'

'I'm interested. What happened next?'

'Well, we had two children, so I spent eighteen years bringing them up and let myself go, then one day, something clicked. In fact, I went into a dress shop and saw myself in the mirror. I didn't like what I saw, so I bought the tightest dress I could find and promised myself that one day, I would get into it.'

'Wow! That's amazing,' Heather said with wide eyes.

'I'd had enough of other people treating me like dirt, but moreover, I was treating myself like that too.'

'But how did you do it?'

'I took a good look in the mirror and told myself I was worth better. And not only that. I told myself that I'd be in that dress within one year and I'd earn enough money to own the dress shop too. So here I am.'

'You're incredible. Look at you.'

'Well thanks. It wasn't easy, but I'm glad I did it.'

'And the dress?'

'It's there on the wall,' she said, pointing behind the counter. 'It's not for sale, but a daily reminder of ... well ... you know. All of this.'

'I'm in awe Lesley. You've done so well and you look happy.'

'I am. It's just a case of flicking that switch in your brain and digging deep enough to make it happen. Anyway. Enough of me. How are you?'

Heather finished her tea. 'I ... well actually ...' Her voice and words were all over the place. Listening to Lesley made her want to tell her how she really was, but years of hiding it, prevented the words coming out. 'I'm absolutely fine. Can't grumble at all,' she said, scrunching up her toes.

'In many ways I'm envious of you up there in that beautiful house with a good man.'

Heather coughed. 'Where is the purple dress?' She blurted out, while taking to her feet.

'Are you alright? Did I say something?'

'Maybe I need to realise how lucky I am,' Heather replied.

Lesley nodded and closed her eyes. It was one of those nods that gave permission. One of acceptance and reassurance. One of knowing and of sisterhood.

'It's on the end of the rack behind you. It's not a sin to feel good about yourself.'

Heather took the dress from the rail and held it up in front of her. It looked sublime. It was the right size, shape and colour.

'It was made for you,' Lesley said with a smile.

In the changing room, the dress felt comfortable. Heather moved around the cubicle to try and see it from all angles, but the mirror was a little too close.

She pulled back the curtain and saw herself in the shop mirror and gasped.

Lesley pursed her lips and nodded slowly. 'Wow!'

Heather pirouetted on one foot and watched her body move freely. 'I'm going to take it,' she said, raising her fist to her mouth and biting her lip. 'And the shoes!'

'It will be a birthday to remember,' Lesley said, wrapping the dress in tissue paper.

'Do you mind if I don't have a bag? I don't want others to see that I've been frivolous.'

'Of course. Straight into your shoulder bag, that's fine, but remember. You are worthy, you know. It doesn't matter what anyone else thinks.'

'I know, but I shouldn't be buying it and it feels very self-indulgent.'

'It was made for you Heather. Wear it with pride. In fact, why don't you apply for the job I have here and wear it then as an advertisement?'

Heather scrunched her mouth. 'What job?'

'Have you not seen in the window. I'm looking for help, one day per week.'

'One day? In the shop?'

'Yes. I've agreed to have my grandson, so that my daughter can continue her studies. It's just a case of opening up and inspiring other ladies,' she said with a wink and a nod to the dress. 'And then adding up the takings and putting them in the safe. That's it.'

'Just one day per week?' asked Heather.

'Yes.' Lesley laughed. 'And I'd pay you cash the following week. You'd be perfect. I need someone I can trust.'

'Cash. One day per week!' Heather said to herself as she headed for the door.

'Just let me know and have a fabulous party!'

15

HAPPY BIRTHDAY

'Happy birthday!'

'Thank you beautiful,' Angus replied.

Heather's heart stopped beating for a moment, but her breathing became rapid. *Beautiful! He never called her that.* But his face looked softer somehow. His eyes showing a little compassion as he spoke. It was in him; she knew it, and as she felt her heart kick back into gear, it felt warm. 'Happy birthday Angus,' she said again while handing him a wrapped gift and card.

He opened the envelope and smiled at the hand-painted cover. A scene of him, fly-fishing and waist deep in the River Spay, she'd painted it on their last holiday. 'I remember that. Caught those two fabulous trout. They were biting that day.'

Heather smiled as she watched him read the message inside. 'To my lovely husband on your special day. Love Heather.'

'Thank you,' he said, kissing her on her cheek.

'That was a fabulous holiday, do you remember? I took the trout into the hotel kitchen and asked the chef to prepare them. They were the best-tasting trout I've ever had, and you did ... painting or sewing? I can't quite remember.'

'Pen and ink sketching with Dougal Mackenzie, the famous artist.'

'Mmm. How did I forget? Too handsome for his own good that man and an eye for more than the local scenery.'

'I learned a lot from him actually.'

'I bet you did. He didn't like me though, and I didn't like him.'

'He was vegetarian, I think. Walking in with two dead fish under your arm was a bit too much for him.'

'Not a real man then. A real man, wouldn't waste his time with vegetarianism. He looked gay anyway.'

'He'd just split from his wife.'

Angus huffed. 'Say no more. You obviously had a deep discussion.'

'You almost sound a little jealous. Would you have fought him at a duel to win me? Don't answer that, just open your present,' she said, not wanting to know the answer.

Angus huffed while unwrapping the parcel. He produced aftershave, woollen socks and a pack of handkerchiefs with his initials ASS. It was unfortunate, but a tribute to his parents, in many ways, having given him the full name of Angus Shaun Sinclair. *They must have had a sense of humour or maybe never realised, thought Heather.* She smiled to herself, and Angus rolled his eyes. 'You must have known I was running low,' he said, holding the aftershave.

Heather shrugged. 'Well seeing as you never buy it for yourself, yes. And you've been complaining about cold feet recently.'

'I must be getting old,' he said, feeling the socks with his hand.

'I know it's not much, but I have another surprise for you later. Something special,' she said, pursing her lips and pushing out a hip to the side.

Angus placed the items on the dressing table and headed to the shower. 'I'll look forward to that,' he said, smirking.

Heather entered her dressing room and laid out her outfit. Her new black shoes, purple dress and a black, cashmere cardigan. On her walk back from the village she'd worked out that the cardigan would work perfectly with the dress and, as she assembled everything, she clapped her hands and felt a tingle in her toes. She was going to his party not only as his wife but also as a confident woman. Lesley had instilled something in her. Compliments about the dress, and the story of her own confidence, made Heather hold her back straight and breathe deeper and slower. She avoided looking at herself in the mirror in her underwear. That might change everything and bring her back down to carpet level, but at least he was in a good mood. It was his special day, and she actually did feel different. *Things were looking up,* she thought.

Making sure the door was almost completely closed; she slipped on the dress and buttoned it up. A slight gap allowed her to see when he was out of the shower and so time the grand reveal. Her heart beat so fast, her calm and considered breathing went out of the window. Instead, she felt a bit giddy. Like a teenager. The thrill of a new dress and shoes was the most exciting thing that had happened recently, and she was having fun putting it all together. She remembered dressing cut-out paper dolls with various clothes on paper tabs, from her *Bunty* comic when she was a girl and loved assembling the different outfits. This was the same, but in real life, and the excitement of the finished look made her jump up and down.

She saw him exit the shower and put on the white shirt

she'd ironed for him and begin tying his tie. 'Are you ready yet?' he shouted.

'Not quite!'

Heather slipped into the heels and looked at herself in the mirror. *Wow,* she thought. She hadn't felt this good in a long, long while.

'I'm waiting,' he said and growled.

'Just finishing my hair and makeup.'

'Don't be too long or I might go off the boil.'

Off the boil? What was he talking about?

Wearing her hair down and with simple but sophisticated makeup, she took one final look at herself and smiled. She would make a thank-you card for Lesley, that's for sure.

'Are you ready?'

'As I'll ever be.'

With one very last look in the mirror, she slowly opened the door and strode into the bedroom like a confident catwalk model, flicking her hair and looking demure.

His face appeared startled. His eyes wide, but then slowly shrinking to a scowl. In contrast, her eyes immediately were drawn to his waist, and the sight of him rubbing his ... erect appendage made her teeter in her heels.

'What are you doing?'

'I thought you were going to wear the black leather bondage gear I bought you for Christmas? Not some boring old dress and a cardigan.'

Heather's heart sank to her knees and then plummeted through the floor. The leather outfit with the metal studs and whip had gone straight to the back of the wardrobe. 'We're going out with your colleagues for your birthday, not to a bondage club!'

'Shame,' he said under his breath. 'I thought you said you had a special surprise?'

'Don't I look beautiful?'

'Well, yes ... I guess so.'

'You guess so? I've made a special effort for your birthday.'

He carried on rubbing. 'Are you going to finish me off, or what?'

Heather's eyes fell with her rejected heart, deep into the ground. He may as well walk all over it. Tread her abandoned feelings into the carpet. She ran back into her dressing room, kicked off the heels, removed the dress and put on her dressing gown before slumping into the corner. 'You're a pig. An obnoxious, filthy pig and I hate you,' she shouted.

'Here we go again! You're always over reacting. Normal people don't react like this. What was I to think? You haven't worn that stuff I bought you and it cost me a fair bit too. There's nothing like being ungrateful,' he shouted.

'Ungrateful! I'm not some kind of back street whore and to spring that on me having never mentioned it. It's not fair.'

'So that's what this is. It's my birthday, and you want to steal the limelight. Can't bear to see someone else having fun on their special day. It's me, me, me, isn't it? I wouldn't expect anything less from you.'

Heather covered her ears with her hands and cried. Her tears, uncontrollable, and her sobbing made her gasp for air. She hated crying in front of him. He said it made her look like an attention seeker, but she felt humiliated. Degraded into nothing but cheap bondage meat. Not a wife. A respected and adored wife, just a receptacle for his depraved fantasies.

'Are you going to carry on with this selfish charade? Because we're going to be late!'

And that was it. The trap. Nowhere to go and no one to talk

to. She was selfish and doing it for attention, and he couldn't see that he'd done anything wrong. It felt like being held against her will in one of those car crushers. Held within the steel jaws, feeling them squeezing the very last fragments of hope and then the inevitable crushing blow from above, as the powerful and relentless steel roof bore down on its painfully slow, but certain path to crush her into oblivion.

He was a past master. An aficionado of control and he thrived on it. His smirking and inability to see anyone else's point of view, let alone feelings, made him king of his arrogant castle.

'I'm not going!'

'Oh yes you are. I'm not having one of your silly tantrums spoiling my day. And everyone will be 'talking' again.'

'What do you mean, talking?'

'They all say that you've been acting strangely lately.'

'Which people?'

'Don't question me, Heather. They're all saying it. That you really do need to seek help. It's only because they care. Like we all do.'

Heather gritted her teeth and put her hands over her ears.

'I don't want to face those people. I'm not coming. Tell them I'm ill.'

Angus opened the door, which made Heather jump. 'Don't come near me.'

'Get dressed. We're leaving in ten minutes,' he said, blocking the doorway. His drooping penis almost touching her face, she turned away into the corner and tried to control her sobbing.

'Do you want to humiliate me? Because that's what you'll do if they don't see us together. The Lord Chief Justice will be there for the first time after receiving my kidney. Can you imagine what that's going to do for my knighthood? Rubber-stamp it. That's right. His gratitude sealing the deal. If you let me down this evening, I'll never forgive you.'

'Please, Angus. Tell them I'm not well or I'm looking after a relative, anything, but save me having to face all of those people when I look like this.'

'An embarrassment. That's what you are. And ungrateful. We could have everything. It's ours for the taking. A knighthood and then the Chief's own job when he eventually pops his clogs. We could move from here, buy a castle, anything.'

'But I don't want to move from here. It's my home.'

She smelt his repulsive breath as he brought his face close. 'Well, maybe you need to think long and hard about whether you want to stay here?'

'I could do it,' she said, clamping hard with her teeth.

'Do what?'

'Leave you. I have everything ready!'

His laughing sent more of his foul-smelling breath up her nose. Sliding her back up the wall, she forced with her feet, until she was upright. 'I could, you know.'

'And where would you go?'

'Somewhere! Anywhere. I don't care.'

'You wouldn't last a day without me. You're going out of your mind. You're sick Heather. Have you not realised that?'

'I deserve better than this fake life.'

'You need to get help. You seriously need to talk to a psychiatrist, because I'm worried about you.'

Heather clenched her fist and wiped her eyes dry with the other. 'I know my own mind.'

He leaned in with his arm against the wall. 'You think you do. But you know, really, you've been losing your mind for some time. That's why I make sure you're safe. So that you don't have to work, or have the worry of paying bills.'

Heather's head began to spin. A mixture of feeling the blood draining from her head and pooling in her feet and his manipulating bombardment. The dizziness exacerbated by his dominant position over her. 'I have a job if I want it.'

'A job! What do you have to offer anyone. You have no qualifications.'

'I've been offered it. One day a week and maybe more in the holidays.'

'Where?'

Heather paused. If she told him, he'd go down there and create some kind of scene. 'A shop,' she said, pushing him away.

Angus grabbed her wrist and pushed her back against the wall. 'Leave me alone. You're hurting me,' she cried as the pain of his tight grip made her hand shake. 'I'll call the police.'

'And tell them what? That a county judge is holding you against your will. They'll laugh at you and probably refer you to a psychiatrist. Do you want that? Maybe it will be a good thing.'

Heather managed to slip from his grip and dash for her phone. He turned his head and stared at her. 'You are going to your party. I'm getting dressed and I'll make up one of the spare beds. Tell them I'm ill and bunk up with whoever will have you. Get drunk, enjoy your birthday without me and we can discuss this tomorrow, when we've both had time to calm down. Okay?'

'You selfish bitch. Don't you care what they'll think if you're not there tonight? Plus, the view of the Lord Chief Justice?'

'I do care, but not while I feel unsafe. Now leave me alone,' she said, opening up her phone.

Jogging bottoms, a fleece and her coat were enough to keep her warm as she headed out into the night. It was one of those walks that had no destination and no purpose. A detachment from what had just happened, rather than stewing in a chair, the fresh air offered Heather an escape. A numb escape, but a chance to flee his brutal negative energy and clear her lungs.

She focused on her breathing as she descended the cobbled road. Benny had followed her to the gate, but had become distracted by something scuttling in the hedgerow. She was alone. She never ventured out this late, and it felt odd. As if she were playing truant or defying her parents. The road was empty. Not a car, nor a person. The shops were all shut up for the night, and it gave the village an eerie feeling. The only sound was of the sea. Two cats startled her as they chased each other and then jumped up on the wall and hissed, with their hair standing on end. At least she wasn't the only one in the village who was on the receiving end of aggression.

The narrow snickets which, in years gone by, would have been busy with smugglers at this time of night, were desolate. Some of them, dimly lit by lanterns and others dark and unnerving. This was the hour of the cat for sure. More of them became evident as she descended further. Each one of them on guard on their territory and with confident tails high above their backs as a sign that no human should stray into their world. The sound of the sea became louder, as did the clinking of the boat masts in the harbour. Maybe the sea could offer some wisdom? It usually had something to say. Its constant force always resonated with Heather, and maybe it was the only constant and reliable thing in her life. She pondered as she walked along the top of the seawall.

Of course, Angus was right. He always was. Where would she go? How could she afford to go anywhere? What about her beloved garden and Benny? There were too many questions, but it didn't matter. There was only ever one answer. He resented her for not providing a family. It always came back to the same thing. Her useless body didn't perform as it should have. He was a proud man, with a knighthood on its way and no heir to carry forth the legacy. He was bitter as a result of her inability to bear fruit. One day a week in a clothes shop wouldn't buy food, let alone accommodation. It was a pipe dream. Delusional, in fact. Maybe she was making it all up in her head? Maybe her quest for freedom was so far-fetched that she was creating the tension between them, just so they could argue? She'd seen it on Jerremy Kyle. A woman created situations in her head, just for the attention of her husband. The lie detector proved that he wasn't actually starving her and locking her in a cage in the basement. Although she did bear the wrist injuries of handcuffs. Maybe she should talk to someone who could help?

Heather jumped down onto the harbourside and examined all the boats as she passed. *She could just take one of them,* she thought. *Who would know?* She could be far, far away by the morning and on to a new adventure and east into Forties, Fisher, Dogger or even German Bight. All easily accessible and funded by painting pictures and selling them in port.

She wandered aimlessly along the sheer wall into the sea. Her brain was tired, and all the overthinking was not even producing anything worthwhile. She eventually sat on a seat used by the fishermen. Some of the old boys, who had retired, rested here during the day, to maintain their connection with the sea and their heritage. It smelt of fish. But it wasn't repulsive. It was mixed with the fresh salty air direct from the sea and the sound of the waves crashing onto the outer wall and the jostling of the fishing boats before her, collectively giving it context and approval. In a way, it was comforting.

It allowed her to switch off her mind. There were no answers. No instant fixes and no real hope for a happy future. She was destined for a life up on the hill, albeit with a man who she didn't love, but was her saviour. Life was never meant to be easy! The words of her mother, never far from the tip of her tongue and ingrained into her being.

The ache within her belly felt raw, and tears flowed freely down her face. This was her soul crying. No sobbing or gasping for breath. No retching or audible sign at all, just her soul, giving in. Waiving the white flag of despair and emptying any courage which might be loitering without intent. In a way, it felt cleansing. Refreshing and liberating to know her true destiny and realise who she really was. A wife, a housekeeper and a gardener. Her duty and her gratitude for what she had and an appreciation of the life she had been dealt.

Seemingly by stealth alone, the moon had moved into full view. Was it waxing, or was it waning? She didn't know. It was one of those in-between moons. Neither fat nor thin, neither full nor empty. She left the seat and walked around the corner of the fish market. There was a light. A solitary light in one of the workshops and the sound of someone sanding wood. Walking a little nearer, it became evident. It was Will's workshop.

16

TURBULENT QUEEN

Heather watched him working in the light of a single bulb, which was dangling from a rafter on an extension lead. The smell of wood shavings and varnish drew her in, to observe him sawing a length of timber by hand. She could see him only from behind. His jeans riding low revealed his Calvin Klein pants, and his vest top allowed his tanned arm to rise up high with every cut. She walked forward, taking silent baby steps. It was beautiful to watch him work. Of course, it reminded her of her grandfather, but there was something enthralling about watching any artisan at work. The nostalgic smell and the rasping sound of a metal saw against the wood-grain took her straight back to her childhood and the comfort and safety of his workshop.

An intoxicating mixture of post-argument numbness, salty sea breeze, oak timber shavings, slow-drying varnish and a splash of young testosterone made her head spin.

'Mrs Sinclair!'

His voice made her jump out of her trancelike hypnosis.

'Grandfather! I mean, you remind me of my grandfather, working late in his workshop.'

'What are you doing down here so late?'

'I was taking a walk and saw the light.'

'You startled me. How long have you been there?'

'Oh, not long. I was reminiscing about the time I used to help my grandfather build his boat.'

'What was her name?' Will asked.

'*Mermaid 11*,' Heather replied.

'I like that,' he said, smiling.

'She was a small boat, but a beautiful one. Does this one have a name?'

'No. Not yet. Well. The story is, she was my grandfather's boat for many years. He used to run seal-watching trips in her and she was called *Turbulent Queen*.' He de-named her after she capsized and nearly killed him. Thankfully, no other people were on board, but he thought the name was bad luck. He had some time away for a few years, and she started to fall apart. I inherited her and found her in a farmer's field just outside Bridlington.'

'Wow, that's quite a story. And you have the privilege of restoring her and naming her whatever you like?'

'Yes. In a nutshell. I feel like I owe it to him. He was a tremendous inspiration and a misunderstood man, in many ways.'

'What do you mean?'

'It's too much to go into now, but he was convicted of a crime he didn't commit and his health suffered as a result.'

'Gosh. That sounds harsh?' Heather said taking a seat on a timber beam.

'It was all sorted in the end, and we did have some very happy years until his death.'

'I'm so glad to hear it.'

'He was a kind man. Never did anyone any harm, he was just in the wrong place at the wrong time. Anyway, at least I have good memories and this great lump of wood, I'm trying to make seaworthy.' He laughed.

'Maybe you should call her *Mistaken Identity* or *Freedom*?'

Will laughed. 'Lovely idea. I think it will just come to me naturally.'

Heather sat looking at the boat in silence while Will carried on with his sawing. It was much bigger than her grandfather's boat. This was a sailboat with enough room for ten or so people, she guessed. And there was a lot of work needed to repair the large gaping holes and rotten timbers.

'Are you alright?' Will asked, wiping his brow.

'Well ... erm ... yes. I guess so,' she replied. Her hand self-consciously went for the pendant, which was usually around her neck.

'It's just, you look a little peaky. Like you've had a shock or something?'

'I ... I ... had—' She was about to tell him everything but stopped herself. He was the gardener, and not even a friend. 'I ... had to get some air. I've had a lot to deal with recently, but I'm fine.'

She saw him look at her with unconvinced eyes. Looking back at her and slightly raising one brow. 'And I'm so glad I've been able to meet your fabulous boat. It's a privilege. It's cheered me up. Anyway, I must go now.'

Will picked up a letter. 'Would you do me a favour?'

'Yes of course.'

'Would you read me this letter?'

'What is it?'

Heather took the already-opened envelope and read his name out loud. 'Wilder Calvert?'

'I have my mother to thank for that! Wilder means untamed, wild or wild animal. I think it's because I never stopped crying as a baby.'

'I like it. It's unique. Wilder.'

Will smiled and anxiously awaited the contents of the letter.

'Dear Mr Calvert, blah blah blah,' she said. Please find enclosed your assessment results for your recent examination.' Heather stopped. 'Should I be reading this?'

Will nodded quickly. 'Please. Would you read on.'

'There are eight or nine pages of results here. Do you want me to read the summary?'

Will nodded again and sat upright on the edge of the boat with his hands under his legs.

'Mr Calvert presented as a polite individual and it was a pleasure to work with him. This assessment confirms Wilder has marked strengths in his non-verbal reasoning skills and his above average general ability indicates he is a capable individual. The assessment also reveals a profile of severe dyslexia. For Wilder, processing language and information, particularly in the written form, is a challenge. As he recognises, activities making demands on working memory, speed of working and literacy are effortful and time-consuming. Clear diagnostic features of dyslexia are seen in the underlying challenges in the speed at which he can process information. A further core characteristic of his dyslexia is seen in his difficulty with phonological processing. This is the ability to manipulate the sound structure of language which underpins the efficient development of literacy skills. In contrast, Wilder's exceptional ability to problem-solve and his determination to succeed in all aspects of the test, combined with an acute determination and motivation to realise his work goals has led to the development of a range of compensatory strategies to support him. The test results show conclusively a very high level of cognitive processing and overall intelligence, which compliment his abilities surrounding practical aptitude, visual awareness and interpersonal reasoning.'

'Is that it?'

'Other than pages of test results and graphs, yes.'

'Thanks. What does it mean?'

'Basically, that you're severely dyslexic, but also very intelligent.'

'Really?'

'Is it a shock?'

Will took a deep breath, pursed his lips and shook his head. 'Not really. But I guess it's confirmation of some things I wasn't sure about.'

'It says you're a very capable and intelligent man.'

'I haven't always felt that way. Especially at school. They told me I'd never amount to anything. Thick, lazy and stupid, which confused me. I always knew, that whatever I did I'd make a success of it though.'

Heather handed back the letter. 'Well look at this fabulous boat for one. It's a work of art and a testament to your skill.'

Will started packing away his tools. 'Thank you for ... you know ... reading that for me. I appreciate it.'

'It's my pleasure Will. You're a very skilled man. With integrity and compassion. That's a very rare thing.'

His eyes were fixed on hers. She saw they were beautiful eyes, like a tiger's, wild and untamed like his name. She felt a tingle run through her body. They had so much depth within them, and the more she tried to look away, the more they drew her in.

'Can I run you home?' he said, pointing up the hill. 'My pickup is at home, it's not far.'

'Where do you live?'

'On Smugglers Row. Behind the church.'

'I know it. Well, how about you walk me to there and then I'll be fine?'

'Are you sure? It's late.'

'Yes,' Heather said. 'I'm enjoying the evening and the walk back up will help me clear my head.'

Will locked up the workshop and they walked up past the ice cream parlour, around the back of the bookshop and into a snicket which involved them ducking their heads. 'I didn't know this existed,' Heather said, with her knees bent and head down.

'It's actually an old smugglers' ginnel. From here there are many others and even tunnels leading to the harbour. You'll be surprised where we come out.'

And sure enough, she was surprised. Will led her down another ginnel and then out through a door onto the main cobbled road. Heather looked back at the door. It resembled the front door of a house, with letter box, handle and number. There was no way she would have known if he hadn't shown her.

'Are you sure you're okay from here?' he said.

'I'm sure. As I said, the walk will do me good.'

'I'll walk with you, not a problem,' he replied.

'I'm fine ... and thank you for ...'

'For what?'

Heather felt her heart rate quicken. 'For ... you know ...' She was in danger of looking a complete fool, and felt her legs start shaking. He had no idea how lovely it was for her to spend time with him and take her mind off her home life. 'For showing me the ginnel!' She blurted out like a nervous schoolgirl.

'That's okay. Goodnight,' he said matter-of-fact.

'Yes. Goodnight.'

'Wait!' he shouted. 'It doesn't feel right letting you walk alone at this time of night.'

'I'm fine Will. I'm a grown woman.'

'Well, not tonight,' he said, moving ahead of her. 'Come on. I'll make sure you get home safe.'

Heather watched him march ahead as he made fun of his over-exaggerated marching.

'Wait,' she shouted after him.

The air was still and silent. Just the sound of the sea in the distance gave the steep, cobbled road a sense of context. Exaggerated marching turned into undeniable trudging and the steam from their panting mouths felt like it was trying to push them back down their increasingly steep ascent.

'I don't think I can make it.' Heather huffed.

'You can. It's mind over matter. Just believe you can do it.'

Her legs felt heavy, and her breathing more rapid. Suddenly she felt his hands on her back and then a surge of power as he physically pushed her up the slope. It felt exhilarating, and she giggled as he helped her. He was pushing so hard, her feet could barely keep up.

'I don't think I can make it now,' he said joking. He was messing around; she knew that. He was young and strong and more than capable, but she enjoyed his playful banter. Another surge had Heather nearly running as they reached the brow of the hill and a grassy patch on the corner of Heather's road.

Will playfully collapsed onto the grass to catch his breath, and Heather came tumbling after him.

Just the faint sound of the sea and their deep breaths in unison, were audible under the clear, dark sky. The rest of the world was silent.

'It's amazing how the old sailors used to navigate by the stars, isn't it?' Will said, pointing up into the sky.

'I wonder how they did it,' Heather said.

'They had good knowledge of the constellations and the movement of the planets. But the North Star, Polaris, was the key to sailing the world.'

'Where will you take your boat?' she asked.

'Seal watching. I want to take people to see the seals and dolphins, like my grandfather.'

'I like that very much,' she said, looking up into the vast sky.

17

MISERABLY ILL

Red roses, white roses, pink roses, white lilies, lisianthus, peonies, eucalyptus, ferns and tulips of every colour imaginable were thrust in her face.

She'd fallen asleep in the armchair in the kitchen and the smell, let alone the sight of the huge bouquet in front of her, not only woke her up, but shocked her.

'I've been a complete idiot,' Angus said, removing his jacket. 'I don't know what got into me last night. It shouldn't have happened. Oh, and I got you this. Your favourite chocolate. It's the 85% one.'

'Thanks!' Heather said adjusting her eyes to the huge bouquet.

'Do we have a vase?' Angus asked as he searched in various cupboards.

'On top of the fridge,' Heather replied.

'Do you like them?' Angus proudly asked.

'Yes! Where did you stay last night?'

Angus reached for the vase and unwrapped the flowers. 'At Helen and Michael's. Their daughter is at uni, so they said I could stay there. They send their love and were sorry you couldn't make it.'

'What did you tell them?'

'That you were miserably ill with a virus.'

'Miserably ill?'

'I wasn't going to say, we'd had a bust up and you were refusing to come to my birthday party.'

'A bust up! Is that what you call it?'

Angus presented her with the full vase. 'Look. I messed up. I know that. You mean the earth to me and I shouldn't have said what I said.'

'Go on.'

'It was Helen who pulled me into line. You know what women are like! She knew something wasn't right and she told me to make this good again. I realised I might lose you.'

'And would you be upset?'

'We've been together many years, Heather, I can't imagine life without you. Shall we have coffee?'

'But would you be upset?'

'You do everything here to keep this house running. Both Helen and Michael said, I wouldn't have got where I have if it wasn't for you.'

'So, you would be upset?'

'I couldn't do it without you and I'm trying my best to make up for last night.'

'So, you're not going to trade me in for a younger model who can bear your children?'

Angus let the water overflow from the kettle. 'I thought we agreed never to talk about that?'

'What! The fact I wasn't able to give you what you truly deserve. A son and heir?'

Angus turned off the tap and stood with the kettle in his

hand. 'Why don't we have a day in Whitby? A change of scenery, walk up to the abbey and get fish and chips?'

'Is this a new start for us Angus? I need to know you're not angry with me because I couldn't be the perfect wife.'

'I told you. I need you. We all say things we don't mean, sometimes and we can turn over a new leaf.'

'Do you truly mean that Angus? Because I'm struggling here. My mind is all over the place and I know I've fallen short, but I don't like it when you're angry with me and it makes me want to leave.'

'I only get angry because I care so much about you. Can't you see that? Most husbands wouldn't even bother to help you get better.'

'So, you think I am ill?'

'I think we should take it one step at a time. It's my job to look after you.'

Heather nodded.

'And now that we have extra help in the garden, we can enjoy some days out. Like today, if we get our act together.'

'So, you're happy for Will to continue? I've asked him to do the mowing. That's always been your job.'

'I hate doing the mowing. Such a tedious job, sat on that mower all day. I need to think about my back or I'll never become Lord Chief Justice. Anyway, we can afford to have staff. Maybe we should get a maid too?'

'I'll get dressed,' Heather said with a huff. 'We don't need a maid as long as I'm fit enough to do the jobs. But I do need to feel valued.'

'Did anyone else comment last night?' she asked.

'It looks like there might be the odd shower today, we might need coats,' Angus said, peering out of the window.

'Did you hear me?'

Angus poured the boiling water into the cafetiere. 'No! I mean, yes! Of course. Let's start afresh, take some time out and draw a line under the last few weeks.'

Heather nodded. 'I'd like that. Thank you.'

'Great. Wear something smartish. I thought we'd call in and have lunch at the new golf club up there. No harm in taking a look.'

18

BAR1

Angus waved and blew a kiss to her before getting into his car.

Their day in Whitby, had been dominated by the golf club visit, but at least they spent some time together and had fish and chips. She felt a warmth in her heart that she hadn't felt in a while. He could be attentive, and although it always had to be some kind of lavish gesture with him, on this occasion, a wave was all that Heather wanted. Benny jumped up onto the kitchen worktop. His purring almost made the china cups jangle with delight, as she stroked him and ran her hand down his back to the base of his tail, which made him roll over for his tummy to be tickled. Her previous cats had never done that, and would have ripped her arm off at the slightest hint, but Benny's loving nature, meant that he was susceptible to a little hands-on affection.

'It's a gardening day today, Benny,' she said, rubbing his tummy and laughing at the depth of his purr. 'I have seeds to sow and tomato plants to prick out and everything will need a good watering.'

She saw Will's truck enter the drive. 'And it will be lovely to have the lawns done too. Come on!' she said walking to the door.

Dressed in his T-shirt and shorts uniform, his tanned, hairy legs looked the part for a gardener. 'Good morning, Heather,' he greeted her.

'Mrs Sinclair!' she replied, glancing up at the camera above the door.

Will hesitated with his exuberant stride. Observed her serious face, then nodded and smiled.

'Are we doing the lawns today?'

'Yes please. I'll introduce you to the ride-on mower and if you can do the smaller areas with the pedestrian one, and then all the edges, too, that would be fabulous.'

'Right you are,' he replied, touching the peak of his baseball cap.

The two of them and Benny entered the garage and walked over to the bright red ride-on machine.

'Are you alright?' Will asked.

'I'm fine thank you. I have much to do myself today, so if you can just get on and do as much as you can, I'd be grateful. There's petrol over there, and you lift the deck with this lever.'

He cut her off. 'I'm familiar with how it all works.'

His abrupt response made her feel uneasy. She could see, he was looking at her as she made a fuss of Benny and collected a few other items, including a trowel from the shelf.

'I mean. Are you really alright?'

Heather turned quickly to face him, holding the trowel close to her body. 'Yes. I'm fine. I'm really fine, thank you.'

The orangery had soaked up the morning sun and was bursting to have its windows fully open. Heather rushed around to allow the outside air in, and Benny followed her.

First, the watering. The days were longer now, and the leaves on the trees were all fully out in all their verdant splendour. Spring had handed over the reins to summer, and the garden was responding with glee.

Filling her watering can, she sprinkled life onto the seedlings and all the other resident plants within the orangery. On went the radio. 'Today, we'll be talking about infidelity and are men and women really that different, when it comes to cheating on their partner.'

Suddenly the red nose of the mower appeared from behind the house, and the noise of the engine made Heather stop watering. It was the sound of summer. The lawns being cut and the anticipation of the fresh-cut smell made Heather smile. Angus always had made a big issue of the mowing. Either huffing and puffing under the bonnet or complaining that the grass was too wet or too dry! She watched Will effortlessly glide the machine around with one hand on the wheel and the other on his knee. He clearly did know what he was doing, and his confidence radiated from his relaxed, yet conscientious style.

Setting out the plastic trays in front of her, she dug her bare hands into the compost and distributed it within them. It resembled a factory production line. The two long benches, covered in trays and compost and various seeds, which she pushed into the divot formed by her finger, then covered over and watered. It was an exciting time, and the preparation and execution, an optimistic summer ritual, which she relished. Concentrating hard, she looked up only when the noise of the mower distracted her. She watched him. He had something about him, which was raw. Untainted, somehow. It was difficult to explain, but it was like he was super confident, but with a beautiful naivety at his core. Anyway, he was the gardener, and he was significantly younger than her. She was a married woman, and thinking about his muscular legs and his cheeky smile had to stop. She remembered thinking exactly the same at school, when she was crushing on Jason Baraclough. In that instance, he was three years older than her, but she recalled the same tingling feeling when he walked straight past her without even noticing her. He had that same ... thing about him. Whatever it was? Boyish, slightly naughty, confident air, but without the arrogance. Anyway, it was going to stop, because, just like Jason Baraclough, it was going nowhere and pathetic, fluttering hearts wasn't going to do anyone any good.

He disappeared once again behind the house, and she set about repotting some sweet pea seedlings and put the kettle on. Not only was she parched, but she hadn't made a drink for Will either, so it was long overdue. Before the kettle had boiled, he emerged on the mower with a bare torso on display. His T-shirt casually draped over the back of the seat, and his hairy chest on full view, was highly inappropriate. *Maybe in his own garden, but not in hers,* she thought. She decided not to look, but simply to reprimand him later. She caught his eye with a wave and placed his tea on the edge of the birdbath, so that he didn't have to come to the orangery and converse. Entering the now roasting-hot orangery, she closed the door and heard the engine of the mower cut out. Keeping her back to him, she continued repotting the seedlings and writing out the wooden plant labels.

Minutes went by and he hadn't come in or knocked, to her relief. But it was killing her. She wanted to look, but also didn't. She would have to tell him to put his shirt on and he might take offence. She pretended to drop her pen and, while picking it up, searched for him out of the corner of her eye. Thankfully, he was back over at the mower and still without a shirt. She watched him adjusting the tracking wheels on the deck and periodically gulping his tea. His thin waist and muscular shoulders were frankly not appropriate for displaying like that, and although he had a body which was ... capable, he had to be told. *Damn,* she thought. She'd crossed the line and admitted that he had a good body and was disappointed in herself. It was akin to drooling over one of her friends' sons. Maybe, she should just tell him to leave. Pay him for the following couple of days, and hire some lovely retired gentleman instead? It would be better for her health and her mind.

Oh shit! He was coming over with his empty tea mug. Thankfully, he was climbing into his T-shirt, but for the moment his head was hidden inside, she looked directly at his six-pack. She actually ogled him. *Disgusting.* Anyway, there was no time to overthink it, he was ...

'Thanks for the tea,' he said.

'It looks like hot work out there?' Heather replied, while digging her fingernail into the palm of her hand.

'It certainly is today. Especially emptying the cuttings and forking them into the compost. I hope you didn't mind me losing my shirt? Oh, and I mended a few divots with some sand I found down there.'

Heather opened her mouth, but nothing came out. all the thoughts about hiring an old war veteran to do the job and reprimanding him, just abandoned her. Like they were having nothing to do with her. 'Oh ... no ... not at all,' she replied! 'We have to keep cool on days like this.' *What a hypocrite.* It was Jason Baraclough all over again!

'That's good. I wouldn't normally, but it is a hot one. I love that green on you by the way,' he said, pointing to her dress. 'What is that, emerald green?'

Heather felt her legs buckle and her heart race. *Why the hell did he say that?*

'It's called Kelly green,' she said in the voice of her fourteen-year-old self.

'It suits you. Anyway, thanks for the tea. I'll finish off the main lawn and move on to the lower areas.'

'Move ... on ... to ... the lower areas! Yes, perfect, that would be perfect.' *Jeez, she was starting to lose the plot, and how dare he be so presumptuous?*

Slapping her hand, hard on a plastic grow bag, she was not only angry with herself, but pissed off that he'd just assumed that it was okay to parade around bare-chested and then have the barefaced cheek to compliment her on her Kelly-green outfit. It was just one of her summer gardening dresses. Nothing special, just one she hadn't had the heart to throw out yet, but it certainly wasn't one that had ever had a compliment before.

It was later in the evening that she found time to wander around the garden on her own. The air was cooler, and the sun almost disappeared behind the North Yorkshire Moors forests to the west. She knew Angus was going to be late, but expected soonish, and with Will paid and long gone, dinner was prepared and she took time to examine his work.

The lawns we immaculate, and all the cuttings, as he said, forked into the compost. He'd even sharpened the blades of the mower and had left them on the side ready for installation at his next visit.

She sat on the wall with her feet dangling, and Benny jumped up to accompany her. His involuntary purring, resonated with hers as she let all her senses take in the beauty of the garden. *This was happiness,* she thought. *This was contentment.*

In drove Angus, and she watched him struggle to get out of his car. It was low to the ground and one of those with the rather stupid aerials on top which looked like a shark's fin. The reason she thought it was stupid was that she knew that it made him feel like a shark when he was in it. He'd said so, and of course it meant that he had a right over everyone on the road, because they were driving in minnows and sprats. Anyway, just in case there were any disputes amongst the other sharks, he had a private number plate that beat everyone else. BAR1. Not BAR2 or BAR3. Number one and the best. Having that badge conclusively made him the top dog, and it was up to all the others to fight it out in anticipation that one day, they might become unbeatable like him. Heather on numerous occasions had pointed out that unless anyone knew what it meant, it literally meant nothing at all and in her mind slightly devalued the top-dog message, but he failed to see her point. Anyway, she observed his belly resting on the seat when he lifted one leg out. He then rolled the other out so that he could face the seat and then climb up the back of it until he was standing. This was a man who wasn't tempting any kind of back-injury fate. At least, when he was behind that wheel, he was not only the most powerful man in the world, but also the most handsome. And red leather seats and matching brake callipers only re-enforced his attractiveness. Fortunately, no one could see his belly bursting out over his trousers and resting on his thighs.

'How was your day?' she asked.

'Two armed robbers and a people trafficker in one day. I'm gradually cleaning up this once-beautiful country.'

"What do you think to the garden?'

'It looks good. Has that young lad been?'

'Will. Yes. He's done the lawns today.'

'Hope he hasn't broken anything?'

'We can trust him, Angus. I just leave him too it and he grafts. Even does extra things without me even asking.'

'Mmm,' he said tucking his shirt back into his trousers. 'I'd still keep your eye on him. We'll see on the cameras if he's stolen anything.'

'He hasn't. I checked. Anyway, dinner is nearly ready.'

Angus gave her a kiss on her cheek, which surprised her. It was lovely, and it actually felt sincere. 'Do you like this dress?' she asked.

He shook his head and pursed his lips. 'It's alright I guess!'

'Do you think this shade of green suits me?'

'Look. Have this,' he said, taking out his wallet and thrusting two hundred pounds into her hand. 'Go and buy yourself a couple of new ones. Save you hanging on to old rags like that.'

Heather took the money and tucked it into her bra. 'Thanks!'

Angus winked and proceeded to the house, leaving her sitting on the wall.

19

DIRTY WORK

Fresh fish straight off the boat was not only exciting, but a privilege. Heather was up early and was determined to get the best of the catch. Two huge lobsters, a crab, and mackerel with eyes brighter than the sun went into her basket. Lobster thermidor for dinner! *Life was on the up,* she thought and Angus would be proud of her.

She worked her way through the mass of nets and buoys and passed Will's workshop. The door was locked, and no one was around. A cheery wave from Margrit, who was walking up from the beach with a towel around her, made Heather smile. If ever there was a woman to be in awe of, it was Margrit. Originally from Switzerland, she had married a Yorkshireman and lived in the village for many years.

'How are you Margrit?'

'The sea is warmer today,' she replied.

Heather didn't believe her. She looked cold and her face was shivering under her blue swim-cap. 'You weren't trying to get back to Switzerland then?' Heather said jovially.

'To the most landlocked country in Europe? I don't think so. I swam in the lake in Zurich most days in the summer when I was a girl though, and sometimes in the winter. You can join me tomorrow morning if you like?'

Heather quickened her pace. 'You're an amazing woman Margrit. Strong and forthright. An inspiration to us all, but I'll leave it to you if that's okay.'

Margrit gave a friendly but dismissive wave and scurried off to her cottage. Heather slowed her pace as she approached Dune.

'Now there looks like a woman on a mission,' Lesley said with a huge smile.

'Oh yes. I'm escaping the invitation to go early morning swimming and I'm going to do lobster this evening and maybe a crab salad for starter, so eager to get started.'

Lesley laughed. 'Sounds lovely. Is there room for another one?' she asked.

'You'd be more than welcome Lesley.' Heather smiled.

'I would, but I'm doing the stocktake tonight. Did you consider the job, by any chance?'

'Yes, I did. I loved the idea but I didn't ask Angus.'

'To be honest Heather, I'm desperate. I had a young girl accept the position and she let me down. Did one day and then gave me ridiculous excuses for turning up late. You'd be perfect. Clothes and shoes at cost price too, don't forget!' Heather's eyes lit up. 'Angus has been in a good mood recently. I'll talk it through with him this evening. Hopefully the lobster will sway things too.'

'Do you have to run it by him? We could just agree now and then I can let my daughter know that I can have my grandson.'

Heather paused and mulled it over in her head. 'He doesn't like the idea of me working. Says it's his job to be the provider.'

'Sounds a tad old-fashioned, if you don't mind me saying. Just thought you might like to have a little extra pocket money and as I said before. The other customers would love you, with your natural look.'

'That's kind, Lesley. Do you think so?' she said, toying with her hair. 'There are some days when I want to earn my own money and then he convinces me otherwise.'

'I guess that's what being happily married means?'

Heather didn't reply, but the cogs were turning in her head.

'Let me know, anyway, I'd be grateful,' Lesley said before slipping back into the shop.

Benny met Heather at the gate pillar. He must have smelt the fish, by his exuberant purring and extended back legs. He would be locked out of the house while the preparations were taking place, that's for sure. Too risky, as she wanted the dinner to be perfect.

Within seconds of entering, the gate buzzer went. It was Sally. She must have been lurking or on another cat visit!

'I thought you'd be in,' Sally said, walking up the steps and giving Benny an indulgent stroke.

'Coffee?' Heather asked.

'I'm parched,' she said, plonking herself at the table. 'Benny is such a lovely boy. You don't fancy another one, do you?'

'I'd love one Sally, but to be honest, I don't think Angus would. He moans at how much we spend on Benny's food and if I don't keep everything clean, he starts wheezing.'

'That's a shame. I have a lovely Persian needs a good home.'

'So, how did it go with Mr Munchkin?'

'Oh! He was a creep. We had our walk and he invited me in for hot chocolate and tried putting his hand up my skirt!'

'I thought you said his mother was there?'

'She was, but she is blind. Sat in her chair opposite us.'

'No way?'

'Yes way! Filthy man. I should have listened to what you said. You told me to be careful.'

'So have you given up on the dating app?'

'No. I've had a couple more dates. Met a very handsome one from Scarborough. He said he was a judge. Or a Barrister, one or the other and knowing what a fabulous husband Angus is, I was hopeful.'

'What was his name?'

'Malcolm.'

'Malcolm! I don't know any Malcolm's on the circuit. Was he nice?'

'He was a total knob. Kept asking me if I'd put him in a baby's nappy and humiliate him.'

Heather raised her eyebrows. 'High court probably! Anyway, don't you think you're better steering clear of the apps? They all sound weird.'

'To be honest Heather, it's getting me down. I don't think there's a decent one out there for me, and I see you up here living the perfect life with a man who cares for you. The ones who like me, I don't like them and the ones I like, don't even reply. What am I doing wrong?'

Heather took a very deep breath. 'Things can be deceptive. If you want my advice. Don't compare yourself to anyone else. Just be you. Maybe you're trying too hard?'

'I just need a man to make me happy. It can't be that difficult, can it?'

Heather took a moment to reply. All the words in her head were not necessarily the words that Sally would want to hear.

'Just be true to yourself Sally. There are some good ones and quite often they come out of the blue.'

Sally nodded. 'I have to go, but say hello to Angus and give him a hug from me. He's a special one. You did well there.'

'I've done crab salad and lobster Thermidor. I spent some of the money you gave me yesterday and thought you might like a treat?'

'It smells good. We deserve to live like kings.'

Angus stopped her by grabbing her wrist. 'You know I couldn't live without you. You know that?'

That was a surprise, but it was a lovely surprise. His lips looked pragmatic as he smiled by pushing them together, and his eyes had a sparkle she hadn't seen in a long while.

'Thanks, that means a lot. Do you want to choose the wine?'

Angus disappeared to the cellar and returned with a bottle of Italian dry white. 'A hint of the Mediterranean, I thought would accompany the fish fabulously tonight?' he said, thrusting the corkscrew into the bottle and pulling it out with vigour. She smiled back at him and reciprocated by pulling the napkins from the goblet glasses with a flourish.

'Bon appetit,' she said, unveiling the stuffed crab shells and presenting Angus with the silver claw crackers and picking utensils.

'Cheers,' he replied.

They tucked into their crabs and enjoyed cracking open the huge claws and scooping out the meat. 'How was your day?' he asked.

'I bumped into Sally. Remember her? She brought Benny to us when we first moved in.'

'The creepy cat lady?' he replied.

'Well, she's actually very lovely. Cares for all those abandoned cats. She went on a date with a judge from Scarborough, Malcolm, I think she said.'

Angus ruminated as he sucked on one of the crab claws. 'Never heard of anyone called that.'

'I thought not.'

'Can you trust her?'

'Yes, she's fine. Just a little scatty sometimes.'

Heather cleared away the starters and produced the incredible-looking lobster from the oven and set it in the middle of the table.

'Wow,' said Angus. 'That really does look fabulous. I wonder if royalty are having lobster right now.'

'Well not this lobster, that's for sure. It was fresh off the boat this morning.'

'Fresh off the trawler this very morning and you turned it into the feast before us. Excellent!'

Heather smiled and felt a lovely warmth fill her chest and heart. That's all she wanted to hear, and her pride in the meal made her giddy. She passed by him to fetch new plates from the dresser and, with her hand on his shoulder, kissed him on his cheek.

'It's a good life, isn't it?' Angus said, touching her hand with his.

Heather smiled. 'Did you know there was a new women's dress shop in the village?'

'No.'

'It's called Dune. I met the lady that owns it, Lesley.'

'Oh, yes?'

'She's looking for someone to look after the shop one day per week, so that she can have her grandson. She suggested that I might be interested. It's during the day. No late finishes.'

Heather looked at him from the corner of her eye and could see he was processing it in his mind. 'Just one day per week?' he said.

'Yes, and maybe the odd Saturday if she's away.'

She could hear his breathing was heavy as she laid out the plates and took her seat.

'And she suggested you might be interested?'

'Yes.'

'Is this the job you mentioned the other evening?'

Heather paused. 'She said she needed someone trustworthy.'

'But you don't know anything about working in a dress shop!'

'No, but I'm a woman, and we know about dresses and the like.'

'Do you know why this is a wonderful life?'

Heather raised her eyebrows.

'Because you are here to look after our beautiful house and maintain the garden you love so much. It means we can continue to live here. If you no longer want to live here or you're bored with it, then we have to discuss it.'

Heather dished up the lobster. 'I don't want to live anywhere else; I do love it here.'

'Well, I think you may need to let Lesley know where exactly your priorities lie and that she pays a professional to do her dirty work.'

'It's not dirty work, its helping her to see her grandson while her daughter continues her studies.'

'Single parent, is she?'

'I think so. She's struggling, but doing her best.'

'So, we bail them out then? They can't commit to a proper marriage and then they abuse your good nature. It's your choice, of course, Heather, but I'd think long and hard about mixing with people like that. She'll take advantage of you.'

20

TORN

Sheer mountainsides, straight into the sea. Winding roads with cream and white houses perched on the most impossible places, all bathed in Mediterranean sunshine. The Amalfi Coast captivated Heather's attention. She scrutinised every photo. Cute balconies and tables with fun cocktails and limoncello overlooking the passionate sea. Terracotta roofs, mosaic-domed churches and bright pink bougainvillea trailing along pristine white steps made Heather gasp. It was the only place a man could wear a suit and no socks. Where a woman could indulge in kitten heels and carefree linen and where love was built into the language and the streets.

The East Yorkshire coast had its places and moments, but this was another world.

Heather's heart sank to her feet as she compared the two. Suddenly, she jumped off her seat.

'Good morning, Mrs Sinclair!' Will surprised her at the door.

'I didn't see you arrive. You scared me,' she said, attempting to cover over the holiday brochure with her arms.

'So sorry. I didn't mean to. My pickup is in for a service today, so I walked here and guessed I'd be using your tools again?'

'Please don't surprise me like that again,' she said, blocking the doorway.

Will held out a white envelope. 'I wondered if you would read this for me? It's from the Maritime and Coastguard Agency.'

'Can you not read any of it?' Heather asked.

'Some of it, but it's too complicated. A straight yes or no would be fine, but it waffles on so much, I just gave up.'

Heather opened the letter and read it. Then took a very deep breath.

'What does it say?' Will asked.

'It sets out all the reasons you failed your Boatmasters Licence. I'm so sorry.'

Will clasped his forehead and then ran his hand over his head. 'I thought so. I passed my practical with a 99% score but it's just the written exam I can't do.'

'You passed with 99%?'

'Yes. I would have had 100%, but I wrote the date wrong on my log sheet.'

'Has anyone ever taught you to read and write?'

'Yes. They've tried. School obviously and my grandad taught me things around the boatyard. I can read all of the signs, because I know them. The other thing, is I panic in an exam. My brain just goes awol and I struggle to read what the question asks and then I become flustered and then its game over.'

'Can you tell me the main safety checks you should do before setting out on a voyage? And explain to me the procedure if someone goes overboard?' Heather asked.

'Well, that's simple. Ensure the boat is seaworthy, check fuel levels, inspect life jackets, fire extinguishers, navigation lights and communication equipment. If someone goes overboard, then I'd alert the crew, throw a life buoy and manoeuvre the boat to recover the person, usually by approaching from downwind. If the conditions make it impossible, then I would put a call out to the coastguard.'

'So you know everything you need to know?'

'Yes. My grandfather taught me everything. I know it in my head.'

'But you just can't sit the exam?'

'Exactly.'

Heather stroked her chin with her thumb and index finger. 'And what are you planning on doing with it?'

'As I said before. Boat trips to see the seals and the puffins. That's why I'm repairing the boat. I used to go with my grandfather. I loved it.'

'What about your gardening business?'

'That's so I can earn the money to do the repairs.'

'I get you,' Heather said, taking a deep breath. 'You'd be perfect at running the tours. I can see your enthusiasm and knowledge being a thrill for your passengers.'

'Thanks,' he replied. 'Anyway, you looking at holidays?'

'*No*!' Heather snapped.

'I saw a holiday brochure; I thought you were planning an escape?'

Heather looked him in the eye. 'An escape?'

'Yer. I imagine you go away for weeks on end, being married to a judge?'

Heather paced uncomfortably on the spot. She wasn't expecting this line of questioning from the gardener. 'I use it to line my seed trays! That's all.'

Will smiled politely. 'What jobs do you want me on today then?'

Heather eased herself through the door. 'I thought you could do some weeding in the borders. The rain recently has made them shoot up. Then perhaps you can help me dig up some of the early carrots and kale for my veg box?'

'Sure,' he replied. 'You not wearing your green today, I see.'

What was wrong with him? Always catching her off guard. First with the brochure and then with her dress.

'I do like the daisies though. Suits you.'

'Oh, this old thing,' she said, stroking her neck with her fingers.

'It looks good. Summery and all,' he replied.

An awkward silence made Heather squirm and her heart race.

'I'll crack on with the boarders then,' Will replied as he turned and walked across the lawn.

Heather watched him walk away. He was just a lad. A gardener with a pipe dream of doing seal-watching trips. *Why did he floor her with his compliments?* They obviously weren't genuine. She was a middle-aged, frumpy, barren and saggy judge's wife. He was charming, that's for sure, but she could see through it. Keep her sweet. Feed the hand that pays and all that. Maybe Angus was right. All gardeners were up to no good. She made the decision to keep a close eye on him and make sure he didn't overdo the charm. In fact, she would tell him assertively that he should remain professional and to refrain from any personal comments that might make her feel uncomfortable. *Yes. Perfect. Decision made,* and with a nod to herself, she turned the doorknob the wrong way and entered the dark store. A quick check of Will's whereabouts, the house and the drive, she proceeded to slide the heavy cabinet and unlock the secret door and placed the holiday brochure on the mounting pile and then slipped in one hundred pounds from the 'dress' money into the plastic box. She closed the lid and slid everything back in place before closing the door and putting on the kettle.

'Why am I doing it Benny? Why do I feel so guilty? I have everything I want here. Angus always says I should be more grateful.'

Benny opened one eye and then curled himself up into a ball. 'Am I being selfish? You'd tell me, wouldn't you?' she said, stroking the top of his head. 'And what about the Amalfi Coast. Would I be happy there? I could visit and see. They say the water is warm? It's hard to imagine, but it looks so clear. Just you and me in a little cottage with a balcony and window boxes full of flowers. Could we do it, Benny? Could we do it?'

He didn't know the answer, and neither did she. The stockpile of brochures somehow made it all seem possible, but also made her feel despondent. She stared through the glass into the garden. Not focussing on anything in particular and unable to think beyond the guilt of just being her! She couldn't help it. Staring into nowhere. Her mind was blank. No answers to the questions, just a sorrowful void of nothingness. That in itself was enough to make her feel even more guilty. She had everything. A beautiful house, garden and a husband who provided all of that. Guilt was guilt, but mixed with the shame, for feeling guilty, that was a perpetual spiral that never let go.

Heather sighed. There were hundreds of jobs to do, but her body had somehow lost the will to move. Her staring continued. Although her eyes were open, it felt like she was looking at the inside of her brain. It was weird and not normal, but after a while, felt strangely cleansing. Her shoulders dropped, and the only thing that was apparent was the slow, steady beat of her heart. Thump ... thump ... thump. Thump ... thump ... thump, it went. It really was the strangest thing she'd ever encountered. Her eyes on the inside of her brain and a thousand thoughts running around inside, like sparks of light. Azure waters, bougainvillea, open toe sandals, swimming in clear water, stripes on the freshly mown lawn, Benny purring on her lap, the cobbled struggle back up the hill, the wind in her hair on the back of a moped, cloudless skies, sparkling prosecco, the cameras on the gate, the shark with his fat belly in the shower, dark nights, carved pumpkins, candles, Christmas Day, sat alone, dreading the new year, chocolate around her mouth and vomiting in the toilet. Boxes of vegetables, the smell of wood varnish, puffins and gannets clinging to the cliff face, foetus photos pushing down on her. Fighting back, her hands bound by fists, spinning chandeliers and out of control, falling. A bottomless hole. Dark, endless and frightening, yet liberating. The wind in her face, the North Star above and the main sail aloft, with doves gliding on the breeze. The sunset burning its way into a new life. The unknown, over the edge and freeee.

A rumble of thunder shook the ground, and one of the orangery windows slammed shut. The sound of the rain on the glass brought her back into the real world, with Benny on his cushion, greenery all around and black seed trays surrounding her. Filling her lungs with greenhouse air, it took her a while to become fully present again. 'That was weird,' she told Benny. 'Feels like I went somewhere, but have no idea where!' He was stirring. His ears twitched at the sound of the rumbling thunder. Then, a flash of lightning and a thunder boom which seemed to come from the centre of the earth and vibrate through every living thing. Heather moved quickly to close the remaining windows as the rain became torrential. Another flash of lightning and 'boom' the ground once again, resonated with fear.

Will! Poor old Will. Where was he? she thought. Running to the door, she scanned the garden. The sound of the rain on the glass was deafening, and was hitting the ground with such force, it was bouncing off, and huge puddles had already formed on the lawn. On closer scrutiny, she saw him sheltering under a tree in just his T-shirt and shorts.

She quickly slid open the door and waved to him to come in and, without any hesitation, saw him run towards her and then stop at the door. He was completely drenched.

'Come in, come in.' Heather shouted above the noise of the relentless downpour. Will did exactly that and for a moment stood dripping with his hands down by his side. 'I thought this was your sanctuary?'

'It is. Only on invitation, but it's dangerous out there.'

Will nodded and looked appreciative. 'The tree gave me shelter at the beginning, but it soon changed.'

Heather closed the door. 'Right! Get the wet clothes off and I'll put them by the heater. I have a small towel for such occasions for myself, you can dry yourself with that and then there's my old coat,' she said, pointing to a wax jacket hung up on the wall. 'It might be tight, but at least you can warm up.'

'Thanks,' he said, removing his T-shirt, dropping his shorts to the ground and grabbing the towel. Heather purposefully didn't look; she caught a glimpse of his solid and hairy upper chest, but then focused on ringing out his clothing and distributing them on the end of the racking next to the heater, which she turned up to maximum.

'They should start drying soon,' she said, turning her head. The shock hit her like a bolt of lightning. A semi-naked man in her orangery felt wrong. His toned and muscular thighs were like nothing she'd ever seen before. The definition of his muscles was ... obvious to say the least, and his ribcage and flat stomach, like something from a Michelangelo sculpture. She turned her head away to allow him some modesty and checked the gate for any early arrivals.

She didn't want him to see her looking at his body. For one thing, he deserved his privacy, and the other was she simply wasn't interested in the body of a younger man. Sheltering from the storm, a good enough reason for him to be there, but it was disgusting to think she might want to ... ogle the body of a man some fifteen years her junior.

Will turned and walked to get the coat. Heather watched his ... his ... well, everything really. He even had the bottom of a Greek god statue from her holiday brochures. She turned her head quickly when he did and busied herself loading the tea mugs and putting on the kettle. She just hoped to God that Angus didn't arrive and start throwing his weight around. It had happened once before when the delivery man had trapped his shirt in his van door and ripped it. Heather had tried to help him with some safety pins and Vaseline for the door, just when Angus pulled into the drive. It wasn't a great outcome, and he made her feel guilty for at least a fortnight after with his silent treatment. Anyway. It wasn't worth testing his jealousy, and the sight of a near-naked man would surely have him reaching for his shotgun.

'Here, give me that towel,' she said as she walked up to him. Her coat did look funny on him; the sleeves were far too short, and he couldn't fasten the zip. Worst of all, it went nowhere near to covering his modesty, and the sight of him in his black Calvin's and what resembled a straitjacket made her giggle. He looked down at himself and shifted sideways until he was partially hidden by a very ungainly, yet perfectly positioned cucumber. He put his hands on his hips and made a funny face, which made Heather laugh out loud. He then laughed, and together they shared the moment. *'Boom'* the thunder once again shook the ground, and Heather jumped. The shock, making her literally leave the floor and then lose her balance, which made her fall against his chest. She felt his arm come across her shoulders and hold her.

'Are you alright?' he said, reassuringly. He was nine or ten inches taller, and as she looked up, he looked down. It was the first time she'd seen his eyes so close, but she was instantly distracted by his lips. 'It's quite a storm, isn't it?' Heather watched his lips move and nodded. 'You're safe,' he said, tightening his arm slightly.

Her hand felt his hairy chest. It was firm, and she could feel his heart pounding.

It didn't last long. Heather pushed with her hand against his muscly chest and broke the ... whatever it was? It wasn't a hug, of course it wasn't, she thought. It was more to do with safety and reassurance in the storm, and that was greatly appreciated, but it certainly wasn't anything more than that. 'Let me see how your clothes are getting on!' she said, walking over to the heater. 'They'll be dry soon.'

Will didn't answer. She just saw him looking at her, so she quickly looked away. It was weird. For a moment she felt self-conscious about her body. He was clearly looking at her. Her dress had taken on some of the rain from his body and was defining her nipples. She had no means of hiding, and that was the weird bit. It felt liberating somehow. She wasn't sure how, but felt like a rush of femininity. Feeling vulnerable in the moment, but liking it. An absolute shock. She hadn't felt that in a very, very long time.

But hang on a minute. This was neither the time nor the

place for feeling vulnerable. The gardener was all but naked in her sanctuary. She'd broken all the rules of entry, and she was justifying ogling his body and pretending there was some kind of 'energy' in the place.

'You have to go now!' she said, trying to pull herself together.

Will nodded.

'How will you get home?' she asked.

'I'll walk. I have to collect my truck anyway.'

Heather nodded and then remembered she hadn't finished preparing the veg box for Zeta.

'Can you remember where Zeta's veg box is, I need to ...'

Will cut her off. 'I did it. Carrots, spring onions, beetroot and a few other things. The box is full,' he said, walking over to his clothes. 'I put it in the garage to keep it dry.' Heather watched him put on his damp clothes and then hang up her coat. 'Thanks for reading my letter by the way.' He reached for the sodden envelope in his pocket and saw it was stuck together. He tore it up and threw it on the compost heap.

'Don't do that!' Heather cried. But it was too late. Will shrugged and headed for the door. 'Wait. Here's your money. I just need your signature.' Will smiled and obliged with a pen.

'Sorry I didn't get as much done today as planned.'

'You really want it, don't you. Your licence,' she said, pointing at the torn-up letter.

'Yes. More than anything. For my grandad's honour.'

'Thanks for doing the veg box ... and for keeping me safe!'

'My pleasure. See you next week.'

21

MASCULINITY

When you're on holiday, a week can fly by so fast, you barely notice it. When you're riddled with guilt that you made someone walk home in a torrential storm in already wet clothes and in the process, made a complete fool of yourself, a week can drag on like a whole year. It was agony. Overthinking everything. Beating herself up that she should have let him stay until the rain had subsided or at least waited for his clothes to dry and offer him one of Angus's coats. Anyway, that was the problem. Or at least the dilemma. Treading on eggshells following Angus's over-reaction to a half-naked man in her orangery or even daring to volunteer some of his clothing was never an option. Those eggshells were brittle and unforgiving. A delicate balance of striding with hope and walking with fear, they were to be avoided at all costs.

'Morning Mrs Sinclair.'

'Good morning, Will. I see you got your truck back.'

'Yes. It's a good old workhorse. At least if it rains today, I can drive home.'

Heather felt her face going red. 'On that note. I'm sorry for pushing you out like that.'

Will looked at her with a stern face. 'I understand the situation with your husband Mrs Sinclair.'

Heather's face became even redder. 'Do you?'

'Yes. He loves you and trusts you. No man wants to see a half-naked man with his wife.'

Heather was stunned. And here was the sting and the knife right into her stomach. Stood in front of her was a man, who first of all, said he understood! That was a first. But then, he'd obviously thought about the consequences and what she might have to go through if indeed, Angus had come home. But there was something else. The twist of the knife. The thing that made Heather squirm and despise herself completely, was that his arm around her felt incredible. His tender, yet reassuring hold, melted her. She didn't want to admit it, and, by God, it would never happen again; she would make sure of that. But his moment of compassion seemed to be drilling its way towards her heart, and it had caught her off guard.

'Thank you. Your parents must be very proud of you. You're a decent young man.'

'I lost my parents when I was six. I can barely remember them.'

Heather wanted the world to swallow her up. *How was it possible to feel every emotion in a two-minute conversation?* Of all the things she could have said, she blurted out the most painful.

Trying to recover some sort of dignity, she responded. 'I guess that's why you had such a good relationship with your grandfather?'

Will nodded with a smile. 'He loved the sea and the wildlife. He gave me that passion.'

Heather's legs buckled. 'I understand that connection. Well, anyway, crack on with the lawns as quickly as possible. No need to do the edges and I'll have a bacon sandwich and a cup of tea waiting for you.'

She saw him move from foot to foot with his head down. 'That's very kind Mrs Sinclair, but I don't want to compromise you in any way,' he said, looking at the orangery.

'Angus is working late. And, it's my way of apologising for the other day,' she replied.

'You don't need to apologise for anything, Mrs Sinclair.'

'Please. Call me Heather,' she said, smiling.

The sound of the mower was in many ways the epitome of a summer's day. The rain of the previous week had given everything a new vigour and the warm air allowed for a more relaxed and philosophical view of the days. More time to enjoy the lighter evenings and relish the surrounding nature. Heather enjoyed selecting more vegetables. The produce was at its best. Juicy, ripe and abundant and she was proud of its contents and enjoying the ... pocket money in return.

With the bacon sizzling under the grill, she watched him from the kitchen window. Up and down he went on the mower. His capable arms tanning with every pass. She tried not to look, while she cut the bread, but the way in which he effortlessly picked up and emptied the grass collection box was akin to a farmer loading a hay bale on his shoulder and manhandling it, like it were a sack of feathers. She could see that he was near finishing and so compiled the sandwiches and headed for the orangery.

Heather had to encourage him in, as he was reluctant to enter.

'Tea up!' she shouted.

Will hesitated by the door. 'Are you sure?'

'Yes Will. Come in. It's granary bread, is that okay?'

He looked agitated as he perched on the workbench by the door.

'The lawn looks fabulous. I'm pleased with the finish now we're cutting it every week. Angus used to leave it, and its condition was nowhere near as good as it is now.'

Will tucked into his bacon sandwich.

'I was thinking about your boatmaster's licence.'

Will looked at her and carried on munching.

'Has anyone tried helping you with your exam?'

'It's a waste of time. I can learn something one day and forget it the next. I struggle to retain it and then get flustered when I have to make it count.'

'What about your grandad?'

'He was the same as me. They didn't have licences back in his day, they just did it with common sense. Did the job and proved they could do it.'

'So, if something has common sense, then it has meaning to you?'

'I guess so?'

'What does it say on that grow bag?' she asked, pointing to the one on the bench.

'It says, tomato grow bag.'

'Is that because you know what it is or are you reading it?'

Will looked at her and fidgeted uncomfortably.

'And what about below that?'

He hesitated, then attempted to read the lettering on the bag. 'For ... tomatoes ... and ...'

Will took to his feet. 'What is this. Some kind of trick?'

'It's no trick. I just thought ...'

'You thought you would patronise me.'

'No! I didn't. I thought I could teach you.'

'It's all right for you in your posh house. It's easy for you, reading and writing. You can have what you want and have a husband that pays for everything. And all you have to do is one veg box a week for some pocket money. It's not the real world.'

Heather stood and gritted her teeth. 'I beg your pardon! This is very much the real world and I resent that. I'm actually saving up for something.'

'Yeh, a new handbag or glitzy shoes.'

Heather felt the tears welling inside. 'It's more important than that. In fact, it's more important than anything ever.'

Will scoffed. 'A holiday!'

Heather looked at him. He'd managed to touch a nerve, even she didn't know she had. 'It's … I can't tell you what it is. That's not fair. I don't have to put up with this!'

'Well, you embarrassed me, how do you think I'd respond?'

'I didn't mean to upset you, Will.'

'Imagine trying as hard as you can and no matter what you do, you always fail, because society says you must be able to read and write. I know I can do the job. Take people out to learn about the wildlife and enjoy the sea. But my reading means I'll never do it.'

'You will do it. I haven't known you long, but I know you are a worthy man. You must do it. I believe in you Will.'

'How can you say that? You have no idea who I am?' he said, heading for the door.

'I can see a very capable man in front of me.'

Will shook his head. 'I have to go. We've said too much. I don't think I can work here anymore.'

She watched him exit the door and walk calmly to his truck without looking back.

'Wait! I'm sorry,' she shouted, but it was too late.

22

CONEY STREET CAFE

The workshop door was locked, and he wasn't around. Heather posted his cash through the letterbox in the door and left quietly. Stomping up the hill, she didn't stop to talk to anyone, and when she got to the top of the hill, instead of turning left to go home, she turned right and headed for the bus stop. It wasn't long before the bus arrived, and on she got, taking the front seat on the top deck.

With Angus away all week on a golfing trip, she headed back to the cobbled streets of her youth, and the Minster, and the Shambles beckoned her. York had been her home growing up, and moving to the east coast meant she had neglected it somewhat over recent years.

Hopping off by the castle gardens, she ventured through the gate and up to the ruined walls of St Mary's Abbey. The sign said that it was built in 1088 and was once one of the wealthiest and most powerful Benedictine monasteries in England. A little further along, she felt the warmth of the stone with her hand. The Multangular Tower was a standing remnant of the third century Roman fort and one of the many reminders of the ancient history of the city. She stood with her back against the warm stone and tried to imagine what life would have been like almost two thousand years ago.

A couple walked past with a young girl, who was running her hand through the flowers as they walked along the path. It reminded her of the days she had spent with her parents in exactly the same place. She would want to stop and smell the flowers, but her mother would drag her along at a pace, even though they weren't heading anywhere specific. The fact was, she didn't know how to stop and take in the splendour of nature and to take a moment to appreciate the things around her.

Heather followed the family discreetly out of the gardens and along the river, running downstream. They would do exactly the same if they were heading home. Through the park and around the duck pond, where she would pull a little sailing boat on a string around the edge. Her grandfather had made the boat for her. A wooden keel fashioned from a sycamore tree felled in his garden and a tall mast with a linen sail. No one else had a boat like it, and she was always proud to launch it on the pond and take it for adventures.

She left the family and headed up a side street to the house they used to live in. A small terraced house with a clipped privet hedge and small rear garden. At the end of the street was the imposing red brick and stone chocolate factory with tall clock tower. Her father worked there and fitted and maintained the machines within the production lines and often came home filthy and smelling of a mixture of chocolate orange and grease. But that didn't put her off scoffing the misfits that he would bring home on a regular basis. The misfits were the misshapen chocolates, which had failed quality control and were not allowed to go for sale, but the staff were able to take them home. She remembered her father saying that he was allowed to eat as much chocolate as he wanted while he was there. She used to imagine how fabulous that would have been. But he said that as a result he never ate any, not one. Well, following the first and only time, when he ate so much, he vomited on the production line and was docked a week's wages.

She sat on the red brick wall at the end of their garden and let her legs swing free, just like she did as a girl. She'd wait for him to come home from work and see what he had in his hand. That was the only time he made time for her, and it wasn't long. He would march out when the whistle blew, pat her on the head and hand over the bag of goodies. 'Don't eat them all at once,' he would say in his deep Scottish accent, and then continue, not into the house, but to the pub at the other end of the street. 'It's my little reward,' he would say.

It was his way of showing love, she knew that, and although it was a small and very fleeting gesture, Heather hung on to it with every bite. Her mother would have tea ready on the table for his staggering return, and then he would further drink himself to sleep until the factory whistle blew the following morning, and he was back in his hobnail boots heading back for a full day.

Turning her head, she could see some of the rear garden. Her mother did all the gardening, and Heather would help with the hanging baskets and the pot plants. It wasn't a huge area, but they made it the best they could. Heather would try to get her mother to open up about life with her father. She thought that they could share the things they had in common, but she didn't want to talk. In fact, she never did until the day she died. Unbeknown to anyone, cancer had spread within her bones, and it was too late to do anything. She said just one thing. 'I named you after the glorious purple hills of home. I should never have left. I followed your father, and then you were born. I should have been true to myself. Now it's too late.' She then closed her eyes and passed peacefully in Heather's arms.

Her mother was a tough woman, and Heather could see the pain within her, but she made her feel unwanted and sounded resentful at her arrival in this world.

Heather pushed herself off the wall and headed to a snicket which ran between the houses and up to the old school. That was the shortcut and where 'the smokers' used to hang out. She hesitated as she looked up the now overgrown path, and a shiver ran through her body. She could almost see her there. The menacing figure of Sharon Sandford with her cutesy blonde pigtails and polished shoes. Her father was the foreman at the factory, and they lived in the detached house in the avenue behind. 'Och aye. Well, if it isn't the Scottish ginger top,' she would say. 'Can't even afford a proper school uniform!'

The sound of her swearing voice used to make Heather's stomach twist with anguish and make her feel sick.

'Why doesn't your dad buy you the same uniform we all have, instead of spending his money on booze? My dad says that he spends more time in that pub than he does at work.'

'He doesn't!' Heather would reply sternly.

'Yellow buttons for ale house gluttons,' was her favourite line as her posh poetic humiliation continued to flow like a vile slick of hateful bile flowing from her thin-lipped mouth.

She hated that blouse, the oversized skirt and the hideous shoes. All she wanted was to fit in and not be a target for Sharon's bullying. Often, she thought about going up to her house and knocking on the door and telling her parents that their delightful daughter was a foul-mouthed, cigarette-smoking, evil bitch. But what use was that? They wouldn't believe her, and in a way, she was right. Her father was a drinker, and maybe if he hadn't wasted his money, he could have bought her the correct uniform and not relied on council handouts. It made her feel isolated. Singled out and open for anyone to fling abuse at her, and what could she do? Nothing. Just take it and keep quiet.

Staring up the snicket, she took a deep breath. The stale cigarette smell of Sharon's breath, somehow still inhabiting the air, made her turn her back to it and, while holding back any kind of outwardly visible signs of utter despair, she walked away feeling as crushed as she had back then.

She continued towards the factory. The air was no longer filled with the sweet smell of cocoa. The building was now smart executive apartments, and the only misfit around there was herself. Abandoned by her mother at the age of forty-eight and then her father two years later on his fiftieth birthday. An overdose of vodka and painkillers finished him off. He just didn't want to do it anymore. People said he was selfish, but Heather didn't understand. She just felt abandoned and unloved. She managed to pay the rent by working in the cafe on Coney Street, and that's when Angus walked in and changed her life forever.

Crossing over the river, and following the riverside path up into the city centre, the memories of Sharon Sandford gradually slipped away onto the York stone pavement with each purposeful stride. She wondered if the old cafe where she worked would still be there. She would pass by, just to see and maybe try and get something to eat. It was a pull up the cobbled street, and when she turned the corner; she saw to her dismay it had been replaced by a vape shop. How different it looked and smelled, but there was a cute coffee shop a little further on with a couple of tables on the street, which took her fancy. A huge slice of carrot cake and a latte felt indulgent but were worth it as she contemplated how some things in York had changed, like the cafe, and how some things hadn't, like the Roman tower and museum gardens. *Some things never change,* she thought. *Was that the same in her life?* Had she become a version of her mother, bitter and angry, but with the added 'gift' of a longer life? Angus's voice filled her head. 'If I hadn't walked in that day, you would still be working in that cafe.' He was right! He did change her life and took her away from near poverty. For that, she was grateful. But the words of her father did too.

'Make sure you're a good wife to whoever takes your hand,' he would say. She hated him, but she missed him. Feeling alone in the world was a frightening thing, but not as frightening as watching him kill himself.

23

SEXTANT

A different woman stood in the doorway of Dune when Heather passed by. The new helper she thought as she waved with a smile. It was open half a day on a Sunday and Heather was glad that Lesley would be enjoying time with her grandson.

The village was bustling with tourists. The holiday season brought them in, in droves. Heather preferred to avoid it at busy times, mainly because everyone now had a dog and not only that, these were pets that went everywhere with their owners and not just one or two, but in some cases in excess of five or six. Those were usually carted around in pushchairs or modified event trolleys, but most others were constrained by meagre 20ft-long leads, which made any haste within the street, into a game of Crystal Maze. She took the secret ginnel to avoid them and scurried along with her head down until she popped out behind the harbour workshops. *Ginnel or snicket?* she asked herself. She had always called them snickets, but Will called them ginnels. A snicket was a cut through, a small pathway, and a ginnel seemed to be more like an alleyway and sometimes surfaced. Well, that was the explanation she was sticking to.

His workshop door was ajar, and she could hear someone singing along to the radio. Obviously, a Harry Styles fan, she thought as she tentatively peered in through the gap in the door.

As the light from the doorway hit his face, he stopped singing. Heather smiled and opened the door further. *It's funny how you can see contempt in someone's eyes so well,* she thought as she put one foot inside. Will said nothing. Instead, put his head down and carried on sanding the keel of the boat.

'I don't want to intrude,' she said softly.

'Well don't,' he replied.

'I want to apologise. You know, for the other day. I was emotional. It caught us both off guard.'

Will carried on sanding in silence.

'I've brought you something,' she said, opening a bag and producing a gleaming, polished brass object in front of him. 'It's a sextant. Saw it in an antiques shop in York, and thought it might go well in your boat. You know, when it's finished.'

Will looked at it and sighed. 'It's beautiful. And it's very kind, but I don't want it.'

Heather paced in front of him. 'It's just that I have had time to think about testing you like that. It wasn't fair, and I'm sorry.'

Will sighed again and nodded gently. 'I over reacted too. It's me who should be apologising. You were only trying to help and I understand how difficult it might be to understand the ridicule and judgement I have received since I was a boy, because I couldn't read.'

'I can see that and I do understand. I was that ginger-haired girl at school that everyone used to tease.'

'You're a very attractive lady, despite the ginger hair,' he said, looking up.

'Well, I'll take that as a compliment.'

'Maybe we both hit a nerve?'

Heather handed him the sextant. 'Well, look. How about we do a deal? You come back to working twice a week as planned and I'll teach you to read, so you can be your own skipper?'

Will took a moment to think. 'To be honest, I've enjoyed working with you in your lovely garden and, have been relying on the income to finish the boat. I've nearly completed the repairs to the hull; it's just the inside now and the mast.'

She could see that his brain was working overtime by the way his eyes rose to the ceiling and squinted. 'So let me get this straight. I come back to work and in return, you get me my certificate?'

'In a nutshell, yes.'

'I don't want to be reciting Shakespeare or anything like that!'

Heather laughed. 'I think *The Tempest* might be a step too far.'

'What do you mean?'

'I mean, I'd love to see you complete the boat in honour of your grandfather and you'd be helping me with my garden and my sanity.'

24

NITROGEN

'The lawns are in need of some TLC. We let it slip and they got out of hand.' Heather said, handing Will the key to the garage.

'No problem. I sharpened the blades, so should make light work of it.'

'Great. With Angus away for another couple of days, I thought I'd make a few adjustments in the house and I'll be out later with a brew, and then if you could help me with some repotting?'

'No problem.'

There comes a time in a woman's life when she has to go through everything. Literally, everything. Clothes, shoes, bags, the lot. Not just to free up wardrobe space. You can always, 'consolidate' your husband's stuff for that. This was an 'out with the old and in with the new' kind of thing. A refresh, a cleansing, almost. Following her trip to York, she felt a new impetus and was going to use it productively.

Heather surprised herself when she opened the wardrobe and instantly grabbed items that she hadn't worn for years and put them straight in a bin liner for the charity shop. Blouses, tops, T-shirts and jeans went in with no hesitation, and it felt good. One pair of jeans had a £10 note in the back pocket, which was a surprise and a little bonus. She felt like she should have done it years ago. Benny joined her on the bed and then decided to 'help' by delving into the bags to make the final decisions! 'What's got into me, Benny?' she asked him. 'Why didn't I do this years ago? It almost makes me feel like I've been living in someone else's house! You don't know what I mean, do you? Well, neither do I Benny. I don't know all the answers, it just feels like I'm claiming back my territory somehow.'

Benny didn't even look up; he was intent on smothering everything in hairs and was doing a sterling job of it.

Next were the dresses. A Dior silver number that was really only suitable for Shirley Bassey and a micro-mini dress, which was only fit for the streets and the back streets at that. There was even one that had been attacked by moths, that she had been wanting to repair, but ten years on, it was time to throw it out. A couple of other dated and worn-out items followed, as they were no good for the charity shop or to make dusters. Everything else was for keeping, she thought, and then spotted the purple dress lurking at the back of the shelf. She reached in and pulled it out. It had felt so good wearing it in the shop. But she could never wear it again in front of Angus. 'I'm being decisive Benny. It's a new start,' she said, picking up the charity bag and shoving the dress in. 'Someone who deserves it can have it,' she said as she was distracted by the mower outside. *Maybe Will could help her take the bags to the charity shop and the recycling centre,* she thought as she looked out of the other window to examine the empty space in the back of his pickup.

The sorting out felt good, and Heather was surprised at how clearer her head felt as a result. Less burdened, more organised and lighter. Tying up the bag, her eyes were drawn to the deep purple dress within. She paused, sighed and then retrieved it and placed it back in the wardrobe. 'Maybe one day Benny. Maybe one day,' she said with a deep breath.

She did enjoy Angus being away. That was one thing she didn't have to think about. She could eat when she wanted and didn't have to cook dinner every night. Instead, simply make some toast or even just nibble on some cheese and pickled onions. In addition, having the garden neat and tidy gave her a sense of pride, and having Will around allowed her to have more time to lose herself in the smaller tasks and indeed, in clearing out her wardrobe.

She took Will a cup of tea and asked him about taking her and the bags to the charity shop. Thankfully, he agreed.

It seemed fortuitous to sort out some of Angus's clothes too. There were items she knew he hadn't worn, and so she set about his side of the wardrobe.

Just how many suits did a man need? Certainly, none with a waist measurement less than 40" and that was being optimistic. Straightaway three suits went in the bag, followed by four wing-collar shirts, which took his total down to six. She knew he wouldn't miss them. Seventeen pairs of khaki chinos seemed a little excessive, so she went through them, looking for excessive wear, damage or just those that would be 'too tight'. One pair were borderline on the waist but had a grassy smudge on the knee. She threw them on the bed for the recycling pile, but then remembered she hadn't checked the pockets.

She was glad she did. Two receipts were stuffed into the back pocket. Dating from a few weeks ago. In fact, not just a few weeks ago, but on her birthday, they caught her by surprise. One receipt said 'Dove pendant £45,000'. She gasped. That was a ridiculous amount of money, but he did say that they were good diamonds. Anyway, £45,000 did have the overwhelming capacity to buy more guilt, that was for sure. Collapsing on the bed, she couldn't believe he'd spent so much on something she hated. In her mind, he'd destroyed it. Either way, ultimately, the purchase was her soul, and the guilt buried deep into her mind. *He was so thoughtless in his thoughtfulness!* she thought, as once again she went to toy with it around her neck and felt lost. *Maybe, she could transform it back to its former glory without him knowing?* she thought.

After a moment of despondent staring at the ceiling, she unfolded the second receipt. She automatically thought it would be the repair cost but was surprised to see 'Diamond ring £125,000'. Her body went into shutdown. No breath, no heartbeat, no thoughts, just shockwaves, like connecting her nerves directly to the mains and riding the pain of 125,000 volts and watching him in control of the switch – smiling.

A diamond ring! There hadn't been such an item on her birthday. They'd fallen out, so maybe he had decided to hold back? They did have an anniversary coming up, but it wasn't a big one. *Maybe he had a lover?* she thought. But a ring like that would be for an engagement or celebration, and he was a married man after all. It didn't make sense and, to top it all, combined they were a lot of money and money she didn't know existed, and cash for that matter.

Flabbergasted and intrigued, she entered his study. *Maybe the ring was hidden in his drawer?* Snooping wasn't her style. If the trust wasn't there, then what did they have? But her curiosity got the better of her. The top drawer in his desk held the cash. Her cash, in an envelope with Heather written on it.

The drawer below had a stapler, hole punch, pens and paper-clips. She moved her attention to the two drawers on the other side of the desk. The bottom one had paper and envelopes, but the one above was locked. She tried opening it by pulling hard on the brass knob, but to no avail. She'd never looked in there. Never needed to look in there nor wanted to look in there. She set about searching for the key, but it was an impossible job. The whole office was cluttered with papers, boxes and files. Heather rummaged in a few box files and tried the drawer one more time with force. *What was she doing anyway, spying on him like that?* The sound of the mower drew her towards the window, and she stepped on the squeaky floorboard, which was under the rug. She jumped from one foot to the other, making it squeak to the beat of her jumps. *She should get that fixed*, she thought as she watched Will almost complete the upper lawn.

Heather rolled back the rug and located the offending floorboard. It did indeed have a slight movement to it, but it was wedged in place and only moved with body weight. With a metal letter-opening knife, she tried to prize it up, but it was stuck. She even put her finger into a small knothole and pulled hard, but it only moved slightly. *It was a job for a professional*, she thought, folding up an envelope and wedging it between the boards to try and prevent it from squeaking. It worked, so she covered it with the rug and headed downstairs.

Tea and three rows of plant pots awaited Will in the Orangery.

Heather tipped a whole bag of compost into a large tray between them and then asked Will to sprinkle slow-release fertiliser in too. 'How much does it say to mix?' she asked. Will looked at the writing on the bag. Five to one rat ... rat ... io. Ratio,' he replied.

'Good, so that's five parts compost to one part fertiliser.' Will poured in the correct mix and looked at her. She knew, he knew, that she was testing him.

'We don't have to do anymore, if you don't want.'

Will nodded. 'I'm fine. I'm keen to learn.'

'Good! What else does it say on there?'

Will attempted to read the words on the bag. 'Gran ... gran ...'he stumbled. 'The other word is fertiliser. I know that!' he said confidently.

'Let's do it together,' she said softly. 'Gran ... u ... lar'

Will repeated it. 'Gran ... u ... lar. Granular fertiliser.'

'I think you're better than you let on,' she said encouragingly.

'Shall we do one more and then get mixing?'

Will smiled.

'What about that word?' she asked.

'Pot ... pot ... as ... ium. Potassium?'

'Excellent. You know what is in fertiliser. It's just a case of not getting flustered and try and say the sounds. Some will make sense, and some we'll have to work on, but well done for trying.'

'Nit ... ro. Nit ... ro ... gen. Nitrogen!' Will said with a huge smile.

Heather smiled back and thrust her hands into the compost. Will did too, and they mixed in the fertiliser together. Heather felt his hand touch hers a couple of times. It was unavoidable. The thing was, she liked it and lingered with her hands hidden within the mix and waited for his hand to touch hers again. Avoiding eye contact, she let him do it again. His hand brushed over the top of hers and then carried on mixing. Heather giggled, and although the compost didn't need any more mixing, she moved her left hand around the edge of the tray but left her right hand buried beneath. Then it happened again. His hand slowly moved over hers. Her face suddenly felt hot, and a tingle went all the way up her arm and then ... deep. To a place she had almost forgotten about. But it didn't stop there. His hand moved partially up her wrist and then slowly back down, before finishing with a very light and tender touching of their fingertips. 'Sorry!' he said, looking into her eyes.

Sorry! They were just mixing compost. *There was nothing to be sorry about,* Heather thought as she diverted her eyes to the floor and felt her heart skip a beat. She blatantly left her hand within the compost again and watched his face for a reaction. He didn't look at her; but instead, moved his hand within the mix and then brought it over hers and pushed his fingers in between hers and connected them by pushing up as if they were holding hands. *Jeez, it felt electrifying.* The shockwaves darted through her body as she let him gently squeeze her hand and then slowly release. He looked at her, and she looked at him. *What was that? A knowing? A moment?* A connection, and once again, she liked it, and the fact it was all hidden, made her feel naughty.

'It's hot in here, isn't it?' she said, moving away to the window and opening it to its maximum.

'How are you doing with your veg boxes?' Will asked.

'Oh! It's just the one veg box. You know for Zeta. But I would like to do more.'

'Why don't you?'

'What do you mean?'

'I mean, what's the point doing one, when you have so much produce?'

'Well, I don't have any more customers!'

'I know at least five people who would love to have one.'

Heather stopped laying out the plant pots. 'I've never run a business, so wouldn't know where to start.'

'You start by doing what you're doing now, just a few more.'

'Yes, but I don't have your confidence, Will.'

'But I know you do!'

Heather was shocked at his direct reasoning. 'Who else would want one?'

'Well, Old Jim Watkins, he has the workshop next to me, he's a pescatarian and loves his fish and fresh vegetables, he's always telling me what he's cooked the night before. And there's Margrit. She asked me if I did them. You know what she's like for anything organic.'

'Wow!'

'And there are some more I could ask. Don't think of it as a business, but a hobby.'

Heather set out the pots with vigour. 'I'm not sure. It sounds like a business to me. No ... I couldn't do that, I wouldn't know what to do.'

Will chuckled. 'You're doing it with one box; you could do it with six. Twenty-six. A hundred and six, it's all the same.'

Heather shook her head. 'Don't be daft! How would I get them out to everyone?'

Will pursed his lips. 'In my pickup. Easy. We just drop them all off at the same time. Even if they're not in, you can leave them on the doorstep and collect the money when you next walk into the village.'

Heather didn't reply and Will started putting compost into each pot.

'Depends on what you want from it? Are you happy with one box for fun and a few extra pounds a week, or do you want to make that holiday a reality?'

'Let's not go down that route again, please Will.'

'Well, it's up to you? I can drop them off and get new customers and we can grow the veg easily up here.'

Heather threw some compost into a pot. 'So, is that what this is all about? It's actually a money-making scheme for you?'

Will took a seedling and plonked it in a pot and then followed it with an enormous amount of compost. 'I'd be doing it for you!'

'How do you mean, doing it for me?'

'As a thank you for teaching me to read and for this job.'

Heather sighed. If he were genuine, that was a lovely offer. She wasn't used to anyone doing anything for her.

'That's kind Will. But as I said, I don't think I have the confidence to see it through.'

Will potted another three plants in silence and then looked at her. 'Of course you have the confidence. Look at you. You're an incredibly intelligent, capable woman. Your veg is better than in a grocer's shop and it's organic, plus everyone gets to see your beautiful smile.'

Heather felt her head becoming extremely hot and fanned herself with her hand. 'I think you see someone I'm not, Will.'

Will leaned towards her, with his dirty hands on the bench. 'I know exactly what I see. If anyone can do this it's you.'

Heather felt her breathing increase rapidly and an emotional response which caught her completely off guard. It wasn't a tear-jerking, welling-up response; it was a 'he sounds like he believes in me' response. Neither of them spoke, but the air felt thick with processing energy, and the windows looked like they were steaming up. They didn't have to speak; they just carried on potting the plants until the compost was used. Will, then filled up the watering can and gave them a good soaking.

'Do you want me to sweep up before I go?' Will asked.

Heather looked at him. Not only was he a handsome man, she was enjoying his positivity and encouragement. 'No, that's it. I'll finish off,' she said, handing him his cash and pointing to the receipt book.

'I'll see you next week then?' he said, turning for the door.

'Erm,' Heather said. 'Are you free tomorrow? I could do with a hand in the veg patch.'

25

OF MICE AND MEN

When a pickup laden with wooden crates pulled into the drive Heather's heart sank.

'Morning Heather.'

'Morning Will. Who are the crates for?'

'You!'

'It's very kind of you to bring them, but I thought long and hard last night and decided I couldn't run a business. I told you that.'

'Well, I know you can. So, if it's a case of you don't want to do it, then I'll take them back. But if it's a case of you think you can't do it, then that's a different kettle of fish. Well, old boxes of fish to be exact!'

Heather shook her head.

'I spoke to Old Jim Watkins and he said yes instantly. Not only that, you know Mrs Srisuwan at the new Thai restaurant?'

'Yes!'

'Well, she said can you do a box, three times a week, with a view to doing more? She's interested in as many fresh ingredients as possible.'

Heather sat on the wall with her head in her hands. 'I can't do it Will. It's too much.'

'Look! You prepare them and I'll deliver them. It's simple, we can be a team,' Will replied.

Heather got up and started walking towards the orangery. 'We're on camera here,' she said quietly, encouraging him to follow her. On reaching the door, she turned. 'Look. Angus will never agree to it. He hates me working. I want to do it and I'm grateful for you asking those wonderful people, but I can't do it.'

Will scratched his chin. 'Well, it's your choice. But I can see a trip to the Amalfi Coast happening sooner than you think.'

Heather paused and scratched her chin. 'They have Limoncello, don't they?'

'And Prosecco on romantic balconies!' he replied. 'Anyway. It can all be done in the daytime and the boxes can go out under my large leaf bag, so hidden from cameras. Just looks like I'm collecting leaves. No weekends or evenings and everything's on a need-to-know basis. And there's only you and me need to know.'

'You're a very exciting man, you know that?'

'Well, you are helping me get my certificate, okay?'

Heather shook her head. 'I don't know why I'm agreeing to this?'

Will nodded. 'Limoncello?'

The boxes were unloaded, and Heather paced the orangery thinking about where they could be stored. 'What are these, anyway?' she asked.

'They were used to pack fish in ice, for transport, but plastic has taken over, so they were abandoned around the back of my workshop. I thought they'd be the perfect size.'

'They are but the plan is foiled at the first hurdle. There's nowhere to store them.'

Will pointed to the sap-green door in the wall. 'What's in there?'

'No! That's private in there,' Heather said in her deepest voice.

'Yes, but what's in there?' he asked again.

'Things! Onions, garlic, seed. Just things.'

'Sounds perfect to me. We can even store the full boxes which are ready to go out, in there. Keep them out of the sun and the cold.'

Heather put her face in her hands. 'This is why I said I didn't want to do it.'

Will put his hands on his hips. 'You said, it was because of your husband!'

Heather put her hands on her hips. 'Well, there are lots of reasons.'

Will stepped forward, held out his hand and thrust a wad of £20 notes into her hand. 'They all paid in advance.'

Heather stared at the money and then at Will. 'Okay. Let's get packing!'

Deep in the vegetable plot, they rolled up their sleeves and got to work digging up the produce and loading the boxes. They didn't speak. They didn't need to. The boxes were the perfect size, and both of them instinctively knew what items were ready and would fit. Will hid them under his giant leaf bag and wheelbarrowed them to his truck, while Heather turned on the hosepipe, as the hot, dry conditions were starting to wilt some of the greens and lettuce.

Will returned and gave a nod. The sign that everything was loaded and ready to go. Heather handed over the hosepipe and began pacing along the edge of the vegetable plot. 'We might need to expand,' she said, mid-stride. Will sprayed water all over the plants, and when Heather came alongside, he flicked the nozzle above her playfully and watched the spray catch her off guard.

Heather screamed and tried to get away, but he sprayed her again. The hedges prevented her escaping, but she made a dash for it. He pretended he wasn't looking, but as she made it to the lawn, he turned quickly and cast more spray her way. 'Stop it,' she cried. 'That's not fair.' It was hot, and secretly, after the initial shock, Heather loved the cool water on her. She ran towards him to grab the hose. *He had to receive some of his own medicine,* she thought. He teased her, pretending he was going to squirt her head-on, and then turned away, so she couldn't reach. Numerous attempts to grab it resulted in her getting wetter, but she laughed, mainly at her frustration, but also in fun.

In a final attempt, she ran at him, and he fell onto the grass, releasing the hose. That's when the real fun started! She opened the nozzle to full flow and hit him straight on, soaking him to the core. She enjoyed hearing him laugh, and it spurred her on to increase the flow, and they laughed together. Eventually and when he couldn't get any wetter, he grabbed the nozzle and returned the spray with full impact. Her dress, dripping with water was clinging to her body. It felt as if she were naked. Carefree and liberated she laughed, and her body was on full display. They both stopped and looked at each other. His muscular chest, prominent beneath his T-shirt, and her breasts, vulnerable, beneath her dress. A bra was an unnecessary hassle, especially at home.

He walked towards her. His face, now serious and his eyes fixed on her like she was his prey. Then, he scooped her up into his arms and carried her to the orangery. 'You've got me all wet again,' he said, lowering her gently into the doorway. She stayed close and looked up into his eyes. With the heat from his body keeping her warm, she wanted more.

'Can we walk and dry off in the sun,' Heather said, removing her hand from his chest.

Exiting the road through the secret gap in the hedge, Heather felt the sun warm her body. She felt safe with him, and she caught him glancing at her body as her dress clung to her curves. It felt naughty and liberating, and she enjoyed flirting with him.

Steam rose from them as they walked higher behind the house onto the heath. Will carefully removed a mushroom from the dead trunk of an oak tree. He tore it in two. 'It's safe,' he said, popping it into his mouth. Heather hesitated and then put her trust in his experience.

'It's an oyster mushroom and good for you. Good for your heart, gut and has vitamin D, as well as many other vitamins.'

Heather ate hers and felt confident in his leadership. 'I thought we might read together,' she said, nestling herself within the heather and bilberries.

'You know I'm not a good reader!'

'I think it will help you learn and we'll do it together.'

Will joined her as she produced a thin book from her bag. 'It's called *Of Mice and Men*.'

Will shrugged and fidgeted.

'It's the story of two migrant workers who travel around seeking work on California ranches. It is about their friendship and the difficulties they face. One of them has a learning difficulty, but is a gentle man.'

Will huddled close and Heather could not only feel the warmth from his body, but she smelled his musky scent. She started to read to him and smiled as she watched him close his eyes and let his head rest against the rough bark of the tree.

Her voice seemed to come alive, resonating with the natural vegetation and uplifted by the warm sun on their faces.

'They have a close bond, don't they?' Will said.

'Yes.'

Heather read some more and noticed that Will was looking over her shoulder. She loved feeling his chin gently touching her neck.

'So, they support each other and in different ways?'

Heather nodded. 'They have a tough time, moving around and are often treated badly.'

Will pointed at the text on the page. 'He says that the work they do can make them the loneliest people in the world, but together, they have strength.'

Heather smiled. 'Can you read the words?'

'When you say them, I can recognise them.'

Heather put her hand on his knee and smiled again.

She carried on reading until their shadows became long and her thoughts stretched way beyond the heath. Will used his hand to make a shadow of a bird flying around Heather's distorted shadow, and she followed suit, flapping the pages of the book so that they could fly together.

26

SPITFIRE BULLETS

Sawing through silver with a hacksaw was not as easy as she imagined, but she persevered. The hideous ring of diamonds felt like they were a cage around the dove. Trapping her and restricting her flight. Heather sawed and sawed, but made little progress. At that moment, Angus's car pulled into the drive. Heather, in a panic, hid the pendant under a cloth and dashed out of the orangery to greet him. 'How was your trip?' she asked.

He kissed her on the cheek. 'Good, yes, all good. A bunch of new lads, but they kept me on my toes, especially at nineteenth hole. Of course I showed them, there's life in this old dog but suffered with a few twinges on the back nine most days.'

'So, you didn't go with the usual crowd then?'

'No, they all shied off, and when this set of younger circuit judges said they had a deal booked at The Belfry, how could I refuse?'

'You never mentioned them before you went?'

'I know. I'd only met them a couple of times, so couldn't even remember their names.'

'Well come in and I'll rustle up some food if you're hungry?'

'I'm starving.'

'I'm defrosting a chicken for this evening, but can make you a sandwich or mushroom omelette?'

Angus turned his nose up. 'I guess a mushroom omelette it will have to be.'

He disappeared upstairs for a shower and Heather took his bag from the hall, and straight to the laundry, where she decanted his clothes into the washing machine. It was strange! Nothing in the pockets, no receipts, no golf tees or even a stray painkiller. The strong smell of his aftershave was on everything, even his golf trousers and shirt, smelt of it all were surprisingly clean, given four days of golf. She had called The Belfry, when his phone was unreachable, to ask him where the harness for the strimmer was, and he mentioned how warm and dry the conditions were, and that he might buy himself some new kit. There were indeed, a new pair of trousers and a shirt, but they still had their tags attached.

Heather remained on her knees and watched the clothes tumble through the circular glass window. Her stomach followed each turn and tumble. *He was definitely having an affair,* she thought. He had been at The Belfry, that was for sure. *But who with?* And everything in his bag was sterile, like he'd made sure there were no traces of anything. Usually, his pockets were full of tickets, cough-sweet wrappers or little golf pencils. *Maybe she was overreacting?* There was no evidence of an affair. But what about the diamond ring? That was suspicious. *Should she confront him about it?* She pondered as the washing machine churned away. There would be an argument, and that was never good, as there was the possibility of him becoming violent, and he would always drag out the misery for days, leaving her feeling sick as a result.

He had always said he would never leave her. She knew that their marriage was paramount to his success in his career and, moreover, he did occasionally show his love for her. Not often and usually in the form of grand gestures, but nevertheless, she thought that overwhelmingly, he needed her, albeit that he was angry that she had turned out to be a less than perfect wife. Taking to her feet, she decided she would push the two jewellery receipts in front of him at the table and watch his reaction.

Chopping the mushrooms, she felt her hand trembling, and pacing from one leg to another was making it worse. Maybe she wouldn't confront him with the receipts. *What if it was a surprise for her?* She cracked the eggs into a bowl and then grated some cheese. *What did she want with a diamond ring, anyway?* The thought came to her as a surprise. She would never have asked that question before; instead, accepting everything that he did. But she felt different, stronger somehow. *What would she do with another diamond ring?* She already had one, her engagement ring and that was enough. Then there were the diamonds encasing the dove. She had more diamonds than Elizabeth Taylor, for heaven's sake.

She heated up the pan and called Angus for his food. Within a couple of minutes, he was sitting at the table, and she served up his omelette. 'I called someone earlier to come and have a look at that squeaking floorboard in your office. I'd been meaning to sort it months ago. There are a couple of other minor woodworking jobs needing attention too, like the bathroom door sticking and the loose skirting board in the hall.'

'I'll do them!' Angus replied. 'Call whoever, and cancel. I'll sort it.'

Heather shook her head. 'You've known about the door and the skirting for some time and done nothing about them.'

'I'll sort them. I'll do it today,' he said thumping his fist on the table.

Heather was surprised by his anger and watched his face closely. 'That would be fantastic. That door has been driving me mad.'

'I'll do it when I've finished eating. *Okay*!'

'Thank you. I wedged the floorboard after I gave it a good old tug.'

The clatter of Angus dropping his knife onto his plate made her jump. Her skin suddenly felt cold as she noticed him staring at her. 'How's the omelette?'

'How do you mean, you wedged it?'

'I put my finger in the little hole and wiggled it. Seemed to make it worse, so I wedged it with a folded envelope.'

'How much worse?'

Heather shrugged. 'Well, more wobbly. I thought it might come up in my hand but it was hard-fast.'

She could see that he was chewing the inside of his mouth. It was always a sign that he was deep in thought.

'What were you doing snooping around my office?'

'I wasn't snooping, I went to the drawer for more cash to pay the gardener.'

'I'll make a drawer in the dining room instead,' he replied. 'And stay out of my office. There are sensitive documents in there and I'd hate for you to get wrapped up in something which could put you in prison!'

'I never thought about that. You mean if I saw something ...'

'Yes!' he interrupted. 'Could be contempt, so be careful.'

Heather nodded. 'I took the liberty of sorting out our wardrobe, while you were away. Moth-eaten, old-fashioned stuff and things we haven't worn for years. I sent a load to the cancer charity and binned some things too.'

Angus shook his head.

'I found these.' Heather slid the two receipts in front of him and took a secret, but extremely deep breath.

The chewing of his mouth continued as he looked at them, and then at her. She felt her eyelids twitch involuntarily and her legs follow suit.

'Yes,' he replied.

'That was a lot of money you spent on the pendant.'

'Shows how much I love you.'

Heather said nothing. Instead, waited for more. *Wow,* she was feeling strong. This was new, and she wasn't sure where it had come from, but she felt like she had him for the first time on the back foot.

'Where is it? The pendant,' he asked.

'I put it away for safe keeping, and I'm glad I did, knowing how much it cost.'

'It's for wearing not for hiding away.'

'To be honest, Angus. I'm too scared to wear it and would rather just have the dove for day-to-day use and the diamonds for ...'

'You sound ungrateful yet again,' he said, standing and scooping up both receipts in his hand.

Heather leaned on the table. 'What about the ring?'

Angus huffed. 'Well, let's just say, you managed to wreck that surprise. I was going to ask you to renew our vows on our next anniversary.'

She scrutinised his face. His eye contact was faultless. 'When were you going to ask?'

'This week. When I'd returned from my trip.'

'Where's the ring?'

'At work. I kept it there so you wouldn't find it and spoil the surprise. But you've managed to anyway, there's no point now. I'll hand it back and get a refund.'

Heather didn't know whether to believe him or not. *Why would he wait to ask, and why do it now after eighteen years and not their twentieth?*

'You could ask me now,' she said.

He huffed again. 'I'm not going to embarrass myself by getting down on one knee when it's not a surprise. You've wrecked it. Snooping around and blowing everything out of proportion, as usual.'

'I haven't blown anything out of proportion. It's you who's doing that.'

Angus shook his head, and then it came. The spitfire bullets, one after the other and aimed directly at her heart, exploded her newfound confidence. 'Tut, tut, tut,' he said. His condescending tongue, simply, and without any actual words, sliced her up into pieces.

'There you go again. Playing the victim. It's me, me, me, every time. Someone goes out of their way to do a good gesture and you manage to spoil it. I'm beginning to think that you're actually programmed to spoil everything. I blame your parents.'

Heather wanted to beat him. He was so unreasonable, and bringing up her parents was the foulest thing to do.

'I have worked on myself beyond recognition Angus, unlike you. Yes, I carry the guilt and the shame of my father's death and my mother's depression, but I've learned to cope and I've learned how to grow. You're still the little boy who is looking for a pat on the head and to be told he's good enough. I see through you.'

He mocked her with his smirky laugh. 'There you go again. Putting everyone else down. The truth is, you mask your own issues and blame it on me, you just can't see it, can you? You're blinkered. In a dream world. If it wasn't for me protecting you and making sure you're safe here, with everything you need ... well, who knows what would happen. You need to think long and hard about what you say to people and how you go about your snooping, because finding things you shouldn't and then making things up to upset others is borderline narcissistic. I shouldn't say this, but I've been concerned for a while now, but I thought it was a phase. I'll take the ring back and we'll forget about this silly little charade. Okay? And, well done!'

Heather's tears ran silently down her face. 'I haven't done anything!'

Angus brought his face right up to hers. 'That's what all the narcissists say. You need to get help, Heather. You seriously do.'

27

GRATITUDE

M*aybe he was right? Maybe she did need help?* She couldn't see that she'd done anything wrong, but maybe she was still harbouring the guilt over her mother and father's deaths. Some mornings she would wake feeling anxious and out of control. She wasn't sure why, but maybe she did need to talk to someone.

The noise of hammering and drilling upstairs brought her out of her thoughts, and then the doorbell rang.

'Heather!' he said with a smile.

'Morning Will. I'm not sure I can do a day in the garden today.'

She could see him examining the tears on her face and then looking at the car. 'Are you okay?'

'I'm not sure. Just in a daze.'

'Do I need to call the police?' he asked as they both heard the hammering upstairs.

'No. He's fixing a loose floorboard in the attic, that's all.'

'Why don't you make a start on the weeding and I'll join

you in a few minutes, if I feel up to it?' Heather said, smiling as best she could.

'I can help. You know that?' he said, looking up the stairs.

'I'm fine, Will, honestly. It's what married life is. The rough with the smooth, and all that.'

Will hesitated, and with a nod, disappeared around the corner. Heather went to tidy the kitchen. On passing the dining room, she noticed Angus's whisky decanter was out on the dresser and next to a glass with dregs of whisky. It hadn't been there earlier, she knew that, because she'd made sure it was tidy. Hastily, she finished off in the kitchen, put on her gardening shoes and headed out with a cup of tea for Will. She found him on his hands and knees in the rockery, pulling weeds.

'Do I have to be worried?' Will asked.

Heather joined him and pulled out a giant dandelion. 'No. He's okay. We're just not seeing eye to eye at the moment and some days are worse than others. He's always the same when he's been away. I found some receipts and asked him to repair a floorboard. He probably just wanted to switch off and have a relaxing day.'

'What do you mean, receipts?'

'It doesn't matter Will. I don't even know why I'm telling you.'

Will took hold of his chin and shook his head. 'And you mentioned a floorboard?'

'Just a lose one up in his office. It was driving me mad, every time I walked over it, so he's mending that and a sticking door.'

'I'm worried about you Heather. There's something not right. You're not your usual self.'

'You don't need to be worried Will. He's like this sometimes, it's part of being married for eighteen years. You haven't had that problem? Sorry ... I assume you haven't.'

'I've been single quite a while. I've dated and was in a relationship for five years, but I haven't found the right person yet.'

'You will. And of course, you'll be wanting children? There are plenty of lovely women out there would snap you up.'

Will laughed. 'Well, she'd have to enjoy sanding down boats and sailing the seven seas!' he said, rocking his head from side to side jovially. Heather said nothing. In fact, an uncomfortable silence shut their mouths tight as they both listened to the loud banging coming from the house.

Will eventually broke the silence, plucking a tall thistle from the dry soil. 'No sooner have we weeded and they're back, these thistles get everywhere.' He laughed.

'I couldn't have children. We tried, but it wasn't to be. He's angry about that,' she said, looking up at the house. 'He wanted a son. I had two girls, but I lost them before they were born. Sorry! I don't know why I'm telling you that.'

'It's fine, Heather. You can tell me anything and it won't go any further. I'm sorry to hear that. Must be tough.'

Heather nodded and smiled. 'I've learned to cope but most days, I don't feel worthy of being a wife or even a woman! Anyway, again, I don't know why I'm telling you this. Sorry.'

'You're a fabulous woman Heather. Don't put yourself down. Life isn't easy. These things are sent to test us, but it's not your fault. Even if you had the girls, they wouldn't have been good enough.'

Heather felt a rush of emotion, which tightened her throat. 'What do you mean?'

'He wanted a son, you said. So even if you'd had children, it wouldn't have been good enough.' Heather didn't know what to say. She sat in the dirt and contemplated his words. No one had ever said that before.

'He's looking.' Will moved his eyes towards the house without moving his head. 'Up in the attic window.' Heather didn't look, but moved slightly to make the weeding operation look obvious. 'When you say… fabulous … what do you mean?'

Will used his trowel to attack another thistle. 'I mean, you have a lovely heart and a kind soul. Look at what you're doing for me. You're confident about helping me get my skipper's licence, but you're not confident about yourself, but you should be. Look at this incredible home and garden.'

Heather blushed. Looked at him and then back at a nettle, which had already stung her.

'And you're beautiful,' he said transfixed on her face. 'I think you're beautiful.'

Heather snapped back at him. 'No, I'm not. Angus says that I'm frumpy and I need my … body improving,' she said looking down at her chest.

Will shook his head. 'You're perfect. You know … natural and feminine.'

Heather felt her face and neck getting hot. 'You say the loveliest things Will. Thank you.'

'I mean it. Wouldn't say it if I didn't.

Heather examined every part of his young face. His eyes were deep-set between his serious brow and his wilful jaw. He looked as if he meant business, with a forthright face full of depth and intention, his nose was flawlessly proportioned, and his stubbly chin formed the perfect backdrop to his friendly, yet cheeky smile. 'What does life have in store for you Will? What do you really want to do?'

He pondered the question for a moment. 'I'd like to sail away. Explore countries that I've never been to. Raise the sail and let the wind take me on adventures. See wildlife in their natural habitat and be free. To grow old with the sea air in my lungs, the sunrises in my eyes and the sunsets in my heart.'

Heather couldn't help but smile. 'Have you ever thought about being a poet?'

He laughed. 'I can't read or write, but I do get words buzzing around my head sometimes.'

Heather let her heavy eyes look to the ground and lifted them slowly. 'Would you take me with you?'

Will looked deep into her eyes. 'You're a married woman.'

The roar of the ride-on-mower at full revs, made them look. Angus appeared from behind the house, riding it like a maverick gunslinger riding into town. Except his weapon of choice was a nearly empty bottle of whisky, which he waved above his head, and he sang 'Scotland the Brave' at the top of his voice, before glugging the bottle dry and throwing it into the runner beans.

Heather felt her lungs deflate as if he'd stabbed her with a knife. The humiliation, in front of Will, inexcusable and downright deplorable. They both watched him drive randomly around the lawn, shouting the rest of the song before disappearing behind the house.

'Would you, take me with you? she asked again.

He deliberated, looking both at her and at the house. Then nodded.

Heather replied with a nod too. 'I'm so sorry. He can be like this when he's had something to drink.'

Will put his hand on her arm. 'Don't worry, it's his house, he can do whatever he wants. I've seen worse.'

'I'm sure you haven't. He'll probably collapse in a chair and go to sleep, but we might have to weather the storm first!'

Angus appeared again. This time, with a can of beer in his

hand and a further three on his lap. He charged around the lawn, throwing grass clippings everywhere and chanting random lines from the song with pride, and occasionally taking both hands off the steering wheel and thrusting them up into the air, like he was at a rave. Yanking at the wheel, he turned sharply and ran down the edge of the lawn and then slowed down, as he approached. 'Thirsty work, this gardening!' he said calmly and then guzzled the beer before tossing the empty can onto the lawn. Another round of erratic driving saw him open another can of beer and dig the mower deck into the pristine lawn, gouging and scalping it.

'I should probably go now,' Will said, pushing up onto his knees.

'Could you stay?' Heather asked. Her voice trembled as they watched Angus dismount the mower and pee up against the cedar tree.

'I'm not sure I want to see this,' Will said, diverting his eyes.

'I haven't seen him drink this much in a while. Please stay,' she said, grabbing his wrist.

Angus remounted the mower and once again headed for them. Another can of beer was opened as he came close. 'Calvert,' he said. 'Will Calvert. I thought I remembered the name. Your grandfather was an innocent man. Mr Harry Calvert,' he shouted.

Another lap of the lawn and he drove by again. 'An innocent man, but not until he came before me. The jury were undecided, but I helped them to realise he was a good man.' He passed by and did a couple of laps while finishing the beer.

'He would have gone down again if it wasn't for me.' The words came out as if he were a Shakespearean actor. One hand on the wheel and the other trailing behind him in the air.

'*Gratitude*,' he shouted. '*Gratitude*! That's what we need.' He drove the machine up to them and dismounted. He stood broad-shouldered with Will. 'You fucking my wife?'

'No sir.'

Angus looked at Heather and back at Will. 'Leave him alone Angus, he hasn't done anything wrong.'

'I'm not an idiot. And no one makes a fool of me, you got that!'

'Yes sir,' Will replied.

'I remember your grandfather. A snivelling shipwreck of a guy.'

Heather saw Will take a step forward. 'He was a decent man, sir.'

'He was a smuggler. A petty criminal. He served his time for that. But he was no murderer.'

'He was a good man. He showed me compassion and love,' Will replied, standing his ground.

'Compassion and love. Huh! You know that when you're married to a good woman. A woman who respects you and understands what you've done for society. He lived the rest of his life in peace, I assume,' he said, moving closer to Will. 'Don't ever forget that, young man. Life can get tricky if you over step the mark.'

'He died not long after. The whole thing destroyed him,' Will said, straightening his back.

'I'm watching you, lad. I'm watching you!'

Heather intervened. 'Leave it now Angus. Will does a fabulous job helping us here. He's an honest man, I can vouch for that.'

'Where's my other beer?' Angus said, slurring his words and staggering back to the mower. 'Where's my goddamn beer?'

'Why don't I make some tea,' Heather said as she watched Angus reel his way up to the house.

Will turned off the mower and made it safe.

'I'm so sorry about that,' she said, heading with him to the orangery. 'He doesn't mean it.'

'Well, he looked like he meant it, and it's a shock knowing he was the judge who set my grandfather free. In a way I owe him.'

'I'm sure he saw that your grandfather was a good man.'

'Are you going to be okay? I mean ... does he ever—'

Heather cut him off. 'I can handle him. He gets a little boisterous when he's drunk. He'll probably sleep it off and have forgotten about it tomorrow.' Will nodded and set off to deposit the mower back to the garage. Heather went to the orangery.

She watched Will return to the rockery and then looked up from her bench to see Angus staggering down the path towards her. She glanced over at Will, who had his back to her, weeding. She raced to the door as he approached, swigging from a freshly opened bottle of Scotch.

'Don't you think you've had enough now?' she said calmly.

Angus sneered. 'So can or can't I have a drink or two in the privacy of my own home?'

'Why don't you have a snooze and I'll have dinner ready later?'

His breath stank of booze, and his words were heavily slurred. Heather didn't want him inside the orangery. He knew it was her sanctuary. He knew not to cross the threshold. They'd had that argument a hundred times before, and she'd threatened to leave him if he ever did.

'What are you up to in there. Your secret den?' he asked.

'Don't you dare step foot in here Angus. You promised me you would respect that.'

'Respect, respect, respect. Do you respect me? Do you even love me? Do you? Do you?' he asked, walking up to the open door.

'Of course I do. Now go and have a lie down.'

'You talk to me as if I'm a dog. What are you doing in here?' He used his body weight to force her backwards.

'Angus, you promised me!'

His shoulder and arm pushed her to one side. 'Heather's secret orangery. What are you hiding from me in here, my love?'

He walked over to the sap-green door in the wall and grabbed the knob. It wouldn't turn. Heather's heart pounded, and she kept her eyes focused on his hand. He tried to force it and then fell against the door, allowing his hand to turn the wrong way. The door creaked open under his weight. She watched him stagger through the door and then stop. The darkness was enough to make anyone stop in their tracks. 'It's just onions and garlic in there,' she claimed.

Her hands were shaking, and her heart was beating so fast, she felt dizzy. He ventured in further and while flailing his arms, knocked over seed trays and packaging. Standing in the doorway, Heather watched with terror as he collapsed against the wooden cabinet. All she could see was her secret boxes and brochures in her mind. *What would he do if he found them?* she thought.

The cabinet moved under the heavy weight of his body. Heather's heart felt like it would explode at any moment, then he pushed himself back onto his feet and headed back to the door. Heather stepped back to allow him into the light. A deep breath calmed her nerves slightly as he moved away from the danger zone. 'I can put the kettle on,' she offered as a further distraction. His silence felt creepy. His face didn't seem to acknowledge her as his eyes searched and scanned around. 'Would you like some tea?' she asked again.

He didn't respond as he made his way slowly towards her. 'You never told me, that you loved me.'

'Angus, I've told you a hundred times.' His face looked evil. His eyes wide and fixed on her, they appeared empty, yet intent on destruction. 'You're scaring me, Angus. I don't like it when you stare at me like that.'

'How much do you love me?' he asked, leaning against her bench.

'I'm your wife Angus. I'm committed to our marriage, that's how much I love you.'

Both dread and fear hit Heather straight between the eyes when she saw his hand reach out to steady himself on the bench. She could see in her peripheral vision his hand moving in slow motion onto the cloth, which was covering her pendant. She'd forgotten all about it. Down went his hand, straight onto it. Following his eyes to the cloth, she saw him feel something was beneath. He pulled the cloth aside and revealed the diamond-encrusted pendant and hacksaw beside it.

He picked her pendant up and examined the obvious cut she had made in the silver housing. He looked at her. 'So this is how much you love me!'

'Angus, I can explain,' Heather said, noticing him making his other hand into a fist. Hemmed in against the sidewall of the orangery and with nowhere to go, he moved towards her.

'I told you it was too heavy.'

'You selfish, selfish bitch,' he said, raising his fist. She could see the anger in his eyes, and he was gritting his teeth as he snarled. 'Will you ever be a good wife?'

'No, Angus, no!' she cried as his fist drew down towards her.

Suddenly, his arm stopped as Will's arm intercepted it.

'No, you don't,' Will said calmly. 'It wouldn't look good, a judge beating his wife, would it?'

Angus tried to fight back, but Will thrust his arm up his back into a half nelson and marched him out onto the lawn, then dumped him onto the grass. Heather followed them and could see Angus lying on his back, crying.

Will looked at Heather. 'Are you okay?'

Heather nodded. 'Not really.'

Will put his arm around her. 'Let's get him up to the house and work out what we do next?'

Will loaded Angus onto his back and man-handled him to the sitting room, where he laid him out on the sofa. *God, he was strong!* she thought.

Heather walked into the kitchen. Her body was shaking and her mouth trembling; she couldn't hold back the flood of tears.

Will wrapped his arms around her. The warmth of his body helped to reassure her, and his strong arms pulled her in tight. 'You're safe now,' he said.

Heather tried to calm her breathing, by blowing out slowly. 'I'm scared Will. What would have happened if you weren't here?'

He raised her chin with his hand, peering into her eyes. 'Don't worry, I'll make sure you're safe.'

His voice sounded so confident. She could see the strength and determination in his eyes as he slowly moved his face towards her.

Thump! Thump! went her heart. He brought her chin up more and wiped her tears off her cheek with his thumb.

Thump! Thump! went her heart. His eyes were focused solely on her, and her legs felt like they weren't in touch with the ground. He hesitated with his hand touching her cheek; which made her feel dizzy.

Thump! Thump! went her heart, and then his lips gently touched hers. His tender lips, the ones she had watched moving with confidence, kissed her right on her lips. She closed her eyes, and as they moved together; she let go. He was in charge, and he knew how to kiss. Gentle, yet with passion and intent. Sensual, but sweet. She didn't want it to end. It was sublime. With his reassuring hand now at the back of her neck and his fingers in her hair, he manoeuvred her into the perfect position, and she was lost. Lost in his forthright embrace, heady with the smell of his masculinity, outraged at his outright contempt, but there was nothing she could do.

Holding her face with both hands, he wiped away the last remnants of tears. 'You're a beautiful woman,' he said softly. 'You need to leave him.'

Heather's head felt light and disoriented. She pulled away from him. *'Get out!'* she said. *'Get out of here right now.'*

28

IMPOSSIBLE DECISION

The cove was a place of absolute contradiction. A place of safety, sheltered from the wind by the towering chalk cliffs on all sides, the sound of the sea echoed against the walls, like the murmuring of monks in the abbey, all consuming, yet muted as the chalk absorbed the tension in the air. The only way in was through the archway. The natural opening carved out of the rock by the relentless sea. Punching its way through and forming a cave that was open to the sky.

Some called it the witches' cauldron, and some called it the gateway to heaven. For Heather, it was all of those as she dug her heels into the sand and lay on her back looking up into the sky. The thought of the sea rushing in was thrilling. It was there, not so far away, tapping on the door, but for an hour or so, kept at bay. The danger was in falling asleep and misjudging the time, because once the tapping was done, it didn't ask permission to force its way in and consume everything in its path, and Heather loved the thought. It could be ultimate freedom, not to be constrained by anything. To let herself go and enjoy the thrill of the unknown and the potential of losing everything.

But that was the problem. Letting go and allowing fate to take you where it wanted was a beautiful thought. The stuff dreams were made of and the epitome of being a carefree woman. The reality was, she wasn't free to lose herself in gay abandon at all. Her head was spinning with confusing contradiction and the more she tried to sort it into compartments, it all ended up flying around her head like irritating wasps. Will's words resonated in her head. 'You can't stay here.' He was right, of course. Angus had slept through on the sofa, but was unaware she was here. There would be repercussions, and not for the first time. Her stomach turned with fear.

She needed to get a grip of reality. She knew that, and as she lay there with her eyes shut; she raised her arms up to the sky and asked for clarity. For guidance and for resolution. She instinctively reached for her pendant. Holding it between her fingers always gave her reassurance, but of course, it wasn't there. Defaced and adulterated, it had lost its simplicity, its femininity and its grounded energy. It was now a representation of Angus himself, with all his extravagance and show. His expensive, generous persona, instead of allowing the dove to be free, now trapping her within the heavy weight of perceived luxury and arrogance. She felt lost without it, and its lack of guidance was troubling.

What should she do? What was the right course of action? It was the impossible decision. How could she make a choice when she didn't know what she wanted? Life was so unfair. *Why did it put you through so much insecurity?*

To top it all, she'd just kissed a man fifteen years younger than her. But it was the tenderest kiss she'd ever known. His warmth and compassion had presented themselves for her and passed between them in a way only a kiss could do. It was a kiss that could take you anywhere. Combat evil and yet celebrate life. Angus had never kissed her like that. Not once. His tongue was like a contained rat scurrying around her mouth as he attempted to eat her.

Could she leave him? That's why she was stockpiling money, but it wasn't enough to support her, and where would she end up? She couldn't afford to rent anywhere or pay the bills. And what about Benny and her plants? It didn't bear thinking about. Of course, the simplest thing was to stay with what she knew. It had worked well for many years. Yes, there were incidents, and treading on eggshells made life difficult, but she had a fabulous home, and her plants and garden were her passion.

She sat up and clutched her knees tight up against her chest and gnawed away at her fingernail on her little finger. It was Will who had to go! That was the simplest decision. He was the reason Angus was angry. He'd seen them together and overreacted, but he was jealous. Will was lovely and compassionate, and she wished she could have taken some of his courage, but things were manageable at home if she kept things simple. Will had overcomplicated her life there. At first, a huge help in the garden, but he had this thing about him which drew her in and caught her off guard. That was the issue. It was side-tracking her and giving her false hope. And false hope of what exactly? Sailing off into the sunset with a boy nearly half her age.

He had to go. It was as simple as that. To risk everything on a kid who couldn't even read or write. Where was the future in that? As lovely as it was, the kiss. It was an invasion of her privacy and her marriage, and she had to be clear, not only in her own mind but also to him, that it meant nothing, and he was not to compromise her ever again.

He'd be in his workshop, she thought. *Now was the time to be assertive.*

Out of the corner of her eye, she saw the sea filling the escape route. Taking a deep breath, she ran to the rocks and clambered free of the rising water. A scramble around the headland, and then she leapt on the partially visible stepping stones back to safe ground. At last, with some clarity in her mind, she had the courage she needed to power through the sand. This was the female pirate talking now, and it felt good, finding the new strength she had inside her. She wouldn't wait for him to come to the house. It would be too painful. *Better to get it over and done with,* she thought as she stood firm on the sand and looked out over the ocean. 'Be brave,' she said to herself. 'Be brave.'

The beach was busy, and negotiating the windbreaks, towels and sprawled bodies meant a meandering route. She persevered and then slipped in the sand, and as she regained her footing. An arm came from nowhere and thrust a kite string into her hand. She felt the pull of the kite as it dive-bombed towards the sea. 'Pull it tight, pull it tight. I can't handle it on my own,' the voice shouted. Concentrating on the kite, she pulled hard, and the kite narrowly avoided crashing into a man jogging on the shoreline. 'Pull again and run,' the voice shouted again.

Run where? she thought, as she took her eye off the kite and saw Will holding on to the other string. He was smiling.

'I don't know what I'd have done without you,' he said. 'Now run!'

Heather didn't stop to think. If the kite were to hit some-one, then it would be her fault. She ran with him, jumping over sandcastles and small children. 'I can't go on anymore!' she cried.

They arrived at the quieter end of the beach with the kite still aloft. Heather stopped to catch her breath and Will thrust the other string into her hand. 'It's all yours now,' he said, stepping away. 'It's in your hands now!'

'Don't do this to me Will, I've never flown a kite before.'

'Well, there's always a first time. You're doing really well,' he said.

The pull of the kite on both strings was difficult to handle. The kite darted to one side and then the other as she tried to maintain the height with subtle pulls on each. 'Don't leave me with it,' she shouted, as the strong wind pulled the kite, and her body, closer to the sea.

'You're doing great. You're a natural.'

'Take it from me, Will. I have something to tell you.'

'I can't. You have complete control,' he replied, and then he did a handstand to prove his hands were not available.

'This is ridiculous! It's not the time nor the place for gymnastics. Take the kite!'

'Not until you say please.'

'Will. I mean it. Don't test me. I have something I need to tell you.'

He came up between the strings and turned to face her. 'Tell me then?' he said with his hands behind his back.

'I'm not joking Will, please take the kite. I'm worried it will kill someone.'

He came closer. Obscuring her view of the kite.

Heather grappled with the strings as best she could as the kite went out of view. *That was unfair and out of order*, she thought.

'I'm going to let go,' she said, gritting her teeth. He came right up to her and placed his hands on hers with his back to the kite, and looked her in the eyes.

She felt the tension of the strings leave her and fell back onto the sand. Will had taken the strings and confidently brought the kite down in a steep dive into a clear area by the rocks. He then placed a large pebble on the ends of the strings to weigh them down and collapsed beside her. Before she could scramble back to her feet, his hand was once again guiding her head towards him, and that was it. His tender lips kissed hers, and the shock waves ran straight to her toes. Their arms intertwined in a passionate embrace. He was sensual and playful with both his lips and tongue. Breaking away to kiss her cheekbones, and he then slid straight back into what was a full-on snog. *Jeez, he knew how to kiss.* Her heart responded by fluttering like a butterfly on the wing – beating fast and stirring up emotions she had forgotten existed. Her hand moved to the back of his neck and could feel the softness of his hair and encouraged him to continue. His body pushed up against hers. He was warm, and he smelt the same as he did when he had carried her to the top of the cliff at the place where they'd first met. She opened her eyes and instantly saw he was looking at her as their kissing became more passionate. She was sailing into the sunset with him. Momentarily, she was able to forget about everything and lose herself in the moment. He did make her feel safe, but not only that, he made her feel wanted.

29

TRUST ME

Secretly, she watched him and the other men erect the boat's mast. The boat was out of his workshop and in the dry dock. With the bodywork complete she looked magnificent. His seal-watching tours would be like no other. The romance of setting out in the hope of seeing dolphins, seals and seabirds in his sailboat was becoming a reality. His grandfather had done it, and now it was Will's turn to resurrect what had been a thriving business.

She didn't want to be seen, and instead watched him from among the crowd of people also curious about what was happening. She'd dropped off some reading cards that she'd made for him in his workshop. They'd discussed what he had to do, and she hoped he would take time out to continue his learning to help him pass his boatmaster's exam.

September saw the hectic chaos of family fun within the village give way to the older and more genteel holidaymakers. The sun was losing some of its heat, but the days were still long enough to be out in the evening.

A huge crane supported the wooden mast as the men fixed

it in place. Will was clearly in charge. *Damn that man! What had he done to her?* she thought as she carried on secretly watching him. The crowd eventually moved on, and Heather made her way out of the harbour. On passing Dune, she barged in through the door and saw Lesley at the counter. 'Fancy that coffee?' she said with a sigh.

'Perfect timing. It's dead today. What's on your mind?'

'Men!'

'They're all bastards, have you not worked that out yet?' Lesley replied. The coffee pot was always on, so it wasn't long before the two of them had each pulled up a stool and were sipping away.

'I thought everything was rosy up there on the hill.'

'Remember the purple dress? He hated it. Wanted me to wear black leather bondage gear instead.'

'No way,' Lesley said, dropping a sugar lump into her cup.

'We haven't been seeing eye to eye for a while now. I've felt like I'm just his slave. Cooking, cleaning and treading on eggshells in case I upset him. He seems to be getting angrier and angrier.'

Lesley took another sugar lump. 'Sounds like I'm going to need some extra energy. Why do you think that is?'

'He works hard. It's a demanding job. I try and make our home a lovely place for him to relax, but he's started taking me for granted.'

'Sounds like a typical bloke to me!'

'Nothing is ever good enough. I try harder and he tells me I'm a failure.'

That's not good,' Lesley replied.

'He tells me I'm not a good wife, which is true.'

Lesley shook her head. 'How do you mean it's true?'

'I couldn't have children. He's made me feel guilty about it and there's nothing I can do.'

'Of course you can do something about it.'

'I can't. He controls everything. The finances, the car, where I go, even our friends. I really wanted the job here, it would have suited me down to the ground, but he wouldn't allow it. He'd make it difficult; say I was neglecting my duties at home or accuse me of flirting with other men. But I've never had my own money, and that was the main thing.'

'Sounds like a narcissist to me.'

Heather shook her head. 'He's just ambitious and a little headstrong, but he's a good provider. I fell short. I could have done better.'

'Why don't you leave him?' Lesley smiled.

'How can I? I love living there. It's my home, my sanctuary.'

'Has he ever hit you?'

'Well ... erm ... just...a. He can be very thoughtful and loving.'

'Really?' Lesley asked, probing. 'Sounds like you're in denial.'

Heather paused and took a gulp of coffee. 'Have you been spending time with your grandson?'

Lesley grabbed the coffee jug and topped them both up. 'You're changing the subject, but he's a smashing little fella. I took him on the steam train; you know from Pickering. It's where they filmed the Harry Potter and Downton Abbey train scenes. Have you been? It's so beautiful chugging through countryside.'

Heather shook her head.

'Well, we had a fabulous day. He's only six and jumped for joy when the driver allowed him on to the footplate.'

Heather smiled. 'Sounds lovely.'

Lesley grinned. 'I'm a proud grandma. Sorry! Anyway. Back to you. Like, I say, it sounds like you're convincing yourself that he's a good man. And if you're telling me about this, then I reckon, you are asking for help. You aren't the first and you won't be the last to have suffered at the hands of a man. And I'm qualified to say.'

'Well, steady on, he's not that bad.'

'You need to leave him Heather. Stop kidding yourself it's going to get better.'

Heather sighed and closed her eyes. She didn't want to start crying, but hearing that made her stomach turn. 'Will said that too!'

'Who's Will?'

'Well, that's where it gets complicated.'

'No shit, Heather. Who is he? Are you having an affair?'

'No, no, not at all. Honestly. He's ... a friend. In fact, he's just a young lad, but ...'

'But what? Do you have feelings for him?'

Heather paused. 'He's beautiful. Kind, funny, strong and ... his kisses are—'

'So, you've kissed him?'

'Only once ... well, twice. But there's nothing going on.'

Lesley opened a cabinet and took out a bottle of sherry and two small glasses. 'This calls for something a little stronger, I think. So where does that leave you?'

'Confused. Giddy, frightened. I'm all over the place.'

'Cheers!' Lesley said, chinking glasses. 'Well, look. There's a place here for you whenever you want it. There's a flat above the shop. I'll rent it out, but it's yours for free if that helps.'

'Thanks Lesley. That means a great deal. But I think it's

just a phase. I'm flattered by the attention, but I think Angus and I should try and work through it.'

Lesley necked back her sherry and slammed her glass on the table. 'You need to leave him. I know you're not telling me the whole story. I used to think I could work things through with my ex, but how long do you keep trying? You need to stick up for yourself, be brave and do what your heart tells you, not your head. Run away with the mystery man if you want, but my advice is, do it for you. Your own pride and your own sanity. Do it Heather, before he goes too far. Do it Heather, trust me.'

30

THE TRUTH

'Is it just you?' the skipper asked. He had an anchor embroidered on his blue and white hat.

'Yes,' Heather replied. 'Will we see seals and dolphins?'

'We can never guarantee seeing anything, madam, but we have heard reports of a pod in the area.'

Heather handed him her ticket and followed the other people onto the boat. She was the only person on her own, and she felt conscious that they were all looking at her. Instead of taking the stairs to the top deck, she remained at the back, where an older couple and a younger couple with a baby made her feel less judged. Buoyancy aids were handed out, and Heather strapped hers on with great anticipation.

The boat chugged out of the harbour and into the open sea. Heather put on her woolly hat and brought the collar of her coat up around her neck. The air was bitterly cold, and the sky grey. It matched her feelings. Well, she didn't know what she was feeling. She had a numbness within her thoughts, which prevented any kind of productive thinking beyond survival.

The boat rolled with the waves. It was neither rough nor smooth. An in-between, 'can't decide' kind of sea, and it was as grey as the sky. Noncommittal and mundane in many ways, and seemingly unsure of its true potential.

Passing the corner of the chalk cliff, the skipper pointed to the mass of seabirds, which not only filled the sky, but also every nook and cranny on the sheer cliff face. *It was incredible how they were able to perch on what seemed like nothing;* she thought. Gannets dominated the area with their enormous bodies and their six-foot wingspans, and tiny puffins darted across the sky and then spread out their stubby wings as they crashed in an ungainly way onto their landing points, narrowly avoiding their neighbours.

It almost seemed impossible that there were so many birds inhabiting the same cliff. *The world was full of impossible things,* she thought. The birds made her think about the impossibility of decision-making, and when faced with a fork in the road, the agony was as sheer as the cliffs before her. Two routes ahead, both with positive peaks and negative troughs, and no clear route, which confused her. She felt sick.

She gazed out of the back of the boat into the unsettling grey water. *What should she do? Run away with a much younger man into an unknown world and risk everything or stick with the devil she knew?* She'd dreamt of running away. A tall, dark, handsome knight on horseback, sweeping her off her feet and defying her husband to set them free and ride off into the dawn with only the clothes they wore, but knowing that their love would bind them forever and keep them safe. Her reality was that she had a life that was okay, just okay! She knew exactly where she was in that life. Angus was working most of the time, or he was away, so her time was filled with the things she enjoyed most. It was merely a logistics operation.

Will had brought disruption to her life, and it was unsettling. Unexpected in many ways, despite being the answer to her dreams, those dreams were never meant to come true. It was merely an escape. A fantasy, a dalliance with romance and a way of coping. *Did she resent him for that? It was difficult to say. Was she glad he was in her life? Yes. That was a definite.* He made her feel worthy. Not a feeling she'd ever felt before. It was a surprise, and although in her mind she didn't really believe it, her heart was in with both feet. That alone was enough to send her into a spiralling mess.

Angus was something entirely different. He'd rescued her from her insecurity, saved her from her shame and given her a life of certainty.

'Seals!' someone shouted, and the boat listed to one side as everyone dashed to take a look. Heather glanced in the same direction and saw the heads of two seals in the water. It was the same couple she'd seen before. They were always together, guiding each other and keeping each other safe. Their faces, looked surprised, yet knowing. Heather chuckled within her body. How wonderful it must be to spend every day of your life in awe of what it brings, but have the wisdom and knowledge that each day brings new challenges, but together, you can face what's coming and have the confidence to know you'll work it out. *That's what a partnership should be,* she thought as she watched them disappear under the rolling waves and then reappear closer to the boat.

Was Angus her seal of life? Was he her protector and her soulmate? He used to be, or so she thought, but maybe she had changed? She had witnessed some growth in her confidence, but in her mind, she was always 'Heather'. But Will had brought a new energy to her. *That's what it was,* she thought, nodding to herself and smiling at the seals who dared to get even closer to the boat. A new energy which seemed to flow into herself. He believed in her. The veg box business. It was his idea that she could do it, and she hadn't realised just how much, he'd influenced her. Not that it made any difference in making decisions. In many ways, it made it more difficult. The younger Heather wouldn't have questioned it. She was grateful for what she had been given, and there was no reason to change that, but now she was questioning everything. *Was Angus having an affair? It certainly looked like it, and what did that mean to her?* Was she upset at the deceit and scared of the future, or was she glad that he might even make the decision for her? It was neither, and it was both. The irony and the agony of rocking the boat. Surely it was better to stop thinking that she had changed and that she had any kind of control over her own destiny. Thinking about it only brought unrest, and it unsettled her to the point that it made her despise herself.

'Dolphin's' someone shouted, and the boat keeled dramatically to the opposite side. Heather turned her head and gasped at the sight of three dorsal fins riding gracefully out of the water. What an incredible sight to see wild animals so close. A fourth fin became visible, and then one leapt out of the water with a playful roll and flick of its tail. A tear ran down her face. *Such freedom, with no constraints, just following their noses and exploring uncharted waters.* Heather felt her fingers and toes tingle with excitement. *Maybe, that's what she was really craving?* In fact, she knew deep down that was exactly what she wanted. Lake Garda, the Baltic Sea, the river Nile, it didn't matter, any free-flowing water would be enough to set her free. Maybe she needed to find the truth? The dolphins and the seals didn't appear to be deliberating about which direction they were heading; they were confident in their ability to just do it. It was time to stop floundering at the water's edge and jump in with faith.

'*The truth,*' she said to herself. '*The truth.*'

31

SECRETS

The wonderful thing about having a husband who was meticulous was that his garage was set out like an operating theatre, with everything in its place. A board on the wall housed all the tools, which were suspended by hooks, and the outline of each tool drawn on so that placement post-use was both easy and clinical. Hammers, chisels, wrenches and saws, all in their correct place and ready for use.

But there was one tool that stood out among the others. A tool that meant business. A tool which offered nothing more than brute force and capability in the right hands and a tool which was able to unearth lies. Heather reached up and grabbed the steel crowbar and examined its swan's neck shape and the claw end and then the chisel at the other. 'Swan neck, I'll call you,' she said, turning her back on the other tools and walking purposefully back to the house.

Climbing the stairs, she gripped harder and harder on the tool and made her way to the attic. Benny followed her. His tail held high with anticipation, but she closed the office door behind her and excluded him from entering.

'Look what I found,' Heather said, brandishing the steel crowbar.

'That's perfect,' Lesley replied. 'I've managed to loosen the screws. We just need to prise up the board and find out exactly what he's hiding up here.'

Heather nodded and slid the chisel end of the bar between the floorboards and began levering. Lesley held the lookout position in the window and offered words of encouragement as she scanned the driveway and road.

'Thanks for helping me. I didn't have the courage on my own,' Heather said as she popped up the end of the nailed-down board.

Lesley come to take a closer look. 'What surprises me, is that this board has been fastened down with screws and nails, but none of the others have.'

'That's because I said I was going to get someone in to repair it, and he went mad. A guilty conscious for sure.'

Lesley shook her head. 'But you said it used to be under the rug and now it's exposed.'

'I know he's hiding something under here, Lesley. I just know it. all the 'late meetings' and the receipts. He's having an affair.'

'They're all the same. No commitment, no balls!' she replied, giving a hand for extra leverage.

The board slowly raised and, with a little more force, popped up, enabling the two of them to get their fingers underneath and open up the void beneath. 'Mmm,' Lesley said. They looked at each other, and then down into the empty space between the joists. They looked at each other again. 'Thinking about it. Was he likely to hide his secrets under the most obvious board!' Lesley said.

Heather bit her lip. 'But I'm sure he's hiding something.'

Lesley scouted the room for other clues. 'You say the rug used to be here but it's now over there,' she said, pointing at the heavy pile rug, which was nearer the door. They both grabbed an end and pulled it back. 'We're looking for scuff marks, chipped varnish, that kind of thing,' Lesley said as she scrutinised the boards.

'This one seems slightly higher than the others!' Heather said.

'And the board next to it seems to be damaged along the inside edge.'

Heather quickly got to work with the crowbar and prised the floorboard so that once again they could lift it and see what lay beneath.

As it popped up, they looked at each other, then again at the void between the rafters and then once more at each other. 'The dirty bastard!' Lesley snarled.

And there it was. A secret stash of four shoeboxes.

'Let's see what he's hiding,' Lesley said, lifting the lid of the first box.

'*Stop*!' Heather shouted. 'I don't think I want to see. What if it's ... you know ... awful?'

'Whichever way you look at it Heather, it's awful. Your husband has a secret stash, and you just want to cover it over and forget it isn't here?'

Heather reached down and removed the first lid. They both looked at each other and then quickly back at the contents of the box.

Bundles of £50 notes fastened with rubber bands filled the box to the lid. Heather gasped and lifted the lid on the second box. Her heart raced as she revealed yet another stash of £50 notes. 'There are thousands here. What the hell is he doing hiding all this money? Who would do such a thing?' Lesley asked. Heather looked at her sheepishly and shrugged, before daring to lift the lid on the third box. The ring! Ten or twelve expensive-looking watches and even a solid gold bar, the size of a matchbox. A black velvet bag revealed a handful of diamonds and, next to it, a very cheap-looking trophy with the words 'Angus MacLeish. Junior Golf Champion 1989'.

Heather sat back on the floor and sighed. 'Do you think he's a thief?'

'Looks like money laundering to me. Whatever it is, it's underhand, or why would he hide it? Anyway, the bottom line is he's keeping secrets from you Heather.'

Heather paused while she contemplated her own secret stash in the orangery and said nothing.

Suddenly, the sound of a car door slamming outside alerted them. Both Heather and Lesley sprang to their feet and raced to the window. Fixing down both floorboards would be a challenge if Angus was about to walk in the door and Heather's hands shook with nerves. She struggled to catch her breath. Lesley doubled back and picked up the boxes and shoved them back in the void, then manoeuvred the floorboard towards the gap.

'It's okay. It's okay. It's a delivery,' sighed Heather.

'A bloody delivery! I thought he was home and we'd both be buried under the floorboards.'

Heather smiled and calmed her breathing. 'It's just some bulk corned beef. I'd forgotten I'd order it.'

'Corned beef?'

'It's one of Angus's favourites and helps to keep costs down,' Heather replied.

Lesley burst out laughing, with tears streaming down her face. 'That scared me. You've told me how physical he gets sometimes. I thought we were doomed. And the irony of you saving a few pounds on corned beef, when there is literally a million pounds hidden in your floor!'

Heather put her arms around Lesley and hugged her tight. 'Shall we have a look in the next box?'

She reached in for the fourth and final box, and Lesley grabbed her arm. 'If this is body parts or some kind of voodoo shit, I'm out of here!' she said, raising her eyebrow.

Heather opened the lid and saw a pile of papers and photographs. Lesley huffed. 'This is where we get the detail. You're going to divorce him, aren't you?'

Heather lifted the photos first. A picture of him at school holding the very same golf trophy. A picture of his graduation day, flanked by his mother and father. Their glum faces seemingly reluctant to celebrate the event. A picture of him receiving his wig and gown in a black suit, contrasting against a bright red carpet. Lastly, a photo of his father in full naval uniform, looking mean and extremely serious. Heather handed it to Lesley and then rifled through the paperwork. Certificates of achievement, degrees and masters, down to his school gymnastics awards and cycling proficiency test. They were all there. Then there were handwritten letters from Angus to his father.

Heather read one out loud.

'Dear Father, I've been doing a lot of thinking recently. It's just that I have been doing really well at school. Straight A's, in fact. I've won trophies in golf and swimming. I've smiled for cameras and heard applause all around me, but when I search for your eyes in the audience, you are never there.

'At home, your silent judgement of how I could do better eats into my heart. I know you want me to join the Royal Navy, but as a cadet, I knew my seasickness would prevent it. I've decided to become a lawyer and, hopefully, a judge. Maybe I can bring justice to this cruel world, and maybe one day you will be proud?

'Angus.'

Heather looked at Lesley and bit down on her bottom lip. 'There's a whole pile of them!'

'This looks dodgy. Money laundering if you ask me or something worse. Why would you keep this secret from your wife. Maybe he's waiting for the right moment and he'll run off with the stash?'

Heather's head rocked back, and she closed her eyes. 'It's a shrine to his father.'

Lesley shook her head. 'What do you mean?'

'It's a collection of all the things to make him proud. He always craved that from him and it screwed him up'

'Bullshit! Heather. There's a considerable amount of money here. He's planning a surprise departure, if you ask me, and he'll leave you high and dry.'

Heather continued to look through the papers and wept. So many accolades, letters and newspaper clippings. Then one caught her eye. She read, 'Judge revokes unlawful imprisonment charge as local seafarer sails freely once again.'

It was Will's grandfather. Wrongly imprisoned and Angus was the judge who set him free. A newspaper cutting which, under any other circumstances would go unnoticed, but for Heather, the weight of this article was comparable to the solid gold bar in the box.

'He's a good man,' Heather said, wiping the tears from her face.

Lesley huffed. 'Don't get caught up in all this Heather. You've told me, he lies to you, and he is mean and cruel sometimes, not to mention his heavy hand!'

'He's my husband, Lesley. I feel his pain. His father and the way he was treated. I feel that. It's one of the worst feelings you could have. It's not his fault.'

Lesley's eyes dropped to the floor and then back to Heather. 'Only you can decide what's best for you. We can all make excuses for other people's behaviour, but at the end of the day, we have to be true to ourselves.'

'It's a shrine. It's his way of proving that he's a success. I know his pain, I feel the same, he's not a bad man.'

Lesley shrugged and shook her head. 'What's that one?' she said, pointing at a newspaper cutting that lay on the floor. Heather quickly scooped it up. 'It's nothing,' she snapped. 'We'd better get all of this put away now.'

'It doesn't look like nothing to me. What is it? The truth? The final incriminating piece of the jigsaw puzzle, which you want to sweep even further under the carpet. Or floorboards.'

'I thought you were my friend? Why are you being so cruel?'

'I want what's best for you Heather. Simple as that. Are you going to show me what you're hiding?'

Heather felt her temples pulsing, and her head felt dizzy. 'I can't. I mean, I shouldn't. It was a long time ago.'

'What was a long time ago?'

Heather reluctantly handed over the cream-coloured, faded newspaper cutting and gulped.

'Speeding Driver Kills Toddler!' Lesley read out the headline and continued. 'A newly qualified driver has hit and killed a three-year-old child on his way to nursery with his mother. The car, which was speeding near the school collided with the boy, who was pronounced dead at the scene. The driver, who lived in the area, was given a custodial sentence and banned from driving for five years.'

'The bastard,' Lesley said, shaking her head. 'Drunk I bet. Has he no conscience?'

Heather's bottom lip began to tremble, and her dizziness made her eyes blur. 'It was me! I didn't see him coming out from behind the parked car. A split second, that's all it was. I didn't mean to do it. He just ran out.'

'But you were going too fast?'

'My mother had called me at work. She'd been badly beaten by my father. I needed to get home.'

'Shit! That's a mess. What did you do?'

'I stopped to help the child, but it was too late and then the police came.'

'I'm sorry to hear that. What happened to your mother?'

'He beat her so hard, she could barely breathe. A broken arm and bleeding from her nose. I could have prevented it getting out of control, but they took me to the police station and I was charged.'

'So that's why you don't drive?'

'I haven't driven a car since.'

'And I thought it was Angus who wouldn't let you.'

Heather shook her head. 'No. I was too scared to even think about it. I could have prevented it. All of it!'

32

GUIDING STAR

'I need to talk to you Will. I've been thinking and we need to have a proper conversation about what's happened recently. I also have exam papers for you. They might help you pass your exam.'

'Meet me at the lighthouse at dusk,' he replied.

'Why the lighthouse?'

'I'm celebrating something.'

'Celebrating what?' Heather asked.

'It's my birthday and you know I don't have anyone else.'

Heather's heart buckled. The tug of war pulled at her heartstrings once again. 'I'm not sure Will. I have things to sort out here at home.'

'Well, you said you wanted to talk to me?'

'Yes! But not on your birthday.'

'Please! I have no one else and if it's the last thing we do, I think we deserve to at least chat.'

Heather huffed.

'I've made food and I'm getting dressed up. It would make my day,' he said.

Heather sat in her chair with her eyes closed and rocked back and forth. She had feelings for him that she couldn't ignore and didn't want to let him down.

Grabbing a generic birthday card from her drawer, she signed it with a kiss and then headed to her dressing room.

There were two men in her life now. But the tables had turned. She sat on the edge of her bed and pictured them both, side by side. The man and the boy. Total opposites and both pulling at her heart, with their heels firmly dug in and their arms hauling in an ironic tug of war. The boy, with his fat belly and his shrine to his father, feeling sorry for himself, with his pathetic, sycophantic offerings of worthlessness. And the man, gallant and honest, his back strong and his moral compass set to rescue mode, he is heart, his driving force and his courage, hoisted high on the mast of adventure.

She was drawn to him, no matter how uncomfortable it made her feel.

Dressed up! What did that mean? Heather searched through her wardrobe and picked out a couple of outfits. *Trousers were probably best suited to venturing into the unknown*, she thought, and mixed and matched a variety of tops and cardigans, but none really seemed to say, celebration.

She tried on a long dress, but it was hardly appropriate for a lighthouse. *Men!* They had no idea what a dilemma it was to choose the right outfit. In complete frustration, she called him.

'Whatever you feel good in,' he said. 'Pull out all the stops, I'm wearing a suit, and we'll be inside and don't forget, I've prepared food too. I appreciate you making an effort.'

Putting her phone down, she was still unsure of what to wear. Making an effort! She didn't want to let him down, of course, but comfort was also a priority. Her gardening dungarees hung on the back of the door. She looked at them. They were the most comfortable item she had, and she felt good in them, but they were hardly celebration standard.

She scrutinised her body in the mirror. *What was she doing? Was she being stupid?* Then, her eyes caught a glimpse of the purple dress, which had been stuffed to the back of the wardrobe!

Perched on the edge of the mountainous cliff, the white lighthouse stood erect and proud. Its base, secured within the rock itself, and the tall, white tower and glorious glass lantern room obvious within its extreme location. A guardian cloaked in white, it oversaw the treacherous rocks of the headland. It's bright light, a symbol of guidance and safety and a beacon of hope and resilience in the darkest of days.

Heather exited the taxi and could see Will in the doorway as she approached slowly in her stilettos. He was smiling and as he'd said, wearing a suit, blue with a white shirt, with the top two buttons open and clutching a large sprig of flowering heather.

'Good to see you,' he said, handing her the heather.

'That's very thoughtful of you, Will,' she said, kissing him on the cheek. 'You look very handsome. Happy birthday."

'It's all around here, the heather. I thought you might like to be amongst your namesake.'

She felt her legs go weak in her black heels and started to wobble. 'I think I wore the wrong shoes.'

Will steadied her with his muscular arm and then produced an enormous metal key from behind his back and looked up into the sky. 'We both did,' he said, laughing. 'But don't worry, we're going up in the world tonight.'

'Up the tower?' Heather asked.

'Follow me.'

Will placed the key in the sap-green wooden door. It was

the door that had inspired Heather when she painted the door in the orangery. It made her smile. The spiral stone steps greeted them as they entered.

'Would you take my coat?' Heather asked as she slid it off her shoulders to reveal her outfit.

Will stopped in his tracks. 'Wow!' he said.

'Do you like it?' Heather asked.

His eyes looked her up and down and sparkled as the light from the tower lit them both up for a few seconds. 'You look incredible. I mean really, incredible.'

'I haven't worn this dress before,' she said, looking down at the way it accentuated her figure before curtsying with her arms out.

'I've never seen such a beautiful woman in all my life. You're like a purple dove. Carefree and ready to take flight.'

Heather looked him in the eye. 'I have to find my strength before I can fly.'

Her heart was beating so fast it made her feel giddy with excitement. When she was with him, it felt right. She was safe and homelife paled into insignificance. *Was it wrong?* she thought. As she followed Will's lead and, in her bare feet, with heels in hand, she climbed higher and higher up the lighthouse.

It was a strange feeling being in the tower. Heather had only ever observed it from the outside, and seeing the steps light up as clear as day every twenty seconds and then plunge into darkness was unnerving, yet exhilarating. On reaching the top they entered the lantern room, and Heather was speechless when she saw the gleaming lantern up close. The beautiful, crystal-like centrepiece, radiating its powerful light across the ocean, made her gasp. Will walked around the glass turret, which offered a 360-degree window to the night sky.

'It's incredible. How did you get the key?'

'I know the keeper. It turns out, he's dyslexic too and he's been helping me with a bit of writing.' Will took her by the hand and led her to the front, overlooking the ocean. Sun-dried tomatoes, black olives, feta cheese, salad and Quiche Lorraine were all laid out on a blanket and surrounded by cushions. It made her heart dance with joy. 'Did you do this?'

Will smiled and added a log to the wood stove. Its deep red glow warmed the tower perfectly.

Sitting on the cushions in a figure-hugging dress was an art, but she felt good. In fact, she'd never felt this good, and although the entire situation was off the wall, Will's chivalry and warm greeting made her relax. With a panoramic view of the night sky and the vast ocean before them, Will invited her to tuck in to the Mediterranean feast.

'I'm not even going to ask how you managed to get all this up here,' Heather said, shaking her head and smiling.

'There's a pulley. Goes all the way to the ground,' he said, looking proud. He leaned over and opened a tiny window and produced a bottle of prosecco from a bucket suspended on a rope. 'Helps to keep the wine chilled too!' They both laughed, and Will's cheeky smile seemed to light up the tower more than the lantern.

'I can't believe you had to go to all this effort for your own birthday!' she said.

Will poured the fizzing wine into the glasses. 'I'm not really celebrating my birthday. I thought, we'd celebrate life. Hope. You know, possibilities,' he replied.

Heather nodded softly and took her glass. 'So, you made me dress up in heels and a dress to celebrate life and hope?'

'No! You chose what to wear. I just said wear something you feel good in.'

'She laughed. 'You're impossible, you know that?'

'Yes! But I'm glad you did. You look radiant and feminine.'

She felt her face getting hotter. 'You make me feel feminine. No one has ever done that before.'

'You're a very beautiful woman, Heather.'

'I nearly didn't come.'

Will nodded. 'I'm glad you did. It's important to me.'

'Why?'

'You mean a lot to me and I'm grateful for you helping me to read. I've booked my boat masters licence exam. I wouldn't have had the confidence to do it again without you.'

'Oh Will. You have the confidence to do whatever you want.'

'And I've never been in love before, until now.'

Heather felt her guard completely drop. He was everything a man should be. Strong and capable, but with humility and a hint of vulnerability. She was falling for him, she knew it, but it still felt wrong.

Heather kissed him on the cheek and handed him the birthday card. 'Here's your present,' she said, opening her bag and handing him a set of papers. 'It's last year's exam paper. I know someone on the inside.'

Will took the papers and thumbed through them. 'Can we go through them together, so that I can feel intelligent.'

Heather paused and examined his beautiful face. 'Will, you are a talented skipper. You always have been. The captain of your own ship. Confident in your ability to navigate turbulent waters and weather the storms of life itself, but with a fine and gentle touch upon the rudder, you reassure your passengers that everything will be okay.'

'Are you all right?' he said with a concerned brow. 'You

might need to eat some food, before you have any more prosecco.'

'Oh, Mr Calvert,' she said, shaking her head. 'You have no idea. No idea at all what a master of your own destiny you are.'

'Cheers!' they both said, chinking their glasses together.

'Well, you are too!'

'I'm not. I wish I had your confidence. You know what you want out of life. I'm such a mess,' Heather said, sipping at her glass.

'You're not a mess. You have complete control of your destiny too. Why are you any different?'

'You're a single man with no ties. You can wake up in the morning and decide to do whatever you want.'

Will looked at her with those stern eyes of his. 'And you can do exactly the same. You chose to live in a beautiful place, you chose to have Benny with you, and you chose to come and meet me here tonight.'

Heather listened to his words. They seemed difficult to hear, jumbled somehow. 'No, I didn't. It's just what happened to me. Circumstances.'

Will shook his head. 'I'm sorry, but you're wrong. My grandfather said to me, life is what you make it. You are not a victim of life; you are the creator of your own reality.'

'What does that even mean?' Heather asked.

'It means, every morning you wake up and flick the switch. You either choose A, or you choose B.'

'You make it sound like it's a simple case of coffee or tea.'

'It is. Just choosing A instead of B, because it's the path of least resistance and then complaining about it, is not a life worth living. You have the power and authority to change that.'

'But what if things stand in your way? Things you have no control of.'

'That is life, and you always have control. Climbing over the things which stand in our way is what make life worth living. It's tough, there's no denying it, but the choice is always ours.'

'I hope you're not patronising me, Will. I hope this isn't some kind of game.'

Will topped up the prosecco in her glass. 'You could leave him tomorrow, you know that.'

'No, I couldn't. What about the house, what about Benny and my garden?'

'You can make that again. It might look a little different, but you'll find and make whatever makes you happy.'

'But I am happy!'

Will didn't reply. He just looked at her with those stern eyes yet again.

'But it's alright for you,' she said, feeling frustrated at his retort.

Will shook his head. 'Would you trade your expensive toaster, parquet floor and your garden for ultimate safety, freedom of your heart and true love? Well, that is the question you have ask yourself!'

She felt as if she'd been told off by her mother. Reprimanded once again for not being good enough. She sat in silence, resenting every word he'd just said.

They both sat looking out across the ocean with their backs against the base of the lantern, and the silence of the outside world, magnifying their thoughts. The only two things that cut through were the sound of the lantern switching on ... and then off, and the squeak of a tiny mouse, which scurried across the floor to nibble on a morsel of feta cheese. Heather watched the mouse. It was so small and timid, stopping to check for danger, and then scurrying across the floor in the hope of finding a meagre morsel. *How did it get all the way to the top of a lighthouse?* She thought. She hated being told off. First her mother, then Angus, and now Will. *Why was it always the same?*

The silence continued, and Heather felt Will's hand touch hers on the floor. It made her heart race. His gentle touch was reassuring, welcome and electrifying, and her guard began to drop again.

'You're the most beautiful woman I've ever known. I can't stop thinking about you.'

That was out of order. It was easier for her to lump all the bad people in her life together and resent them en masse. Then he goes and says that!

'I mean it. From the day we first met. Here, below this lighthouse. I was captivated by you.'

Damn him! Why did he have to say that? The tingle was coming. In fact, it was too late! It had already entered her hand and arm and was working its way towards her heart.

She couldn't look at him. Instead, she let her eyes wander across the ocean and, between blinding flashes from the lantern, picked out the lights of ships way out on the horizon.

'Your hair in this light. Any light. The way your lips move. The way you walk and the way your dimples get bigger when you're thinking.

Her heart thumped hard and fast. His words sounded genuine. But no one had ever said things like that to her. She deflected his attention by standing and pointing out into the sky.

'Which is the North Star?' she asked, feeling relieved that she had halted his charm offensive.

Will joined her and pointed into the sky with one hand and put the other arm around her back and held her waist with his hand. She felt safe and wanted.

'It's easy to find,' he said as the lantern lit up the sky and then plunged them into darkness. 'Well, usually easy to find, if you're not in a lighthouse!' Their eyes adjusted, and he located the star again. 'Look for the two stars at the end of the Big Dipper's bowl. They point to the North Star. It's pretty much always in the same location, so that's why it's been used for navigation for so long.'

Heather nodded. 'I noticed you had the mast installed in your boat.'

'Yes, she's looking really good. Should have her in the water pretty soon.'

'Do you have a name for her yet?' Heather asked.

'Not yet. It will come to me. I'll let nature decide her name.'

Putting his hands on her waist, he turned her slowly to face him, and then combed his fingers through her hair, pushing it behind her ears to reveal her neck. She could see his eyes were serious and full of intent as she relished his hand through her hair and then momentarily at the nape of her head. He did it again, this time gently tugging her hair as it tangled between his fingers. It made her shiver, but shiver with release. His touch was sublime. Gentle, yet strong. Looking into his eyes, the silence between them felt dangerous and exciting. He gently pulled her towards him and hesitated. His eyes never faltered as they drew her in.

And that was it. He brought his lips to hers and touched them softly. It was a reassuring and respectful kiss, one that encompassed both their gratitude and their longing. She could feel it. He was kind, and he was gallant. He was romantic, and he was exciting. Her legs felt weak, and he kissed her again, this time tilting her head so their lips met like they were soulmates. Equal, playful and intoxicating.

She felt safe within his kisses as they took her spiralling out of the tower and up into the night sky. Kissing with their eyes open felt liberating and enthralling. Watching his eyes penetrate deep into hers, her heart pounded as if it were pushing liquid concrete around her body, but at a fast pace. It was the heartbeat of change. It was the heartbeat of liberty, and it was the heartbeat of desire.

'Run away with me Heather. Run away with me,' he said.

Heather bit her lip. 'It's been wonderful, but I think I should go now. I've loved every second of being here with you, I really have, but I must get back.'

Will held his gaze and then smiled. 'I understand. I loved it too. Thanks for celebrating with me. I'll call you a taxi,' he said, before kissing her again.

33

ALWAYS

Things had happened fast at the lighthouse. Their kisses were like nothing she'd ever known, and she loved it. Above all, he made her feel good about herself. Feminine, desired and respected.

Driving back in the taxi, Heather's mind was on his smile and his hands touching her. He was amazing. Different from any man she'd known, and he meant what he was saying, she could not only see it, she could feel it, but it felt so wrong. So, earth-shatteringly right, yet wrong on every level. She felt numb and longed to be held. To have protective arms around her, showing the way.

'Turn around!' she said calmly. 'Take me back to the lighthouse.'

The door was open as she approached. The sap-green, turning orange as the lantern lit up the coastline. Heather walked slowly up the steep steps and, on reaching the top, saw Will with a blanket around him on the cushions nibbling olives. 'I didn't know if you'd still be here,' she said, warming her hands by the wood stove.

'I didn't expect you either,' he said opening the blanket for her. 'Will you keep me safe?' she said.

'Always,' he said, wrapping the blanket around both of them. Heather rested her head on his shoulder and relished the warmth from his body as he wrapped his arm around her and held her tight. She'd never felt as safe; she could feel his love pulling her in close to his body and knew he was honourable.

'Always,' he repeated.

Waking as the sun warmed the lantern room, she felt disorientated. Not exactly sure where she was. Will was stoking the stove which had kept them cosy all night. She watched him and admired his gentle movements and felt her mind clear, like a sea-fret fading and the sun rising in her soul. He was in her heart and deep. Like never before, a feeling which excited her and filled her with compassionate warmth. She had changed. He had influenced that. He had made her realise what was important in life. It wasn't a house or status; it was all about love. True love. *You almost didn't need food, if you could feel truly desired,* she thought. It was a feeling unlike any other, and she was in with both feet.

She refused his offer of a ride home. It was safer to get a taxi than risk him being recorded on camera. She walked to the gate; her heart sank like a lead weight into the ground. Angus's car. Unexpected and glaringly obvious in the drive as she walked in after being out all night. Her body jerked, and a shiver, like the devil himself was crawling through her bones, made her stop and stare at the lawn. There he was! Sitting in his armchair by the orangery, smoking a large cigar and brandishing a half-empty whisky glass. He looked smug as he puffed smoke into the chilly air. Then, suddenly, she felt a pain as strong as a punch straight to her stomach as she observed the debris surrounding him. The whole orangery had been ransacked and strewn all over the lawn. She felt another blow as her lungs were unable to draw air and her organs felt like they had been punctured. The sap-green door, lay on the grass. Ripped from its hinges, it housed a pile of objects that hadn't seen the light of day for a long time. A display of guilt like an island amid the upturned seed trays, discarded plants, papers, pots, watering can, tools, her crumpled sparkly windmill and broken furniture. He'd emptied everything and, central to it all, were the pile of holiday brochures, a plastic tub and a shoebox.

'Glad you could make it,' he said, smirking.

Heather's legs gave way as she staggered towards him. Collapsing onto her knees, she saw him lift her passport and flick through the pages. 'Thinking of going somewhere?' he said, kicking over the pile of brochures and causing the contents of the boxes to spill out in front of her.

Heather shook her head. 'I had to dream. Where's my pendant?'

Angus shrugged.

'Where is it Angus?'

'You hated it?'

'Where is it?'

'You tell me? You've hidden it, like everything else. Like this, hiding it from me, so you could get away. What made you think you could do it? You can't even drive,' he scoffed, waving her driving licence and then throwing it into the flowerbed. 'Dangerous driving won't get you far.'

She crawled on her hands and knees to retrieve it. 'I did it for my sanity. You've no idea what it's like.'

'And congratulations are in order too.' Reaching into the

envelope, he revealed her certificate. 'Maritime navigation! Who knew you were a sailor? You're quite the mystery woman, aren't you?'

'You hid things from me and I hid things from you. That makes us equal,' she said with a tear rolling down her face.

Angus took a long, slow puff of his cigar and then exhaled the smoke before glugging his whisky. 'Yes. Equal, except you don't know what you're doing, do you? Holiday brochures, really! You know you can go anywhere. All expenses paid. All you have to do is ask. Anyone would think I'm some kind of ogre.'

'I was just thinking ahead. Maybe a change from Scotland.'

'And I thought you loved it there.'

'I do, I'm not ungrateful.'

'I don't blame you, Heather. It must be tough living with me.'

His turn of phrase caught her off guard. 'Do you think you deserve better?' he said, finishing his cigar and throwing the butt onto the lawn.

'Sometimes! I'm scared of you when you're drunk.'

'Do you hate me?'

Heather closed her eyes and felt her lungs filling with air. 'Of course not. You've given me everything Angus. Do you think I don't know that?'

'I thought we were there for each other, but you've changed.'

She took to her feet and inhaled another deep breath. 'I've tried to be a good wife. It hasn't been easy. I know I fell short of your expectations, but I've tried, I really have.'

She could see he was chewing the inside of his mouth as he stroked his chin. 'And I've supported you in your career and made sure we have a beautiful home.'

He nodded. 'If you want, we can put all of this to one side. Draw a line under false hope and make a fresh start.'

'What about the ring and all the things you hid from me? Is there anyone else?'

She saw his eyes look down at the floor. 'Proof. Proof to the world that I'm doing a good job, that's all.'

'You don't mean the world you mean your father.'

He clenched his fist and bit down on it with his teeth. 'I am better than he was. He is a nothing to me. A nobody. I have more than he ever did, and I have you. A loving wife, who adores me,' he said, taking to his feet and grabbing her by the arm. 'You do love me, don't you!'

Leading her to the house and up the stairs, her arm hurt with his grip. He opened the bedroom door and threw her onto the bed like a rag doll. 'It's time to draw a line under everything,' he said, exposing her legs and dropping his trousers.

She might as well have been dead. Her mind was numb. Empty and desolate as she lay there with his weight fully on top of her. The dutiful wife at his disposal, yet again and no better than a piece of meat, grateful for everything he had provided. Of course. *How lucky was she to have all of that? How lucky was she to have been saved, and how lucky was she to know, he was truly there for her?*

His grunting shifted her indifference to relief as he claimed his feast and then rolled over onto his back, panting.

Heather walked straight into the shower and let the warm water flood her skin. It poured over her face, and her open eyes stared at his grotesque body on the bed like a gorged maggot. She wanted the water to wash her away. Cleanse her from the inside out and let her disappear through the plughole and not have to face him again.

He lay there while she silently dried herself and put on her joggers, T-shirt and fleece. Men were disgusting. Playing with her emotions, like she was a puppet. They were foul beasts with no care for anyone's feelings and he was the worst.

34

THE COVE

'Need a hand?' Will's voice behind her made her heart jump and her skin turn icy cold. The steps down to the beach, where they had first met, were steep in places, and a steady arm would have been perfect.

'No thanks!' Heather replied as she carried on walking. 'I said to meet in the cove.'

'I never did what I was told. You seem anxious?'

Heather didn't reply. Instead, she concentrated on reaching the beach. Will caught her up and placed his hand on her shoulder, and she instantly dropped it to release his hand.

'Is your exam soon?' she said.

'Next week.'

'How are feeling about it?'

'Nervous. I've been there before and it's daunting.'

'You'll be okay. I know it.'

'Thanks to you.'

Heather walked to the edge of the water. The waves tickled the sand and then retreated with force. 'Looks like the tide is going out,' she said, turning to look at him.

'You look stern, but beautiful,' he replied.

'Don't do this to me Will.'

'Do what?'

'The charm offensive. You know I'm a vulnerable woman. I need stability and reassurance not love-bombing.'

'I've never love-bombed anyone. You know what I say is genuine. Anyway, what's got into you?'

Heather jumped up onto the rocks and negotiated her way around to the cove entrance. Waiting for the sea to relent, she made a jump for it and landed on the sand, then ran between the chalk cliffs. Will followed and dashed ahead, forcing her to stop. 'I'm grateful, you know that? I'm reading more now. It's all because of you.'

'I'm glad to hear it Will. You've done well, but there's something I need to tell you.'

'What is it?'

Suddenly, a wave rushed into the cove and soaked their feet. 'Damn it,' Heather said, moving towards the back of the cove, where the tall cliffs felt protective.

'Are you running away with me?'

Heather bit her lip. 'I'm not the woman for you Will. I can't have children. You deserve better. I'll hold you back.'

Will looked her straight in the eye. 'I love you. I want you by my side'

Her breathing quickened, and she could feel her throat tightening. 'You don't love me Will. You barely know who I am.'

'I know how I feel. I'm not a child.'

'You're fifteen years younger than me; you're just a boy.'

Will grabbed her by the arm. 'Get off me!' she said, pulling her arm from his grip.

'Do you think I don't know my own mind? There isn't a day

since we first met that I haven't wanted to be with you. Yes, you've helped me, but it's more than that. Much more. Chemistry, magnetism, call it what you want, but I've felt it and so have you. I'm not some kind of heartless narcissist, I feel it and I feel it deep in my core.'

'I'm leaving him!' she blurted out.

Will said nothing, just stared at her.

'I've decided to leave him. But I'm doing this for me. Not for you, but for me. I need to feel strong.'

'I can help you,' he said, smiling.

'I need space Will. Time to work it all out. Come to my own conclusions.'

Will picked up a pebble and threw it with force into the water. 'I don't want you going back there.'

'I'll be fine, Will. I'm stronger. Things have happened. I feel different, and that's because of you. I'm grateful, but I have to stick up for myself and I won't let a man decide what I do or what's best for me. You understand?'

'I'll have the boat ready in a couple of weeks. We can sail away together and leave all of this behind.'

Heather's heart twisted, and the pain within made her well up. 'Stop it, Will. I've made up my mind. Whatever path I choose, I have to do it without you. It's like having an affair, and I can't live with that on my conscience.'

Will picked up another pebble and threw it with frustration through the arch and far into the sea. 'I have to respect that, but it's not easy for me. I won't let him hurt you, but it's your choice.'

'It's not easy for me either. You are a beautiful, beautiful young man. I have to do what's right for me for a change and although it breaks my heart, I have to let you go.'

She could see the tears running down his face, and it set

her off too. The sorrowful energy between them seemed to pull them together closer than ever as they wrapped their arms around each other. They sobbed and squeezed each other tightly. Their tears mingled together as their lips touched. 'I love you,' he said. 'That will never change. I'll be waiting for you.' Heather's tears streamed uncontrollably. 'Don't say that. You have to go and live your own life. Find a beautiful girl and make a new life and have children.'

'I'll be waiting for you, Heather,' he repeated and then broke their hold.

Heather nodded and wiped her tears on her sleeve. 'I'm sorry Will.'

He controlled his tears with all his might. 'I love you Heather! And always will. I understand that you need to find your own strength. But I see it in you. Your search is over. You're an incredible woman and it's there within you. If you need me. Show me a sign. You know where I'll be.'

Heather watched him leap up onto the rocks and disappear around the corner. Her sobbing made her stomach ache with bittersweet pain, as if she had been stabbed repeatedly, and then she collapsed onto the cold sand.

What had she done? She'd broken his heart. He didn't deserve that, but she had to be true to herself. Lesley had taught her that, and it was no use pretending that she had any kind of future with him. *Better to deal with it now than leave it, and then suffer greater pain later,* she thought as her tears continued to flow. He was a beautiful man, but the complications of children and stifling his life didn't bear any further thought. *It was best. It was done.* It felt like she'd done the right thing.

35

WHEELBARROW HELL

One veg box fit perfectly into her wheelbarrow. Its squeaky wheel, virtually unnoticed on the short trips within the garden, was now irritating as she approached the top of the hill. Heather dropped the handles, rested it on the cobbled road and took a deep breath. It wasn't, an everyday deep breath. This was a defiant and rebellious one, and even more powerful when you're pushing the world up, off your shoulders and building your strength. She knew it was there, hiding. It had first become evident when spiteful Sharon used to bully her in the snicket and the breath helped her to absorb the pain and try and make it look like she was rising above it. Anyway, wheeling a fully laden wheelbarrow down a near-vertical road demanded an element of control, and she was determined not to be beaten. Well, at least hang onto it and try not to kill anyone on the way down.

She couldn't help but notice Will's pickup parked near the bookshop, which made her more determined. She dropped the veg box off at the hairdresser's, gritted her teeth so much, it started to give her a headache and set off up the hill for the next box. 'One down, eight to go!' she said to herself.

It wasn't long before Heather realised that forcing a wheel-barrow with a squeaky wheel up a near-vertical hill was not only sheer hell, it was a fantastic way of trudging through your mind and punishing yourself with the agony. All those foul memories from her past and the guilt she had held deep inside her. *What if her father had got home later that day? What if she had set off earlier? What if she took a different route?* All questions that she'd asked herself over the years, and never an answer. But this time it was different. She'd read about 'being empowered' but it never meant anything to her, she'd never been empowered to do anything. *Was the determination within her, changing everything?* She had no clue, but something had changed, and as she trudged against the hill, she imagined all the people she most wanted to bludgeon to death with a pickaxe and mentally carry out the act with the least amount of guilt. Her mother and father, Angus, Sharon Sandford, Amy Armitage, Mr Parker her old Headmaster, Bertie the dog, who took her toy sailing boat from the pond in the park and destroyed it before burying it in the woods. All of them, metaphorically bludgeoned and dealt with so that her mind could be free.

She reached the top of the hill, stood up straight and took in the deepest of deep breaths and while putting her hands on her hips, screamed at the top of her voice. The echo against the cliffs, reverberated within her soul.

She didn't need a man. They caused her nothing but heartache and trouble. The thought of her pathetic father was clear. Moaning about his miserable life and blaming her mother. They were both to blame. Victims. Sorrowful victims of their own lives and with lack of courage or conviction.

Wallowing in the mire of self-pity and blaming everyone else. Heather had carried not only the responsibility of her father's death, but her mother's insecurity and negativity. '*Enough*', she shouted as she witnessed a mother usher three small children away to the other side of the street and two old men shaking their heads. 'What's up, never seen a grown woman stick up for herself before?' she bellowed at them.

There was something religious about setting off again and again with the heavily burdened wheelbarrow. Almost akin to sitting in church with her mother on a Sunday morning and contemplating their sins. There was nothing quite like creating gratitude by persecuting yourself. Telling yourself that you weren't worthy, and that you had to strive to become a better person, and that one day, the powers that be, if you'd sinned enough, might just forgive you.

Old Jim Watkins, went some way to cheering her up as she dropped his veg box off.

'I never thought I'd see the face behind the fabulous veg box and what a beautiful one it is,' he said, winking at her. Jim was not a man to mince his words, nor to tell lies. He was as open as the sea and as honest as the deep-set wrinkles on his face. A grafter, a celebrity among fishermen and a true gentleman.

'I'm so glad you're enjoying it, Jim. I'll try and keep it going as long as I can!' Heather said with her fingers crossed behind her back. *How could she ever think of letting these people down now?* she thought.

'Do you still have a boat out there, Jim,' she asked, pointing to the array of boats before them.

'No lass. Them days are long gone for me. I'm ninety years old next month, and the sea gave me everything, but it's time for the younger ones to reel em in now,' he said, pointing at Will's boat, which looked ready to sail.

'It's a beautiful one is that,' Heather replied.

'Restored it himself, he did, Wilder. Incredible hands and a craftsman, despite borrowing most of my tools.' He laughed.

By the last barrowful, she was on her knees, crawling up the hill, but she had a business. Earning her own money and feeling proud of herself. She sat within the barrow overlooking the village and the sea beyond and opened a can of lemonade. 'Cheers!' she said to herself, and then burst into tears. But not sorrowful tears. They were tears of relief. It was looking like she'd initiated a plan. A life-changing plan, and it felt big. *Could she really do it alone? Did she have the courage to see it through?* She shrugged. *How did you actually know if you had the courage or not?* she thought. The thing was, and whether it was courage or not, she felt she had changed, and that in itself, felt liberating.

Heather tidied the lawn of all the debris and placed everything back into the orangery as before. Broken furniture went on the fire pile, and her passport, driving licence and cash had already been stowed carefully in the house. Benny helped by pouncing on anything that moved in the breeze and chased fragments of bedding fleece across the lawn. 'We're moving to a new home,' she said to him but he didn't hear. Instead, left her feeling mean about moving him to a flat in the village. It wasn't ideal, but she couldn't leave him in the hands of Angus.

36

FESTIVAL BLUES

Red, white and blue bunting zigzagged across every street. The white rose of Yorkshire punctuated almost every house, and the sound of folk music filled the harvest festival air. Everyone came to the festival. It was your duty. The young and the old, from the salty sea dogs to newborn babies. If you lived or worked in the village, then you were the village. It was a celebration of the sea and gratitude for all it provided. Dancing in the street was compulsory, and eating and drinking your statutory duty.

Heather wove her way through the revelry and stopped in front of Dune. She looked up to the window above the shop. 'We're going to be safe, Benny,' she said, stroking his nose through the bars of the carrier.

Lesley opened the door and gave Heather a hug. 'You've done the right thing you know!'

Heather sighed and smiled, as Lesley took them up to the flat. 'Stay as long as you need,' she said, handing her the key.

The flat was small, but self-sufficient, with a bedroom,

bathroom and studio kitchen. 'I took the liberty of getting some cat bowls, food and a litter tray,' said Lesley.

'That's so kind of you. It was all too much to carry. I will have to go back for more clothes later.

Lesley nodded. 'I'll give you ten minutes to get sorted and then you're coming with me.'

Heather scowled. 'What do you mean?'

'The festival. No one misses the festival, not even you.'

'I don't want to go. Leave me here. I'm happy, just Benny and me.'

Lesley grinned while shaking her head. 'You're coming with me and we're going to show the world that we are strong.'

'I'm grateful for the flat Lesley, I truly am, but I don't want to leave Benny, and I have things to sort out.'

'Nothing that can't wait until tomorrow. Benny has food and water and his cushion, he'll be fine.'

A variety of stalls lined the street, and fairy lights lit up their wares as the stallholders tinkered with their displays and chatted enthusiastically about their craft. They strolled arm in arm along the Main Street and lingered at every stall. Dressed crab, prawns and cockles in plastic pots were popular, and Lesley treated them to one of each to share. The pub had a stall on the street selling local cider and beer. 'Two pear ciders please,' Lesley ordered as Heather rolled her eyes.

She held on to Lesley's arm as they watched a fiddler play his intoxicating and fast-driving reel with a supporting band of accordions, harmonicas and guitars, and Heather's feet tapped to the beat, and her body began swaying to the rhythm.

Heather bypassed the handmade jewellery stand and lingered by the hat stall. She tried on a pink and white woolly one and rejected it following Lesley's comments about looking like a marshmallow. Moving swiftly on, the next stall had an array of books and a sign saying 'Meet The Author'. Heather picked up a book with a green cover and read the back page. 'What kind of things do you like to read?' asked the author. 'Romance, true crime?'

'You love a good romance don't you Heather?' Lesley piped up.

The author's eyes lit up. 'Well, this one is a love story. Unhappily married woman, seeks solace with a rugged and handsome odd job man and is torn between the two.'

Heather placed the book calmly on the table. 'Sounds horrific... What happens?'

The author chuckled. 'Well, I'd be giving away the plot, but let's just say, she has to bury a few skeletons in her cupboard, overcome huge obstacles in her life and find the courage she needs to be true to herself.'

'Sounds like utter clap-trap... How much?'

'You hoooo,' a piercing voice shouted. They both turned to see Amy teetering on her impossibly high heels and heading towards them. 'Hello darlings, how are you?' she said, kissing Heather on the cheek and then Lesley.

'And where's the most handsome man in the village? You didn't leave him at home did you? Haven't seen him on the thirteenth tee for a while, but I sometimes take a different route, you know with the dog.'

Heather glanced at her seamed stockings and totally inappropriate footwear. *'Trollop!'* she thought and then wiped her lipstick off her cheek with a tissue from her pocket.

'You on your own?' Heather asked.

'I left Neil at home with a twelve pack and a Second World War film. You know what he's like, as much use as a floppy anchor. He never comes to things like this. Anyway, saw you in a taxi the other night, looking smart. Go anywhere nice?'

Heather coughed and stumbled off balance. 'Must have been someone else. I don't go out much myself.'

Amy nodded silently. 'Ri-ight!'

The music became even louder, and more revellers took to the street to dance. It was difficult to hear Amy talking. Something about Neil and his dodgy hip and Heather's gaze wandered to the band. *Wouldn't it be lovely to dance,* she thought, and then something caught her eye. Will! chatting to a girl over by the fudge stall. They knew each other, obviously, and she kept putting her hand on his shoulder and laughing.

'I said, Angus promised to come over and give me some advice on the neighbour's new wall. I'm sure he's taken some of our garden.' Amy shouted. 'He's a judge, not a lawyer. Anyway, we've split up.'

'What?' Amy shouted.

Heather looked back to the fudge stall. Then, a gut-wrenching blow to her stomach. The sight of Will and the girl dancing in front of the band. He was confidently twirling her so that her dress spun up to reveal her legs, and the two of them were laughing. *Not that she was bothered.* Of course not. He was a free agent, as was she. He could dance with whomever he wanted.

'Can we go now?' Heather asked.

'What's got into you? You're behaving very oddly.'

Heather closed her eyes and shook her head. She felt a coldness within her feet and hands, but moreover, her heart felt it too. She looked up the street to see Will spinning the girl around and smiling with joy. Her stomach churned, and the coldness quickly turned into an impending heat. Beads of sweat ran down her forehead, and before she could scurry into a corner, she vomited all over Amy's shoes.

'Tea solves everything,' Lesley said, pouring them both a cup back at the shop.

'Are you alright?' Lesley said, handing Heather the tea.

'I'm so sorry. I don't know what happened. I'm a mixed bag of emotions.'

'Was that him, with that girl?'

Heather nodded. 'It's okay. We had a discussion about me doing this alone. I don't want him mixed up in it all, especially if Angus gets wind of it.'

'So, you're protecting him?'

'I guess so. He's has his own things to deal with and he's young enough to have children.'

'But you love him?'

Heather struggled to reply. 'I ... I ... can't be held responsible for someone else's lack of offspring. I can't have that on my conscience.'

Lesley topped up the cups. 'But he said that he loved you?'

'Yes.'

'Well don't you believe him?'

'I'd feel guilty holding him back. I can't live with that, Lesley. It's worn me into the ground, since I bore the responsibility of my father's death and my mother's misery.'

'None of that is your fault, Heather.'

'I know that now, but it doesn't take away from the fact I can't have children. Will deserves more than that. He'd make an amazing father.'

Lesley put her hand on Heather's knee. 'It sounds to me like you're punishing yourself.'

'I'm doing this for me Lesley. You taught me that, you should be proud.'

'Lesley flung her arms around her. I am. I know how hard it is, but I see the spirit in you now.'

Heather went up to the flat and cuddled with Benny, who purred and nuzzled her with love. She unpacked some personal items and started to make the flat feel homely, then sat in the chair by the window and looked at all the missed calls and texts from Angus. 'Let's talk. Come home. I'm sure we can work this out!' And more. Many more. They were overwhelming and some of them nearly compelling, but Lesley had said not to respond. Instead, she sat in the window and watched the party continue in the street.

A text from Lesley drew her attention back to her phone. 'Stay strong and don't give in to him! XX'

37

SUBLIMELY PERFECT

It was the same place as her navigation exam – the Maritime Institute building, behind the town hall. She hung back within the shadows of the pine trees on the other side of the road and watched them congregate outside. Will sauntered up and chatted with a couple of the other young lads. She watched his expressive face as he pointed over to the harbour and as the group laughed together. A man in uniform came to the gate and opened it. That was her cue to cross the street. 'Hey. Good luck,' she said, walking by him and not intending to stop.

He grabbed her arm. 'Thanks. How's it going up there?' he asked, stopping her in her tracks.

'It's going okay. I just wanted to let you know that I'll be thinking about you in there. Stay calm and make sure you read the questions fully. You know the answers.'

Will, pulled her closer. 'Thanks. It means a lot. Did you get the parcel I left you in the orangery?'

'When did you leave it?'

'Yesterday. Don't worry, I sneaked in the gap in the hedge. Looks like you had a change around in there?'

'Something like that. How's the boat?'

'Almost done. Just rigging the sails and loading the fridge and she's ready.'

Heather smiled. 'I'm happy for you and your grandfather.'

'Mr Calvert?' The man enquired whether he was going inside.

'Yes! I'm coming.'

He let go of her arm. 'See ya.'

Heather raced past the harbour. A quick wave to Old Jim Watkins as he dragged a couple of Marlin across the compound and then she climbed the hill. It never got any easier. In fact, it felt like it had grown and become steeper. Out of breath, she maintained a decent stride and then dived behind the bus shelter. She saw Sally walking towards her on the opposite side of the road. She'd probably been loitering near the house. Anyway, today was not the day, for filling anyone in on recent events, and she didn't have the energy for, just chatting. Edging around the wooden shelter, Heather timed her moves to hopefully stay out of sight.

'Damn!' Heather shouted. She stepped straight into a steaming pile of dog mess. That's just what she needed, she thought as she peered around the corner.

'Is that you Heather?' Sally's voice came from the front of the shelter.

'Yes, it's me,' she said, creeping out onto the edge of the path and vigorously wiping her shoe in the grass.

'What are you doing behind the bus shelter?'

Heather shrugged and laughed, then smiled and rocked her head from side to side while pursing her lips. 'You know me. I think I spy an unusual plant and I'm in there!'

Sally's eyebrows raised as she watched her systematically clean her shoe. 'What plant was it?'

'It ... erm ... wasn't in the end. No plant, in fact ... just a beer can, you know, caught my eye.'

'You seem flustered, are you alright?' Sally asked.

'I'm fine, honestly, I'm fine. Here ... for the cats,' she said, handing her a £20 note.

'You don't have to give me money every time I see you, Heather.'

'I know, I know, it's just, you do such a fabulous job.'

Sally took the cash. 'Well don't feel guilty if you don't next time.'

Heather felt like she had slapped her in the face. *Guilty! That was it.* She was paying for guilt she didn't even know she was feeling guilty about. The irony was shocking. 'Thank you, Sally. You've really helped me today.'

'I haven't done anything!'

'You have, you have no idea, how much you've helped me. Anyway, got to dash, got to dash.'

Heather marched away and headed for the house. At the gate, she looked up at Highcrest in all its glory and wondered why she'd never stopped to look at it from this angle before. *I guess you don't when you live in it and see it every day,* she thought.

Walking in felt strange. No Angus, no Benny and an eery silence. It almost felt like she was trespassing! Opening the front door, she paused and peered in. It was her home, but she felt like she was merely visiting. She immediately turned and headed down the path to the orangery. Again, an eery silence accompanied her as she opened the door and walked in. It was unusually warm for early December, and some of the plants looked dead. Her heart sank as she walked between the benches and pulled plants out of their pots. She'd neglected her pride and joy and felt sick. The watering can was half full, and she emptied it among the plants that had managed to hang on.

Turning on the radio, she spotted the parcel on her bench. It was wrapped in black plastic and had a sticker on it, saying, 'Seed'. Heather sat at her bench and proceeded to open it. A brown cardboard box, about the size of a shoebox, with a lid intrigued her. *What was it?* she thought as she tentatively lifted the lid, and then instantly closed it. *What the hell!*

Heather sat in a daze. Unable to move and shocked at the contents. Plucking up the courage to look again, she opened it and took a closer look. Money! And lots of it. A ridiculous amount of £50 notes bundled together and an invoice. She took it out and scrutinised it. Sale of diamonds £45,000. A handwritten note at the bottom caught her eye. 'It was the best I could do.'

Heather felt her shoulders being pressed towards the ground as if the surrounding cliffs were weighing down on her. There was one thing left in the bag. A purple velvet jewellery box. She hesitated and breathed deeply before scouting around to see if anyone else was there. *Old habits and all that,* she thought as she double-checked the driveway. She felt vulnerable with such a large amount of money in her possession, and reaching into the box made her hand shake. She held the box in the palm of her hand, she could hear something rattling inside. She partially closed her eyes and nervously opened the lid.

She gasped! It was perfect. Sublimely perfect. The simple circular pendant was restored to its former understated glory, and in the middle, the beautiful dove with its wings aloft and its diamond eye dazzled her. Her grandmother was back with her, and it felt incredible. Squeezing it in her hand, she let her grandmother back into her thoughts and deep within her soul. 'It's good to have you here. I need you,' she said.

The repressive weight felt like it was being lifted from her shoulders as she fastened it around her neck. Heather pressed her finger against the diamond, and let it cut into her finger. The words of her grandmother came straight into her mind. *'When challenges come, face them head-on. They are the times when we learn and grow. Embrace change and you will live to be grateful, but also fly with absolute freedom.'*

Her words seemed meaningless at the time. Wise words into young ears, but she had remembered them, and today, they had incredible relevance and meaning. 'Not so easy, though,' she said out loud. 'You wouldn't wish it on anyone else, would you?' She continued looking up into the sky and pressed hard on the diamond.

What a thoughtful man! Will had not only taken care of it for her, he had realised the importance of the simplicity and brought it back to its former simple glory. She'd never witnessed that level of kindness before. Thoughtful kindness, unconditional kindness and a sentiment which made her mind, body and soul feel warm and loved.

She brought the pendant to her lips and kissed it. The time was right. She had money to make change, and she had love within her heart. 'Embrace the change,' she said and rose to her feet.

38

BEAST CLIFF

'What are you doing here?' Angus's voice scared her to death.

'I was making sure the plants were okay,' she said, covering the box with a newspaper.

'I want you home, where you belong.'

'It's gone too far Angus. I've been treated badly and I have to stick up for myself.'

'I miss you. This isn't a home without you. We've been together a long time and, yes, we've probably taken each other for granted ...'

Heather butted in. 'Too right you've taken me for granted. I've done my best to make this a happy life. I trusted you and you betrayed me. I'm not a skivvy or a punch-bag. I'm worth more than that Angus.'

'Can we go into the house and talk?' Angus said, smiling.

'I think we've said all we can.'

'Please! I owe you an apology.'

Heather paused and nodded. 'I won't stay long, just five minutes.'

In the kitchen, Angus poured her a glass of white wine. 'We've hidden things from each other, secrets we should have talked about. I should have been more honest.'

Heather refused the wine and stood up straight. 'Now we're getting somewhere. Go on.'

'Golfing and working late. I realise I should have been at home. I neglected you.'

'Don't stop there Angus,' she said with her sternest face. God, she felt strong.

'It's what everyone else was doing. I thought it was normal.'

'Now that looks like a step backwards to me Angus. Are you sure you don't want to rethink that?'

'You've changed.'

'No shit, I've changed. You've put me through an emotional rollercoaster and you expect me to not have changed?'

'Look. We've both changed. I thought you were happy and I made sure that I provided the best life for both of us ...'

Heather butted in again. 'Three of us!'

'Yes, yes, Benny, of course, the three of us, and I was only trying to do my best.'

'But why did you lie to me regarding the shrine to your father?'

Angus slammed his glass down on the table. 'It's not a shrine! It's a collection of good things. Achievements, investments, keepsakes. Everyone has those.'

'Not hidden under a floorboard Angus. Other people are proud of them and display them on a shelf or in a glass cabinet.'

She saw that his breathing had become more rapid and his voice was shaking. 'My father never showed me the respect I deserved. I wanted him to be proud of me.'

Heather nodded, but kept her back straight.

'I've been proving myself to him, since I can remember.'

Heather sighed. 'I know that. But you didn't have to! We are all seeking validation from our parents, whether they are dead or alive. It's what screws most of us up, have you not realised that? I had the same with my mother. Her unhappiness was passed on to me. By offloading the burden to me, it validated what she had been looking for with her mother.'

'But did it make her happy?'

'Of course not. It made us all unhappy. It was selfish.'

Angus's eyes looked weaker than usual. 'How do you know all this. I've never heard you talk about it before.'

'I've done a lot of processing Angus. Trying to work out what is going on here.'

'Are you proud of me?' he asked.

This caught Heather by surprise. It wasn't a side of him she'd seen before. A vulnerable side. 'Of course, I am. I've supported you all these years and never faulted. I've seen you working hard, but ...'

'But what?'

'I need more.'

'More? I had your pendant fixed with eighteen 1.5 carat diamonds, you live in the best house in the village and you say you want more?'

'That's exactly my point. You don't see it do you? It's not about the diamonds, this house or the five-star hotels in Scottish glens. It's the little things which matter. Intimacy, affection, kindness and trust.'

'But I give you all those and more.'

Heather shook her head. 'I think we've just come to the end of our journey. We've done what we can. We've given it our best shot and maybe it's time to think about other options.'

She saw him look her up and down with his eyes casting under his heavy brow.

'You really have changed,' he said, huffing.

Heather closed her eyes and sighed. 'Exactly! I've grown Angus. I've learned. Albeit the hard way, but I've learned to listen to my heart.'

'You make me sound like a heartless idiot.'

Heather didn't reply. Instead, raised her glass of wine and took a large swig.

'It's that young lad, isn't it?' he said, raising his voice.

'No Angus. It's not. There's nothing going on between us. I'm doing this for me, for my own sanity and my own worth.'

'I tried to protect you from other people. I know how dangerous they can be. Especially, that Lesley from the shop.'

Heather shook her head. 'She's a good friend Angus. One of a kind and she's been through a lot herself. I respect her and she does me.'

'They all want something from you. I've seen it all before me in the court.'

'No Angus. There are some genuinely lovely people out there. The trouble is, your view is skewed.'

He shook his head vigorously. 'I know the truth. I saw you with that lad. You laughed together and he was here more than he wasn't. I'm not stupid.'

'He brought light to a dark place. He's a compassionate man, that's ...'

Angus cut her off. 'Exactly. Compassion! Is that what you need these days to sleep with someone else's wife?'

'*Slap*'. Her hand responded without hesitation and slapped him across his face. 'I have not slept with anyone but you, and I resent your accusation. I'm standing up for myself here, I don't need anyone else fighting my corner.'

Angus emptied his glass in one gulp. 'So that's what it's come down to is it. Fighting our corners, like boxers vying for the medal. Well, let me tell you, I always have the last punch. No one humiliates me ...'

This time, she cut him off. 'I'm leaving you Angus. I want a divorce and I want it with no fuss. Half and half. I realise we will have to sell this place, that's regrettable, but we can both move on and live happier lives.'

He grabbed her arm and twisted it until it burnt through her skin. 'Get in the car,' he said, forcing her out of the door.

'*No Angus! You're hurting me*,' she shouted, but it made no difference. He dragged her to the car and made her get in.

'Stop it, Angus. You're scaring me.'

He locked all the doors and remained silent.

'Where are you taking me?'

Turning his head, he stared at her, before reversing violently into the road without looking, and then sped off towards the cliff tops.

'I'll call the police,' she said as she gasped for air.

'Your phone is on the kitchen table,' he replied calmly.

'This is it, Angus. My trust will be gone forever. You can't scare people like this. Where are you taking me?'

'To the end! Where else? You made me do it, remember that, it's your fault.'

'What are you talking about, the end?'

He stopped the car, and it skidded on the gravel at the top of Beast Cliff.

'I'll scream if you get out of this car.'

'There's no one around. Scream as loud as you want. Now get out.'

She clung to the seat and closed her eyes. But Angus was already around by her door and opening it.

'I'm not coming. I'm scared.'

'We're doing this together,' he said, grabbing her arm and pulling her out onto the gravel.

'If this is some kind of game. It's not funny.'

'We're just going to take a walk along the cliff. Like husbands and wives do. You said I should spend more time with you.'

'Not like this,' she said, squirming.

Beast Cliff was one of the tallest along the coast, and its near-vertical face plunged straight into the sea, with jagged rocks directly below. Angus maintained a tight grip on her arm as he marched them to the highest point.

'Dramatic, isn't it?' he said, smirking. 'Dangerous and mysterious. A bit like you.'

'What are you talking about?'

'The writing was on the wall, wasn't it? I should have realised before I married you.'

Heather tried to break free from his vice-like grip. 'What writing?'

'Your father. You driving him to his death. You do it to everyone eventually. I can see now how he must have felt before he killed himself.'

'Don't you dare do this to me Angus. You know damn well, his death was of his own choosing.'

Angus laughed out loud. 'And this is of my choosing, thanks to you. What else do you expect me to do? A divorce! Public humiliation and the loss of my knighthood. It's all part of your conniving scheme.'

'I would never do that to you. Never!' she replied.

'Well! That's what you tell yourself. And that's why you're so good at it. Convincing yourself that you're right and then manipulating everyone around you. I told you; you needed help a long time ago, but you ignored me. You're selfish, arrogant mind, set firmly on destruction. They used to put people like you in mental institutions. Keep everyone else safe.'

Heather couldn't believe what she was hearing. He sounded so convincing, and even made her consider whether she was a controller. *Was her 'thing' with Will, part of a selfish game?* It was confusing to hear, and it made her feel dizzy.

'I wouldn't have said anything, but you've driven me to it. What hope do I have now that you have taken everything from me. I trusted you and you let me down, just like my father. He was a selfish man and never thought about anyone else.'

Heather searched for the grounded reassurance of feeling her pendant around her neck. The diamond was there, and she needed it like never before. She squeezed it between her thumb and index finger and relished the stabbing pain.

'See!' he said, looking at her with steely eyes. 'Yet another secret.'

'It's not what you think. It's my saviour.'

'And you are mine!' Angus said as he pulled them to the very edge of the cliff. With the wind buffeting them, and the sound of the sea crashing onto the base of the cliff, and almost deafening in its relentless barrage. Angus turned his back to the sea and pulled Heather close to his face, while maintaining his firm grip.

'It's time to bring this to an end. I tried to save you. You were a nothing when I first met you and you flourished in my arms. I didn't judge you on your inability to bear us offspring. I could have resented you, instead, I bottled in my feelings, all for you. And this is all the thanks I get.'

He leaned back.

'Don't do this Angus. I'm sorry. I'm truly sorry. Don't take us over the edge.'

Angus laughed and relaxed his grip. 'You're not coming! This is my party and your responsibility. You decide whether I live or die. The waves sound like your father pleading, don't they?'

'No, you don't. This is not fair. You're doing this to hurt me.'

'I'm doing this for me. Be true to yourself, have you ever heard that phrase? You decide.' His heels were over the edge as he looked deep into her eyes. 'Push me! Finish me off. Discard me forever,' he said, rocking his head backwards. 'Or save me. Take me back to the safety of our house if you really care.'

Heather grabbed his collar and held him there. She could feel his weight in her hands.

'You decide!' he said, looking deep into her eyes.

The sound of the seagulls drowned out the crashing waves below. They sounded as if they were mocking her. Laughing at her as they flew close by and making her unsteady on her feet. Every second in her mind, a year of their marriage, ticked slowly and painfully. Flashbacks of his poisonous mouth and his tightly gripping fingers, strangling her spirit and stifling every ounce of joy. She loosened her grip and felt the wind pushing him into her. His eyes now closed and his fate at her fingertips, she felt her heart pummelling her lungs and regularly missing a beat. Its irregular pattern, unnerving and weird. She let go and saw him slowly move away from her. Her pounding heart was in her feet, hands and temples, as she grabbed hold of him, and with everything she had left, pulled him to the ground, clear of the edge and collapsed on top of him. Tears surged down her face and dripped onto her fist as she attempted to thump his chest, but didn't have the resources to follow through.

'Take me home,' she said, sobbing. 'Take me home!'

39

CROAK OF CROWS

Angus's breath in her ear woke her. Their spooning position made her squirm and instantly want to move, but it meant at least they were both still alive. Heather gently removed his arm and slid out of bed unnoticed. In the bathroom, she examined her face. Her skin was pale, and her eyes red with exhaustion. It seemed almost unreal, the two of them defying death, high up on Beast Cliff. *She couldn't live with his death on her conscience,* she knew that, as she noticed the increase in deep crow's-feet by her eyes. The guilt would have been with her forever, and would have destroyed her. She knew he could manipulate her; she wasn't stupid, and this time he had pushed her to her limits. The reality was, she had a fabulous home. The three of them had coexisted well over the years, and it was she who had mixed things up. She'd done the wrong thing getting involved with Will and pretending that she had changed and deserved better. Her mother had always drilled into her that she didn't deserve to find a loving partner and therefore should be grateful to anyone who would have her. Life was intended to be tough, and to think the grass could be greener was a recipe for upset. Brushing her hair, she pondered what lay ahead and, putting on her dressing gown, quietly headed to the kitchen.

A new kitchen was the first item in her notebook. Followed by a new king-size bed. His snoring and foul after-drink breath made it challenging in a double. As the coffee percolated, she sat at the table and doodled in her notebook as she thought some more.

New linen, obviously for the new bed and maybe a different colour in the bedroom? Out with the old and in with the new, was becoming the emerging theme.

She poured herself a coffee and wondered how they would cope with the garden. Angus would obviously have to trim down and get his back strong again. They would have to be a team to maintain the splendour of the property.

A car! Wow, that was a surprise thought. She wrote 'car' anyway and then thought about how she could be ready to drive again after all these years. A bit of independence was going to be essential moving forward. She could buy herself a car, given the money from the diamonds, so it was possible.

Taking her coffee with her, she put on her slippers and exited the back door onto the patio. The lawn was looking unloved and a couple of dead branches from the cedar had fallen and were lying on top of the lavender. She placed her coffee mug on the garden table and went over to remove them. It was a full-time job maintaining everything, but it did give her a sense of pride and purpose.

The vegetable garden was looking good despite weeks of weeding neglect. She sat on the edge of the birdbath and, without really thinking about it, worked out how many veg boxes she could get out of what was there. The air was freezing cold, and her dressing gown offered little in the way of insulation. Opening the orangery door, her body shuddered. It was cold in there too. The heated bench had not been on, and the remnants of Angus's rant were still obvious. She sighed. It felt different in there. Unwelcoming and sterile. More like a huge glass store than a sanctuary. She glanced at the bottle of antifreeze, which ran through the heating system. 'POISON' it said on the side in bold lettering. She looked up at the house and wondered if Angus was up and out of bed yet. *Better take him a coffee*, she thought and then sat at her bench, staring out into the garden and resting her hand upon the box full of money.

The deep croak of crows high above her in the chestnut trees echoed against the glass. The air was perfectly still, emphasising the calls of seagulls in the distance and the faint brushing of the sea, audible, as she recalled Will thrusting the kite into her hands and them running along the beach. She was terrified of allowing it to crash into someone, but it was fun and exciting. He did those kinds of things. Despite the responsibility, they laughed and shared the moment together. Him, teasing her and she hating him for putting her in that predicament, yet falling madly in love with him. *It wasn't all about him! That was the difference.* She sighed. It had just dawned on her that, that was the case. Selfless fun, was the best fun.

Resting her elbows on the bench and her chin on her hands, she sighed again. He was too good for her. His positive, carefree nature, opposite to her responsibility as a wife and the gratitude she was constantly being told to acknowledge. Magazines, TV, radio, all celebrating the gratitude revolution and any modern woman chastised for not recognising what they had, and proving that they were happy because they accepted their lot. *Did it make her a modern woman? Was being grateful, truly the gateway to happiness?* None of it actually mattered when you felt worthless. Worthiness was not a feature of her upbringing, and any sign of holding your head high was soon brought down to the chocolate factory floor and cobbled street. She was bolder, that was for sure, she would push for new home improvements and tell herself that she was worthy of a new car, but above all, she knew that Angus would provide stability and comfort, albeit, at a cost sometimes, and if she were a good wife, and stopped kidding herself that the grass was greener elsewhere, it could work as well as it had before.

Heather took a fresh coffee up to Angus. He was sitting upright in bed. His pinstripe pyjamas made him look like a public schoolboy, with greying hair. She placed his coffee on the bedside table, kissed him on the forehead and then sat beside him.

'Thank you,' he said, smiling. 'You saved me. Without you, I'm nothing. Promise you'll never leave me?'

Heather smiled, then stood and loaded the laundry into the basket and opened the curtains to a brand-new day.

40

WILDER

Bacon, sausage, black pudding, eggs and tattie scones looked like individual fairground attractions against the drab kitchen walls. The cupboards were dull, and the air was thick and grey. It was business as usual. His hand periodically appearing from behind his *Financial Times* to spear a sausage and although she couldn't see his face, the wet slapping of his mouth, put her completely off eating anything. 'I need to take Benny to the vet's to look at his paw,' she said, looking at the front page of the paper 'Interest rates drop as futures and guilts underperform!' the headline read. 'I also have a bag of clothes to take to the charity shop.'

Angus grunted from behind his paper.

'I'll take them down in the wheelbarrow. Will be good to get some fresh air and stretch my legs.'

'Will you bring me a bottle of Scotch back with you. Get the best you can find. You know what I like,' he said, reaching into his pocket and throwing a wad of cash on the table without dropping his paper.

'Sure. Anything else?'

His smiling face slowly appeared. 'Some cigars. Havana, Cuban? Get the best.'

'Sure,' she replied. 'Finish my breakfast, if your still hungry.'

He said nothing, just grabbed a sausage and continued reading.

'I'll get everything together.'

Angus grunted and Heather prepared the cat carrier. She worked out that she could accommodate the cat, within his carrier and the bag of clothes in the wheelbarrow together. It would be a test going down the hill, but she was up for the challenge.

'Bye,' she shouted from the kitchen door. He was still engrossed in his paper. 'Bloody share prices are down again,' he mumbled.

Heather responded with a huff and put on her coat, hat, scarf and gloves.

'Don't forget the cigars!' he shouted.

On her way out, Heather opened up the orangery and watered all the plants. She coaxed Benny into the carrier with some tinned mackerel. His deep purring made her stop for a moment and toy with her pendant.

'Sorry!' she said, locking him inside. She walked down the central aisle and unplugged the radio, grabbed some teabags from the tin by the kettle and shoved them in her pocket. Stopping once again to look around the beautiful Victorian ironwork, she nodded to herself, then ran her hand over her workbench and sighed, before bundling Benny and the bag into the barrow and exiting via the gate. She looked back at the house and smiled.

The bag kept rolling off and tumbling down the steep hill, but Benny remained calm within his carrier, as she walked straight past the vet's. She didn't even stop to look as she diverted to Sally's house. There were three cats sitting on the doorstep as she rang the bell.

'Sally. I need a favour,' she said, handing her the carrier and Benny.

Sally was still in her dressing gown and scowled. 'What do you mean?'

'I wouldn't normally spring this on you, but I'm going away for a while and I can't get him in at the cattery.'

'Are you going on holiday?' Sally asked.

Heather smiled and removed her engagement and wedding rings. 'Here. Have these as payment. Sell them,' she said, turning her back and sobbing.

'Are you okay, Heather?' she shouted.

Heather kept on walking. 'He loves mackerel!' she shouted.

Speedily and forcefully wheeling the barrow, she headed for Dune. Lesley was just opening up. 'The flat is yours whenever you want it you know,' Lesley said.

Heather walked up to her and kissed her on the lips and held her head between her hands. 'You're fucking amazing. You know that.' Heather said, dashing upstairs and grabbing her heavy rucksack. 'I owe you everything,' she said, handing her a sizeable wad of money.

Lesley fell back against the doorjamb and refused the money. 'Where are you going?'

'I don't know, but I have a purple dress, my compass and a whistle, so anything is possible.'

'Have you gone mad?'

Heather ran down the stairs. 'Yes! And the best thing is, I'm not feeling guilty about any of it and I'm doing this for me. Wish me luck.'

Lesley laughed and threw her a beach towel with a palm tree and sunset into her arms. 'You might need this!'

Heather tossed it in the barrow and set off walking, then stopped, turned and ran back, kissing Lesley one more time and giving her a lasting hug. 'Don't cry. I'm doing it,' Heather said, breaking their embrace and grabbing the barrow. 'Thanks for everything!' And with that, she disappeared towards the sea.

The industrious smell of the harbour made her eyes light up. The sun was rising above the tall sails, and the tide was high. The fishermen were busy, as always. Loading and unloading their boats. Heather skipped, trotted and gambolled her way towards the workshops. There was a frivolity in her step, and it felt good. She stopped by a stack of lobster pots and breathed deeply. Taking in the maritime air and running her hand on the barnacled pots, feeling the twisted hemp between her fingers, made life seem real and tangible, yet she felt like she was in a dream. Strange really. Such a huge life-changing decision, and, for the first time in her life, she felt like she was at the helm. Making the choices and plotting a new course. Scary! Oh yes, it was scary. She'd done the impossible. Fought her demons, confronted Angus and challenged his bullying. *Why had she let it go on for so long? Why didn't she realise sooner?*

She sat for a moment on a bench and took another deep, salty breath. Will had changed her life. Set her on a new bearing and given her a confidence she never knew she had. She wondered if he had passed his exam and whether the boat was complete and ready for its maiden voyage to watch the seals. He deserved everything, and with her fingers crossed; she ushered positive thoughts towards his workshop. She was in love with him. She'd never felt such a feeling before. That's what was confusing. *Everyone thinks love is happiness and joy, but really, it's all of your emotions,* she thought as she watched the seagulls swoop and rise high into the sky on the generous breeze. The air was icy, but the sun took away the edge with its glowing optimism. She was glad that she had found such a beautiful soul. Without Will, she wouldn't have taken the path, let alone tackle the crossroads. He took her there, and he encouraged her to choose a path that was true. Not the easiest path, but a path that had integrity and honesty. 'None of it is your fault, so why persecute yourself,' she remembered him saying. She didn't understand what he was saying at the time; in fact, she felt patronised by his flippant tone, but now it resonated deep within her. He was right. None of her mother and father's prejudice and hatred of themselves had anything to do with her. They'd passed the negativity down to her to ease their own selfish insecurities, and that was wrong. Abuse no less, and nearly forty-seven years on, it was time to throw it all back at them and through the evil channel they themselves had created. Angus – if she wasn't so desperate and insecure herself back then, when he strode into the cafe, she may never have even given him the time of day, and instead, found herself a humble, strong and handsome gardener in which to build a happy life.

Anyway! It was done. She'd given her best; she was sure of that, and although moving away from Highcrest was a wrench, she knew it was really a prison in Victorian wolf's clothing. *She had a maritime navigation certificate anyway, and a passport, so what more did she need?* She thought as her hand was already toying with the pendant Will had lovingly restored.

It was time to go and get him. Show him her true feelings and set course for new horizons.

She stopped outside Will's workshop, which was locked up.

Leaving her barrow, beach towel and bag of clothes, she skipped across the yard and onto the harbour wall. She was excited to see the boat. He'd said it was almost complete, and the excitement made her heady with thoughts about what he had done inside and its new name.

The harbour was heaving with boats, and as the sun rose higher, she found it thrilling but difficult to see each boat clearly. Which one was his, she kept thinking as she progressed systematically around the wall. She searched eagerly for his young face, craved his strong arms around her, and the touch of his incredible kisses.

She reached the far end of the harbour and saw no sign of him, so she set off walking back. With the sun behind her, it was easier to see the boats and, more importantly, the occupants. She looked over to his workshop and spied that her wheelbarrow and contents were still at the locked door. She carried on and felt a downhearted wave of disappointment at not being able to see him. *Maybe he was in the dry dock, fixing something?* she thought.

'Morning Heather. It's a beautiful day.' Old Jim Watkins greeted her as he lugged a huge anchor chain along the slipway.

'It really is, but should you be hauling that chain? It must weigh a ton?'

Jim laughed. 'Been doing it all my life. The day I stop is the day I throw in my sou'wester and sleep with the other pirates.'

'Were you once a pirate?'

He looked her up and down. 'You're never 'once' a pirate. Lovely beetroot by the way, had it with some Dover sole and samphire.'

Heather squirmed and shuffled from foot to foot. 'I might

not be doing the boxes for a while,' she said, fiddling with her pendant.

'Shame! You did me proud with those leeks and garlic, as well.'

'Have you seen Will?' Heather changed the subject before he made her feel completely guilty.

'Yes. Saw him first light, loading up.'

'Do you know if he passed his exam?'

Jim scratched his grey, wiry beard.' He certainly did, 99%.'

'Wow, that's impressive,' she replied.

'Spelled his name wrong on the front or would have been 100%.'

Heather shook her head and laughed. 'I'm pleased. We worked hard on it.'

Jim took off his sou'wester. 'You helped him, did you?'

'Not really. He did it himself. I just gave moral support.'

'He had no one after his grandfather died. Did everything himself and as honest as you'll find anywhere.'

Heather nodded. 'Where is he?'

Jim stroked his long beard and looked her in the eye. His eyes were multicoloured, like individual planet earth's spinning with worldly experience. 'You just missed him. Set sail just after sunrise. She's a mighty fine boat.'

'Missed him? Where was he going?'

'Dun know? An adventure, he said. Sold his pickup and gardening gear to young Marcus Jones,' he said, pointing to the other side of the harbour at a lad loading the truck.

'What about his workshop?'

'Spotless! Not a wood shaving nor a cobweb, and all my tools back in my place.'

'But, how long did he say he was away for?'

'Said he was done here. Nothing to keep him on these shores.'

Heather's legs buckled. The weight of his words hit her with a tsunami of emotion. *She'd missed him! Left it too late.* Instead of having breakfast with Angus, she should have been down at the harbour apologising and celebrating his achievement.

Staggering to a pile of heavy-duty fishing nets, she collapsed onto them and burst into tears. She was a selfish bitch. She should have run away with him when he asked, instead of rejecting him. The worst thing was, she really wanted to congratulate him on obtaining his boat masters. His grandad would have been proud, and she wanted him to know that. Her tears dripped continuously onto her hands. Her heart shivered with cold, and her stomach ached with bitter disappointment. She was in love with him, and she had messed it up. Overthought it and gone back to her stupid old ways. Missing the opportunity of a new life full of love. But, moreover, she was hurting for him. Not because he needed her; he was capable on his own. He understood himself and had done all the hard work. Not many men could say that, but he had processed everything, and it meant he knew his own mind. He was free now. Free to sail and free to live and in a beautiful boat, which ultimately was the freedom of his grandfather. Heather whimpered at the thought of the pride he must have to stand at the helm of everything he had created.

Her breathing, heart rate and sobbing contradicted each other. Her body and soul out of sync and her mind spinning.

'Go for it Wilder,' she said. 'Go for it and seek new adventures with the pride you deserve. My love is with you although you will never know what you did for me. I'm grateful for our time together and I wish you every happiness and a wonderful life ahead.'

'Are you okay?' Old Jim Hawkins asked as he checked on her again.

Heather smiled. 'He taught me that I can do it on my own. That I am brave enough to do this. I realise now what a wonderful gift he bestowed upon me. He saw the strength in me, even when I couldn't myself. I'm grateful and I'm honoured to have known him.'

He looked at her with his worldly eyes, shining bright in the flame of the oil can. 'If you believe that in your gut, then you've won the race! Happiness comes from within, not from outside. My lovely Betsy used to say that all the time, and she was the most beautiful soul I ever knew. God bless her.'

Heather watched his eyes become washed with tears as they shared a smile together.

'It's times like this when you realise, that you are your only saviour. I will miss him dearly, but I now have the strength to seek my own path, thanks to the many people around me, including you, Jim.'

He put his hand on her shoulder. 'If you trust your heart, your head will follow. The sea will look after you. I'm sure of that.'

41

PURPLE DOVE

The sap-green door's paint was peeling off and collecting in a soggy pile on the ground. The brass handle, stained with salt-crystallised rust, looked like it was about to fall off. In the cold light of day, it appeared uncared for and neglected. It was slightly ajar and Heather saw her opportunity to enter and squeezed in, without alerting anyone. There was one last thing to do!

In contrast, the pristine lantern sparkled and radiated its bright light for the world to see. The last time she had stood here, he had had his arms around her and she had been kissing him. His picnic, cushions and sheer audacity of getting them into the lighthouse was the most romantic gesture she'd ever experienced. Watching his lips move as he spoke about the stars was enthralling, and listening to his jovial cockiness when he produced the wine from the suspended bucket made her smile.

She walked around the tower, looking out in all directions. *Where was he? Where had he decided to go without her?* She checked her phone-nothing! *Should she send a text? She knew it was too late, but what did she have to lose?*

'Hi, hope you're, okay? I hear you passed your exam. I'm proud of you. Wish I had come with you on your new adventure. Try not to forget our evening in the lighthouse. It meant the earth to me and I want you to know, that you changed my life beyond compare. Sail your heart to new shores and know that you will always be within mine.

'Love Heather x'

Her throat and cheeks hurt as her tears dripped onto the phone. He was a beautiful man and deserved to live his life to the full, and although inside she felt empty, she was happy for him. Truly happy that he was honouring his grandfather and free to find his true love. Removing her pendant from around her neck, she held it in the palm of her hand. The diamond in the dove's eye sparkled and then dazzled her in the light of the lantern.

'Now I am free,' she said out loud. '*I am freeeee!*'

Looking down, she could see Highcrest. Obvious from the tall cedar tree, which dominated all the other trees. She could just make out the white pinnacle at the top of the orangery roof. It was no longer her safe place. It didn't even feel like it belonged to her. Angus had soiled it. Raided its contents, and raped it of its soul. There was no going back despite his threats. He was no longer her responsibility.

'*Fuck you Angus*!' she shouted. '*And fuck you too, Dad*.' She was completely done with the two men who had worked her into the ground. Pressing the diamond into her finger, she pierced her skin and felt the tingle of release. Her grandmother was her father's mother. She had lost him to the drink. It was not her fault, although it destroyed her. She was a hardworking woman, and her husband had set the scene for controlling destruction. But she held her head high and passed her love in the only place it could go, and that was to Heather. Her father was a weak man. Hiding from his father and the truth. Unable to drag himself out of his sorrowful mire of self-loathing, she knew deep down he was a good man and loved her. Each bag of chocolate misfits and walk within the park, his signs of love and a symbol of his own inadequacy.

It was no wonder that she sought solace with a man who kept her just above the filthy floor of humanity. Just enough to breathe, but constantly reminded of her place within society and the respect she had to show to the underside of everyone's boots.

She had been pathetic. She'd allowed them all to grind their insecurities into her and force her down into the ground.

They were all bastards! Each and every one of them, but she, had seen something she was never supposed to see. The contrast. The flip side and the stark reality of self-respect. The man who couldn't even read and write, the humblest of men and the kindest of hearts, had nurtured her with his confident hands and poured nature's lifeblood onto her unconditionally. He had shown her how to grow; she could feel it deep down, and he had enriched her soul with simplicity and hope.

This was true gratitude. Without him, she was laid bare, but he had equipped her with courage, and now was the time to take that courage and free herself from the disgusting shackles of other people's insecurity and set a course for her own truth.

Heather kissed the pendant and fastened it back around her neck. Then, removing the purple dress from her rucksack, held it up against her body. Femininity didn't have to come with compromise. She didn't have to hide her vulnerability behind iron gates. She could be strong in the knowledge that in the right hands, she could be herself, let down her guard and revel in the knowledge that one day she would unfold her petals and shine in the glorious sunlight of worthiness.

With both hands gripping the dress, she tore it down the seam and opened it out. He told her she was beautiful in it, and she felt it in her bones. The power of his honesty thrilled her, and now he had passed on his wonderful optimism, and it was time. Time to make the change.

Draping it in front of the glass, the lantern shone with purple resonance out across the ocean. Her sign of thanks and her beacon of love to the man that changed everything. 'I love you. Now sail and know I will always have a piece of you in my heart. I am free and today; I will spread my wings and fly.'

~

She wasn't going back to the house. She was never going back. It wasn't her responsibility, and neither was that foul walrus. Heather walked briskly past the gate, took in the Victorian facade and then headed down the steep cobbled road. Arriving at the newsagent's, she picked up a gold, sparkly windmill and took it to the desk. Afternoon, Heather, Mr Biernacki said. 'Do you want the *Financial Times* as well?'

'Not today, thank you, or ever again! I have my own headlines to write.' And that was it. She was off down the road, making the windmill turn with vigour as she blew optimistically into its sails. It was time for a journey of her own, and the harbour felt like the best starting point.

'A one-way ticket to ...' Heather paused. 'Where do you sail to?'

The man behind the ticket office window scratched his head. 'Hull, Edinburgh or Rotterdam.'

Heather thought about it. She'd been to Hull, great aquarium, and Edinburgh was too much like going back to her roots. She'd never been to Rotterdam though! She moved her hand to the side pocket of her rucksack and ran her fingers along the edge of her passport. *What would it be like to go abroad?* she thought.

'Rotterdam, please,' she said matter-of-factly.

'You've just missed the Rotterdam, but there's another one in two hours,' the man said.

'Damn. And the Hull?' she asked.

'One and a half hours.'

Heather toyed with her pendant. *She could catch the ferry to Hull and then springboard from there,* she thought. 'No, Rotterdam it is please.'

The man smiled politely. 'Return, madam?'

Heather paused again. 'No thanks.'

She turned towards the cafe and felt her phone in her coat pocket. *Angus!* Her heart beat rapidly as she pondered. *What he might be doing? Or what was he about to do?* She couldn't bear to ruminate and slowly walked to the edge of the harbour wall. The light was fading as the wintry night descended fast. The harbour lights reflected upon the rippling water. She looked up to see the purple glow of the lighthouse beam and smiled. It was then that she gripped her phone and hurled it into the watery depths below her. 'Goodbye', she said softly and then confidently walked to the cafe. Her only concern, was that Angus might try looking for her, which made her neck twitch.

With a strong coffee in hand, Heather entered the cold, now dark street and wandered slowly over the cobbles. *She was doing it.* Forging ahead with ... she didn't even have a plan. This was instinctive and raw and felt exciting, but it was frightening too. The unknown city of Rotterdam. She hadn't seen it in any of her brochures, but at least from there, the gateway to Europe and the azure sea and golden beaches were not only accessible but positively welcoming.

Old Jim Watkins' oil drum outside his workshop, was alive with flame. The glow of radiant heat attracted her, and she positioned herself upon the fishing nets and sipped her coffee. Heather watched the comings and goings of the harbour start to quiet down for the night. It was only 4.30pm, but the stars were out in full splendour. She chuckled as the purple glow of the lighthouse was still projecting her message of freedom and thanks to the whole world. *He must never go up there,* she thought. *The lighthouse keeper.* She dozed in the comfort of the warmth as Jim occasionally and silently checked on her.

The last call for the Hull ferry came over the loudspeaker, and Heather tussled with the idea of ditching Rotterdam and getting out of the village as quickly as possible. But Europe was beckoning her. *No half measures,* she thought, and it wasn't much longer to wait. In fact, as the Hull boat departed, the Rotterdam came in to dock, and people and cars began offloading and a pedestrian queue started to form by the ticket office. She took her place and eagerly awaited the call to board. The cold bit into her face as she watched smaller boats come in and leave the safety of the harbour. *Other people are doing it,* she thought. *Having lives and setting off on adventures. She was as strong as they were, and this was it. A new start and a new heart.* 'Boarding will begin in ten minutes.' The voice announced over the Tannoy.

Heather smiled as she watched a sailboat elegantly head out towards the open sea. It was a calm night, thank goodness. *I wonder where it is heading?* Her mind pondered the myriad of possibilities. Suddenly, there was an altercation with an incoming sailboat. The harbour entrance was tight, especially when outgoing and incoming boats jostled for position. Then, a shock wave hit her straight in the face. Not a ripple of shock, but a full-on tidal wave of complete surprise. The incoming sailboat looked familiar and not only that. Her skipper had the most beautiful face. A man who knew the stars. Had handcrafted the magnificent wooden hull and had personally installed the tall, proud mast. He looked right at home, standing confidently at the helm with one hand on the wheel.

She couldn't move. Frozen to the spot, her heart resonated within her entire body. 'Boarding for Rotterdam, boarding for Rotterdam.' The voice said as she felt a gentle push on her back. She moved forward with the queue and lost sight of Will in his stunning boat.

'I'm not waiting all day, luv.' A voice behind her urged her to take the loading ramp to the ferry. She moved with the crowd and looked back once again, but the side of the boat obscured the moorings.

What was she even thinking! Will knew nothing of her plans, and she wasn't even on his mind. He was a free agent, and she had to let him get on with it. 'I don't want to push you luv, but there's a queue behind you.' The man behind her, once again, urged her on.

'Passports please,' a man in uniform shouted as she approached the border kiosk.

Heather took one more look back and then clenched her fist. There was no backing out. She handed her passport to the guard and heard a voice yelling her name. She looked and saw Angus! 'Heather, wait,' he shouted.

The guard handed her passport back and cleared her way to the dockside. 'Wait!' a different voice said calmly. 'You're coming with me.' Heather turned her head and looked straight into his eyes. His beautiful eyes.

'Will!' she shouted as he scooped her up into his arms, just like he had when they first met.

'How did you know?' she said, wrapping her arm around him.

'I saw your sign,' he replied, gesturing with his eyes to the lighthouse. 'I said I'd be here for you.'

'But you'd gone.'

'I thought you had. But I couldn't leave behind my most precious cargo.'

He brought her face close to his and stopped by his boat. He looked deep into her eyes and kissed her passionately. His lips tight against hers, joining them together and connecting their hearts.

'*Heather!*' Angus shouted from the other side of the barrier.

She didn't look. Instead, she continued kissing Will and lost herself in his eyes.

'*Heather*!' Angus shouted again.

Will placed her gently back on the ground, giving her a chance to respond.

Heather never faltered and looked at Will. 'I love you,' he said. 'Run away with me.'

She looked down at the side of the boat. Its name, beautifully handwritten on the bow. '*Purple Dove*.' She flung her arms around him and felt his arms squeeze her tight.

'I have my navigator's certificate,' she said, grinning.

Will nodded. 'Happy to have you with me, shipmate.'

Offering his hand, Will helped her onto the deck and put her hand on the wheel. 'Greece or Amalfi?'

Heather looked at the sextant mounted on the helm and

giggled. 'I love you Will. I'll go anywhere with you,' she said and kissed him.

They didn't wait to see Angus wrestle with the border force guard. He didn't have a passport to get to the dockside. *Shame! He could have thrown himself into the harbour,* she thought for a split second and then watched Will undo the ropes and cast them off from the dock.

'Set a course due south,' Will said, tossing Heather her bag of clothes.

'How did you find my bag?'

'Old Jim Watkins tipped me off,' he said, grinning.

Heather didn't look back. Instead, she took her bag and ducked below deck to where the glow of the wood burner met her with a welcome warmth within the cabin.

Watching the green harbour light pass the porthole, she knew they were heading out on an adventure, and she took a breath which tingled every vein in her body.

Will appeared at the door. 'We're on course, and it's a quiet night. Are you okay?'

Heather nodded. 'Purple Dove?'

Will smiled. No matter what, you were always going to be with me.

He took her hand and kissed her, both of his hands cupping her face and sealing his commitment with his kisses. Heather relaxed and felt her heart race like it had never before. She felt him remove her coat and fling it towards the hook on the wall, she heard it land on the floor and he smiled while still passionately kissing her.

He lifted up her fleece and threw it on the floor, which made her smile. Kissing and smiling at the same time was just the most divine thing. He then removed his Arran sweater to reveal his bare chest. 'What about the boat?' Heather asked.

'I've anchored us just off the coast. We're with the seals now.'

Heather kissed him and put her hand on his muscular chest, and she felt the hairs between her fingers.

Releasing her bra in one movement impressed her. He was masterful and sexy, and those capable hands of his, which had crafted the very boat they were in, were now focused on her.

Kissing her neck and playfully nibbling her ear made her quiver. 'You're safe now,' he said, holding her face in his hands and following the contour of her cheekbone with his thumb. 'You're safe.'

His reassuring voice let her heart detach from her mind. His confident tone instantly penetrated her defences and the joy of letting go felt new, liberating and exciting. His beautiful lips were now touching hers gently, reassuring her further and magically winding down the drawbridge of her castle wall defences. Her knight on horseback galloping toward her with conviction and honour from the battle, and sweeping her up into his arms. She'd dreamt of this moment and then locked it away, in the hope that one day it might come true, but the reality, the ruthless king, had kept her imprisoned and declared romance, hope and desire were testament to treason.

Still cradling her face in his hands, and focused entirely on her eyes, his kisses were humble and respectful, yet bursting with passion. She could feel it in the way he was gentle, and at the same time, playful and confident. Heather trusted his intent and followed his masculine lead, losing herself in his kisses as they became stronger and passionate. Her heartbeat changing from skittish excitement to pounding with emotional connection, she was in. Casting away the shackles of her imprisonment, and riding with him out of the castle into the unknown.

Handcrafted woodgrain and the smell of seasoned timber, laden with bed linen, blankets and cushions, formed the bed and radiant heat from the wood stove, relaxed Heather to the point her head was spinning, with a heady mix of carefree abandon and excited optimism. 'You're an incredible woman, you know that?' he said. His eyes conveying his sentiment, and his brow confirming his sincerity. So that was it. She was galloping with him and at speed, trusting his leadership and faithful in his ability to take her anywhere.

Tracing his jawline with her fingers, his stubbly chin felt rugged and defiant. 'And you are a remarkable man. I'm sorry!'

Will shook his head. 'Don't ever be sorry. Together, we can learn and grow. Together we can do anything,' he said, caressing her neck with gentle kisses, and by the time they were along her collarbone, her entire body was warm and receptive. His tongue running around her nipple felt sublime. Reluctant in the past to celebrate her breasts, she watched Will tease her now erect nipples, concentrating on one and then moving his attention just at the right time to the other. A complete contrast to the grabbing and heavy sucking of her marriage, Will was playful with his tongue and naughty with his flicking and sensual sucking. If this were heaven, she was a convert.

The exquisite tingles in her breast worked their way down her body as Will continued kissing her stomach and even her side, down to her hip. That was a first and although it tickled, it sent the tickles to all the right places. Sliding off her trousers and shoes, he did the same and held her tightly in front of the warm glow of the wood stove. They were naked, together and for the first time, she felt safe in his hands and open to his advances.

'Are you okay?' he asked.

Heather smiled. 'Where are we heading?'

'A place beyond holiday brochures. Somewhere we can flourish and I can see you drink limoncello on a sun-drenched balcony.'

'I'm yours Will, take my there.'

And so, he did. Riding the waves together, up and down, holding on tight as he pushed forward in his quest to make her his. Taking her to the edge of the world and then bringing them back on course as he navigated skilfully with his commanding leadership. Then, every star in the night sky filled her mind, floating on the rhythmic swell and knowing there was no turning back. He set his course and showed her the way to freedom. Every lighthouse across the world lit up in a blinding array of blissful celebration. Her body engulfed within a super-storm and with a tsunami building within her core, she succumbed to the deep waves and held on tight until thunder and lightning lit up her mind and earthed her soul. Writhing within the electric storm of his passion, her body gave in completely, letting the shockwaves lift her high above the boat and into the night sky, and let true love guide her like a shooting star.

The End.

EPILOGUE

Dear Lesley,

I'm writing this postcard to thank you not only for encouraging me to find my truth, but for being a true friend. Will and I sailed away to the Mediterranean. Not easy through the Bay of Biscay, but we made it to Spain, Italy and Croatia, before settling in Greece. Building a new life from scratch has been the hardest thing I've ever done, but every sunrise I share with Will, makes it all worthwhile.

The picture on this card shows our new home. Not the stone house with the donkey outside, but the whitewashed house with the olive tree overlooking the ocean. (Your beach towel comes in handy every day when I swim in the clear, clear sea.) The olive tree is one hundred years old and we are surrounded by orange and lemon groves. You can just make out my little car in the background too!

Moving on from Angus has been tough, I won't deny it, with some days being harder than others, but Will's patience is as endless as the sea itself.

Will runs dolphin and turtle watching boat trips, and I sell my art and olive oil to tourists in the local village. We have four cats, including Benny, who was shipped safely to us last month. And sometimes a goat! (Not enough room to explain!)

I'm in love with the scenery, the climate and the beautiful man, who brings home fresh fish every day and tells me to apply my sunscreen. The pitfalls of auburn hair! I am learning to read and write Greek, and Will is already communicating with the other fishermen in the way he knows best, his smile and generosity.

How is your grandson?

Much love, Purple Dove x

ABOUT THE AUTHOR

J A Crawshaw was born in Yorkshire, England, in 1969. He is the father to two grown-up sons and a passionate environmentalist and tree lover. His struggle with dyslexia and reading and writing meant that he was never meant to become an author. He now writes to free anyone who might be held back by a lack of self worth, like he was.
'We are worthy of ourselves and should celebrate our differences and unite in the knowledge that it's okay to be proud to be you.

More information can be found at
www.jacrawshaw.com

youtube.com/Authorlife_JA_Crawshaw
tiktok.com/@j_a_crawshaw_author
instagram.com/j_a_crawshaw_author
facebook.com/jacrawshawbooks

ALSO BY J A CRAWSHAW

An exciting and spicy journey of self discovery, empowerment and search for true love. Follow Charlotte's turbulent mission to find her truth, and rebel against her childhood conditioning to happiness and true love.

A Rollercoaster Trilogy

Plot twist & passion. Start the trilogy here.

I COULDNT DO IT WITHOUT YOU

Feel like leaving a review? I'd be incredibly grateful.

AMAZON - J A Crawshaw

FREE BOOK

Want to be the first to hear about new books before anyone else?Claim your free book when you join many others in my VIP group www.jacrawshaw.com/freebook

Cover reveals, giveaways, insider information and more.

Don't forget that review 😍

Printed in Dunstable, United Kingdom

78040652R00190